The Sto...

Philip Gross

OXFORD
UNIVERSITY PRESS

Great Clarendon Street, Oxford OX2 6DP

Oxford University Press is a department of the University of Oxford.
It furthers the University's objective of excellence in research, scholarship,
and education by publishing worldwide in

Oxford New York

Auckland Cape Town Dar es Salaam Hong Kong Karachi
Kuala Lumpur Madrid Melbourne Mexico City Nairobi
New Delhi Shanghai Taipei Toronto

With offices in

Argentina Austria Brazil Chile Czech Republic France Greece
Guatemala Hungary Italy Japan Poland Portugal Singapore
South Korea Switzerland Thailand Turkey Ukraine Vietnam

British Library Cataloguing in Publication Data

Data available

ISBN-13: 978-0-19-275464-6

ISBN-10: 0-19-275464-5

1 3 5 7 9 10 8 6 4 2

Typeset in Meridien by
Palimpsest Book Production Limited, Polmont, Stirlingshire

Printed in Great Britain by
Cox & Wyman Ltd, Reading, Berkshire

1

The Eye of the Storm

He comes out of the night. Think of a moth—the way it picks up a scent, just one trace in a million, and reels it in across the miles of darkness. For him, the boy in the black coat, it's that *glow*. It's something *happening*—like news, like headlines in the papers, cameras, lights! Once he's seen it, it's as if there's nowhere else for him to be.

The brand-new leisure complex is a blaze of neon—red, white, and electric blue. The heads of the crowd are silhouettes against its sheer glass walls, its lamps and hanging gardens. Chain stores, ice rink, burger palace, galleries, and see-through lifts all float reflected in the still dark waters of the harbour, with the famous brand names upside down and inside out. Now there's the *'testing-testing'* of a PA system, getting ready for the moment—the Grand Opening. Compared to this, the rest of Milbourne is as dull as something from your grandma's photo album.

Out in mid-harbour something moves. Just a swan. The image shivers, like a moment's interference on a TV screen.

And this is just a reconstruction. If it *was* television, you'd see the word RECONSTRUCTION in the corner of the crime scene, so you don't forget. The one person who could *really* tell you won't be telling. And the rest . . . ? They'll have their stories, afterwards . . . but who can you believe, these days?

There he is. He's walking quickly in his long black coat. The crowd is full of families. For the smallest children it's past bedtime but they've stayed up for the Christmas lights. Slightly bigger ones, dressed up for the pageant, have been practising all afternoon, while the older girls are gathering in groups, in the skinniest tops they can get away with in November. They're here to see Cara Sanderton—that's Maylene from the soap of all soaps. The boys are mostly here to see Kieran Scott, local striker made good. He's in a bigger league than Milbourne Town these days.

A Mickey Mouse stilt-walker stalks through the crowd. The huge head peers down above a family, grinning, till a toddler in his buggy starts to cry. This is carnival night, and the black coat moves in among them like a shadow. No one sees him. He's not famous yet.

But this is just a reconstruction.

Cut in jerky clips of CCTV footage. They'll have reels and reels of it to hunt through later. That's him, there. Catch the back of his head among the hundreds in the car park jostling for a view. That's him again—inside now, moving through the concourse. Somehow he's got past the bouncers with their bow ties and shaved heads. Search hard and you might find a still of it happening: he's not wheedling and shoving like the others; no, he's casual, like a mate from way back who the bouncers can't quite place. Now he's made one of them laugh: the man nods and the boy in the coat slips through.

Inside the concourse are people who *matter*—business people, the MP, the mayor in his gold chain . . . Further back are others who'll be made to matter for the evening: old people, people in wheelchairs, carefully-picked chil-

2

dren from the local schools. You might catch a glimpse of *him* amongst it all—just mingling. There he is, on the edge of a group of old ladies: *such a nice young man* . . .

For a moment he looks up, straight at the camera, almost as if he felt it watching. His eyes seem to meet yours for a moment and he gives a quick *Can't-talk-now-catch-you-later* kind of smile.

Almost at once he's deeper in, where the school parties are. In this frame his back's to the camera, but you see a girl, one of the older ones, who turns towards him. She's a face you'd notice in a crowd—not *pretty* in the ordinary Maylene sort of way, but that rush of black curls, those dark eyes under strong brows, and a profile like a painting in a pharaoh's tomb . . . all that would make you look twice. You can see her face, lit-up and interested, over his shoulder, from behind. If a teacher looked now, she'd think: *Oh, Clio's bumped into a friend*.

When Clio tried to remember, later, this is the moment she'll replay again and again.

Hush. Everyone looks up. With a clatter of drums the majorettes come high-stepping down the mall: little girls in fishnet tights and pink satin uniforms, twirling batons. Their families glow with fondness as the girls march by, keeping their chins up, with the smiles they've been working on all week. They *Halt!* beneath a Christmas tree as huge as a space shuttle launcher.

And where is *he*? Not in the concourse any more. He must have found the back stairs, because now he's on the first floor, following the scent that drew him here. There's nothing obvious to show it, unless you count an extra *No Admittance* sign or two, but up here is the *real* thing. This is where the true VIPs will be—not downstairs making small talk with the mayor. The names. They're waiting for their moment to appear and wave like royals from their balcony.

3

He's in the corridor. Now there's only a frosted glass door between him and that glowing inner room. *Celebrity*—so near, he could get a tan from it just standing here . . . And that's when one of Maylene's minders, built like a bull, with iron eyes and no expression, steps forward, blocking the young man's way.

Outside in the crowd, people are holding up placards with '*Maylene We Love You*', or chanting '*Kie-ran, Kie-ran*'. Inside, the famous people notice something slightly wrong. Is there some hitch in the schedule? Suddenly, a scuffle . . . For a moment, the young man has forced himself halfway through the door. He just has time to look around, to take in the faces of the actress and the striker, their make-up artists and wardrobe people and somebody's agent on his mobile phone—then a scrum of minders close in round him, and the CCTV doesn't show him any more.

Three minutes later than advertised, Maylene and Kieran step out to acknowledge the cheers. Whatever Maylene says is lost in echoes but it doesn't matter. She gives her wide, slow, famous smile and throws the switch.

On cue, press cameras swivel upwards. A giant sleigh comes juddering along the wires strung from the second-floor balcony, with its two-dimensional reindeer and three-times-life-size Santa. *Now!* someone whispers backstage, and the lights go out. For a second, there is only the glow-worm green of the Fire Exits, and . . . '*Aaah!*' says everyone as the fairy lights blossom—a dazzle of red, white, and blue.

There is a loud *crack*. Something shudders. For a second people grin, uncertainly, as if it might be fireworks. Then flame rips upwards and, my God, it's not. Outside, the live sound relay cuts out and the crowd can see the glass walls shiver, then come shattering slowly outwards. The tree is a flaming torch already, real fire.

From the long view, over the harbour, the building seems to stagger and recover from the blast. Then, perfectly reflected in the water, it begins to burn.

Dear M . . .

I must be mad to be writing this, like you'll ever read it. But I can't stop the thoughts in my head. That night, that was the beginning . . . and I didn't even know. Did you? Did you even really notice me?

The police came round taking statements — about four hundred, they said, and I must have been number three hundred and ninety-nine, they looked so worn out and fed up. They asked about you. Yes, I said, we chatted — yes, he seemed OK — nothing, you know, strange — I thought he was somebody's friend. And no, I don't remember what we talked about. That's all I can think of, I said. Sorry I can't be more help.

And all the time I was thinking: this is not exactly true. I did remember something. Not what you said, or looked like. (We both know how you could change when you felt like it, shape-shifter!) No, it was in that moment when everybody went on talking round us, mouths moving, words coming out, but where we were it was quiet. The eye of the storm. I didn't say that in my statement.

I don't tell fibs. It's as if my name was a kind of a truth spell Mum and Dad put on me. Clio. <u>Clio-with-an-I-not-an-E.</u> I used to tell people they'd named me after the car, but no: they meant the old Greek Muse, a kind of minor goddess of . . . wait for it — history! I mean, poetry, I

5

could understand — you need a bit of inspiration. But history? That was just the stuff that _happened_. Facts. Me, I could never make things up to keep the grown-ups quiet, like my friends could. I had this thing about it. I'd be found out, something terrible would happen. So the only thing I didn't tell the police, that one small detail, kept on coming back to me. I hadn't told a lie, had I . . . so why did it feel like I had?

Besides, I couldn't have described you. Even now, the more I try to see your face, the more I can't. It's like a blank spot on the film. I know what he meant, that spokesman in the local paper — though everyone thought it was a bad joke at the time . . . 'Somebody's missing,' he said. 'Trouble is, we don't know who.'

2

The M Files

Afterwards, there was no problem finding witnesses who had seen him. Most of them seemed only too glad to talk about it—though quite why, they could not say.

Witness A: the Force Ten security man:
'Yeah, I knew there was something about him, right away. The way he was walking . . . No, he wasn't *running*. Not *as such*. But everyone else was trying to *get* there. Him, he was going in *the opposite direction*. You learn to notice things in this job. My name's Clive, by the way.'

To be honest, Clive had been fed up. The biggest event of the year, and he and his mate Ryan were stuck in the back car park. Ryan was double pissed off because Jade, his little sister, had been showing off her uniform all week—what with her being a majorette, and in the big parade. From out here round the back, he and Clive weren't even going to see the Christmas lights go on, and he was sulking in his hut.

Clive had been gazing out towards the Complex when suddenly he saw this young bloke—fair hair, long coat—coming through the cars, in his direction.

Then the flash. Weird silence after. The first curl of smoke.

'Jesus!' That was Ryan, from the hut. 'What was that?'

But Clive was staring at the figure in the greatcoat. At the sound of the blast the kid had turned, mouth open . . . not in shock, but in a grin, a big grin. As Clive watched, his fist came up—*Ye-es-sss!*—in a little air-punch, like you'd do for a brilliant goal.

That was out of order, Clive thought. That was very wrong.

'Hey, you!'

The kid looked round just as Clive piled into him, ramming him up against a white van. 'Quick,' Clive called to Ryan. 'Get the Bill here. Say we've got one of them.'

'One of who?' Ryan was staring at the orange flicker that was rising now inside the smoke. 'Christ, Jade's in there . . . !'

'One of the bombers,' Clive said. 'That's a sodding *bomb*, you mark my words. Ryan . . . Ryan?' But Ryan was gone, barging his way through people flooding from the building. Family came first, with Ryan. All around, the shouting and the screaming had begun.

Clive held on. He wrenched the boy's arm up behind his back, like he'd learned in the Territorials. But the kid wasn't struggling. He had a smooth kind of face— the sort your mate's kid brother might have. He didn't look like a bomber. Then again, Clive thought, the clever ones wouldn't, would they, and he jerked the arm again.

The kid gasped, then he sort of . . . smiled. 'Bomb? Did you say *bomb* . . . ? Why not?' As cool as anything. Something about this kid felt not quite right to Clive. People react to the sight of a uniform, even if it's only Force Ten. Some of them get lippy, most go cowed and meek, but this one . . . ? He was *watching*—the way you watch a film you're not sure you're going to stay up for—giving it the benefit of the doubt. It was doing Clive's head in, and he nearly punched him, but lights were flashing round them: the cops had arrived. Later, Clive tried to tell them about the feeling, but all they wanted was facts. When the local press caught up, a little later still, Clive told them again and again.

Witness B: the policewoman:

When WPC Dawn Grey reached the pair by the white van, she thought: we're wasting our time. She'd never had much time for these Force Ten cowboys—failed crooks or bent ex-coppers, mostly. It only took a glance to see excessive force was being used. 'OK, I'll see to him now,' she said.

The boy's nose was bleeding slightly from one corner. He was shaken, all right, but no structural damage. As he looked up she clicked through a description in her mind: *white male—late teens—fair hair (longer than average)—black coat (long)—white silk scarf (posh affectation)—middle class look (student, question mark)* . . .

'Well,' she said, 'you got yourself into a spot of bother.'

Usually at this point people launched into the accusations and excuses, or they clammed up. This young man looked at her with a shrug and smile.

'Watch him!' the Force Ten man shouted behind her. 'That's your frigging bomber!'

A crowd was forming. 'Hold it right there,' WPC Grey said, loud enough for everyone to hear, 'We have no, repeat *no*, information about any bomb.'

Bomb! The word went round the crowd in whispers. 'Please move along,' she said. 'There's nothing to see.'

Her pocket radio crackled. 'Yes,' she said. 'Soon as we can.' Somewhere, a new set of sirens—fire, or ambulance—cut through the hubbub. And the young man watched her, head on one side, his very pale eyes hardly blinking, taking it all in.

'This man says he saw you acting suspiciously . . . *Running away from the scene*, in fact.'

All round them cars were revving, people calling to each other, weeping out loud as they walked. The young man didn't raise his voice at all. As WPC Grey leaned towards him, it was as if they'd ducked beneath the surface of the noise.

'I wasn't running,' he said.

'Where were you going?'

'Nowhere. I'd had enough, that's all.'

'Had enough . . . Just before the opening, right? The moment everyone was waiting for?'

'Yes, but I'm not *everyone*.' It should have been cheeky, but he said it like a simple fact. 'I couldn't get in.'

The radio crackled again. 'Look, you'd better beat it,' she said.

'Wait . . .' He hadn't moved. 'I did see something. Two men, by the loading bay . . .'

That stopped her.

'Probably coincidence,' he went on. 'They stopped and sort of looked both ways. Then the bomb . . . Sorry, *explosion*.'

'These men . . . could you describe them?'

'It was dark. I'd have to think.'

The radio crackled, losing patience. WPC Grey glanced at the squad car officers who'd just arrived. 'Better get this one to the station,' she said. 'Just in case.' And then the press arrived.

There was a rush of questions, all together. The word *bomb* was in most of them. 'No comment,' she said, as the flashbulbs flickered. In the prints they published later, the young man was clearly visible behind the WPC's back. He held his face up boldly and, depending how you looked at it, that half-raised hand could have been shielding his eyes, or it could have been a small clenched-fist salute.

* * *

10

'Within the last few minutes, police have refused to confirm or deny that they are holding a youth in connection with the suspected terrorist incident at the opening of the multi-million-pound Harbourside Complex. Emergency staff have been drafted in to Milbourne General Hospital to deal with injuries from burns and broken glass. A spokesman said it was a miracle that no deaths had occurred. Concern has focused on international football star Kieran Scott, rushed to hospital with cuts to his right leg. It is not yet known if he will be fit to appear in next week's game against Portugal. Meanwhile actress Cara Sanderton is understood to have been allowed home, but is said by close friends to be in shock. Police have issued a number for relatives to . . .'

Witness C: the social worker:

The first thing Stella Horton heard was the newsflash, as she soaked away a day's stress in the bath. It was her evening for herself: Toby was at his father's overnight and if she wanted to lie back and sip a small Bacardi in the bubbles, why not? It was the word *Milbourne* on the radio caught her attention, that and the grave tone of voice. Stella sat up. They were talking as if it was Milbourne's 9/11. For a second she caught herself thinking she could go and take a look, then frowned at the thought. She couldn't stand the kind of ghouls who stare at accidents and fights. Stella lay back. Be honest: did she care if Kieran Scott missed the game? Years ago she'd had a rather special holiday in Portugal. Stella rather hoped they would win.

It was after midnight when the phone went. 'Nnnn?' she said, reaching for the bedside table. It was Dawn's voice—her voice in uniform, as WPC Grey.

'Look, Stel,' her friend said quickly. 'I'm really sorry, but we need some help here. An emergency.'

'I heard. Sounds like you need firemen, not social workers. I was asleep . . .'

'It's a bit unusual. We're holding this kid.'

'I'm not on call, Dawn. Where's his parents?'

'Search me. Nothing on him—no papers, no ID. Can't trace parents, teachers, care workers, anyone. They're already trying Missing Persons. Thing is: he keeps saying he's eighteen—I'm not convinced—if he's not, and if he doesn't have an *appropriate adult* with him—you know, PACE procedures . . . Get that wrong, they'll string us up in court.'

Stella groaned. She was awake now, hopelessly. 'Why me?'

'This one bothers me, Stel. You see, I brought him in, volunteering evidence. Volunteering. And suddenly . . . they're saying he's *confessed*.' At Dawn's end, the background clatter of the station went muffled. Dawn was shielding the handset, speaking close and low. 'I don't know what they did to him, Stel. He seems a decent kid. Bit smooth, but bright. He's no bomber.'

'*Bomber?* So it's true, then?'

'Look, I can't talk. They've got Anti-Terrorist Branch people on their way from London. This kid's got to have an adult with him—someone respectable—someone not connected with the police. If you won't do it, they could get anybody . . . some retired colonel who'll sign his name to anything they do.'

'I'm out of my league here, Dawn . . .' There was an awkward silence. Even down the phone, two miles away, Stella could see the look on Dawn's face. She knew what her best friends always said: *That's your problem, Stella: you just can't say No.*

And she couldn't say No.

Witness D: Clio:

A light came on and glimmered through the trees at the end of the garden. Clio gazed out. No one's sleeping

12

tonight, she thought. That light was Mrs Horton's, Stella's, where she went to babysit. Toby must have had one of his dreams: he was scared of the dark. Not Clio; she liked it. Some nights, when things got a bit much—too much school, too much Mum and Dad, too much friends, even—she would stand with the bedroom window open so she could feel the cool air on her face. If she was still she could hear the sounds of after-midnight—little rustles in the darkness, now and then a yelp or hiss. Just the week before a thin fox had limped across the garden, looking greyish in the moonlight, and though Clio kept very still it seemed to stop and look in her direction.

A tap on her door . . . When Clio didn't answer, her mum came in anyway.

'Clio, darling, you must get some sleep. Try to put it all out of your mind.'

'I'm fine, Mum.'

'It was terrible,' her mum went on, as if she hadn't heard. 'Just think . . . No, don't. You mustn't dwell on it.' Clio bit her lip. Why did people, mothers especially, always think they could see inside your head?

'It wasn't *that* bad. It happened really quickly—like a fire drill at school, except there *was* a fire, that's all.'

'Oh God, when I think about it . . . You're a lucky girl, you know that.'

'I know.'

'Won't you lie down? You look pale. I'll get you a nice hot drink. Or . . . I've got some pills I take when I can't sleep.'

'Thanks, Mum, but I'm fine, really I am. I'll get into bed in a minute, promise. *You* should get some sleep.'

'Well . . .' Her mother backed off. 'If you're sure . . .' She stopped in the doorway. 'I don't mean to fuss. It's just that . . . well, you're very special. You know that, don't you?'

'Of course, Mum. I love you too.'

'I know. Night night. And close that window. You'll catch your death.'

'Yes, Mum . . .' But the window stayed open, and she didn't move.

She was special. That was what people had said for as long as she could remember: special and lucky . . . She had a lot to be grateful for. Sometimes, she thought, a bit too much. At the end of the garden, the light in Stella's house went out. Toby must be asleep. Clio gazed out, listening, and wondered where the hungry fox would sleep tonight.

3

An Appropriate Adult

'Shouldn't you be home in bed?' said the young man in the holding room.

Wait a minute, thought Stella. *I* should be saying that to *him*. She did not know where to begin.

How old was he? Young, said his face—smooth, not an adolescent spot in sight. His hair was so fine it was almost white. His body language, though . . . He leaned back and swivelled to face her, like somebody in the media business, used to granting interviews.

The PC by the door looked on, impassive.

What am I doing here? Stella wondered. This boy wasn't a terrorist. He didn't look like someone who'd had a confession beaten out of him, either. In fact, he looked rather at home.

'Sorry,' he said. 'Didn't mean to be rude. They keep saying I've got to have somebody *with me*, don't know why. But thanks.' He smiled. 'You're allowed to sit down.'

'Thanks.' Stella fingered the papers she'd been given by the sergeant at the desk. *The Role of the Appropriate Adult.* She wished she'd stopped to read them before she came in. 'Uh . . . You know you don't have to say anything if you don't want to . . . er . . . and any time you want to talk to me alone, you've got a right to . . . and . . .'

15

Her little speech trailed off. What a difference it made, she thought, being in your teens or your late thirties. When had *she* last looked that fresh in the small hours? The young man's eyes were clear, and . . . it was hard to say what colour—slightly greenish, slightly grey? When they met hers he didn't blink.

'Would *you* like to?' he said.

'Sorry?'

'Talk for a bit on our own.'

Stella looked at the PC by the door. Without betraying that he'd listened to a word, he put one hand on the doorknob. 'Yes,' she said. 'I think I would.'

'Do you think they've got this place bugged?' said the boy as the door closed. 'I would, if I was doing an inter-rogation.'

'I don't think *interrogation*'s quite the word.' Stella had a sneaking feeling that he might be right about the bugging. He didn't look bothered.

'Call me Max,' he said. 'Good to meet you, Stella.'

'Mrs Horton.'

'Sorry. I was talking to your friend Dawn. She's nice. I'll call you Mrs Horton if you like.'

'No, no, it's OK. Have you got everything you need?'

He shrugged.

'They said you didn't have anything with you—no bag or anything.'

'I had a bit of bother earlier—got mugged by some blokes in an alley. Don't get me wrong, I can look after myself, I know a bit of kung fu—but they nicked my bag.'

'Have you told the police?'

'It doesn't matter. Didn't want to waste their time. Oh, and another thing . . .' He leaned closer and lowered his voice. 'You know I confessed?' He paused.

'Yes . . . ?'

'Well, it's true. I did it. As simple as that. This isn't a frame-up. Do you want to go home now?'

'No . . . I mean: I don't get it.'

'There's nothing to get. Were you *there*, at the Opening?'

Stella shook her head, with just the slightest wrinkling of her nose. He noticed.

'Uh-huh . . .' he said. 'Not your kind of thing?'

'It's just shops, for heaven's sake! Same old chains, same old brand names, just like everywhere else in the world. And as for Maylene . . .'

'She's a bitch.'

'You met her?'

'Oh, yes, I dropped in at the party. But I didn't stay.' He chuckled, and she found that she was chuckling too. Somebody tapped at the door.

'Look,' said Stella quickly. 'There must be someone I can contact for you. Mum and Dad? No? Friends, then? Oh, come on, there must be. Just so I can tell them not to worry.' She dropped her voice. 'I don't have to tell the police.' He smiled to himself, as if he'd won a private bet.

'What are they saying on TV?' he said. 'Did we make the national news?'

'For God's sake . . .' said Stella. 'This isn't a game. The police are taking this very seriously. They've got someone coming from the Anti-Terrorist Branch.'

'I know,' he said. 'Detective Inspector Wayland. That'll be because I mentioned the Angry Brigade.' Stella fished in her mind. The words brought back something . . . when? Way back, in the 1970s. Even *she'd* been a child at the time.

The knock at the door was firmer this time.

'What do you mean, the Angry Brigade?' said Stella. 'You weren't even born then . . .'

'Sounds like time's up.' He got to his feet. In the doorway, he turned. 'I *know* it isn't a game, believe me.'

Raised voices met them in the corridor. At the desk, the sergeant was trying to make himself heard above a hubbub of reporters. *No comment . . . No comment* again . . . Max headed towards the crowd but two constables moved in, steering him the other way. Dawn took Stella to one side. 'Did you get anything out of him? About his parents? Did he mention . . . Swindon?'

One look at Stella's face gave her the answer. 'Oh, never mind. But before you go in, Stel, there's something else you ought to know.'

He was a big man, DI Wayland. He sat in his big chair like a man carved out of stone. He had a weathered look, as if he'd waited in that chair for thirty years and could wait another thirty if that's what it took.

'The Angry Brigade . . .' he mused to the ceiling. 'Nasty bunch of cranks and misfits—playing at *urban guerrillas*, as I recall. Hmm . . . But that's ancient history. A bit like me . . .' His gaze snapped back to Max. 'Read a lot of history books, do we, sonny? Study Modern Crackpot Politics at your posh school?' He was twisting something in his big hands. Stella thought it was a white silk scarf.

She looked at Max. In the holding room he'd seemed grown-up, *in possession* of himself. He hadn't needed her. Now, beside the granite Wayland, he looked fragile. Sensitive, thought Stella. She imagined Toby, a dozen years on, sitting where Max was sitting. She would be there for him, whatever he'd done. Where were this boy's family?

And another thing . . . She could hardly bear to sit and watch. She needed to ask him something—about

18

Swindon. She wanted him to say the story Dawn told her just now wasn't true.

Wayland held them in a long pause. The recorder was whirring. The words of the caution had been spoken ten minutes ago. Since then, he and Max had been sparring, just limbering up, while a couple of officers stood by each door, just in case. Now the interview was under way for real.

'Everything you've said so far,' said DI Wayland, 'is in print somewhere. Quite easy to find it, for someone like you—bright . . . bad attitude . . . Internet access . . . time on his hands. A waste of education, I call it.'

Max didn't argue—just looked back at him.

'Oh, come on,' said Wayland. 'What's in it for you? I mean, pretty inoffensive affair, wasn't it? Bit of a party for the kiddies, a few fairy lights, dressing up . . .'

'Window dressing,' Max said. 'It's just shops, for heaven's sake. Same old chains, same old brand names, just like everywhere else in the world.'

Stella felt as if the whole room turned her way, though no one moved. Those were *her* words. Wayland gave a contemptuous grunt. 'Give me patience,' he said to himself. 'Look, kiddo, the one thing we know about you is that you tell porkies. First, that cock-and-bull about the two men in the loading bay . . . Then when no one can corroborate your story suddenly it's the Angry Brigade. You tell me: why have I come all the way from London just to listen to this stuff?'

'No reason,' said the young man, mildly. 'I confessed. That's all there is to say.'

'Maybe,' said Wayland. 'Maybe not. Tell me something I don't know already—anything, go on—just to make my journey not a waste of petrol.'

Max frowned, thinking. 'OK . . . The Stoke Newington Nine . . .'

'Eight,' Wayland said.

'Nine. With the one who wasn't mentioned at the trial. The one you didn't get.'

'Hold it, kiddo.' Wayland was paying attention now, all right. 'If you're winding me up . . .'

'Excuse me,' Max said, articulating clearly for the tape machine. 'That's my scarf you're twisting in your hands.'

Wayland glanced at the recorder and threw down the scarf. 'I don't like people playing games with me—spoiled brats in particular. I don't take kindly to it.'

'Excuse me.' Stella's voice came out fainter than she'd hoped. 'I don't think you should . . .'

'Excuse *me* . . .' said DI Wayland, massively. 'And who are *you* in this investigation?'

'I . . . I'm . . .' Stella clutched her little wad of papers. *The Role of the Appropriate Adult* seemed very flimsy suddenly.

Then the door opened, and a plain-clothes officer slipped in: 'Sir . . .'

'Not now, man. Can't you see we're interviewing?'

'Sir . . . It's urgent. It could make a difference.'

'It had better,' Wayland muttered. 'Concluding recording, 02.43.' Click. 'Well?'

Nobody breathed as the two men put their heads together. 'What . . . ?' A long pause. Wayland's face darkened, all the creases in it deepening. He let a long breath out through clenched teeth. 'Right! Somebody . . .' He scanned the room. '*Somebody's* going to sweat for this.' He heaved himself up. 'Just get that little liar out of here . . . before I knock his bloody head off. And make sure he goes down for Wasting Police Time, top whack. Now, I'm going home to bed.'

* * *

'So it wasn't a bomb,' said Clio's mother. 'One moment it is, next moment it isn't. You can't believe a thing you're told, these days.'

The smell of fresh coffee had drawn Clio in from the garden, and she waited, listening, just outside the breakfast room. There was Mum, in full flow. Now she'd got over imagining Clio dead among the rubble she was telling the story to anyone and everyone, as if she'd been there herself.

'Yeah, well . . .' Her father leaned back, with his knowing look. 'It all sounds a wee bit too convenient to me. Sorry, some builder just left an oxyacetylene cylinder on the scaffolding, and who should come along and knock it off but Santa!'

'You know what these contractors are like. Everyone knew they were doing the job on the cheap.'

'Even so . . . I'm just saying it's *convenient*. Terrorism's bad for business. You bet the powers-that-be in Milbourne pulled some strings. What do you think, Stella?'

Stella cradled another black coffee. She wasn't coping well with last night's lost sleep. 'Me? I was just glad it let that poor lad off the hook. They were starting to get really heavy on him.'

'Hmmm,' said Clio's father. 'He sounds like an odd case to me. I wouldn't waste my *poor lad* on him.'

'He's not a criminal, though, is he?' Clio came in.

'Oh, hi, Clio love,' said Stella. 'Your mum says you were *there*, at the Opening.' Not for the first time, Stella smiled at the contrasts of this family—Jen, tall and angular . . . Mike, like a rather balding cherub . . . and Clio. The changeling. She was something else again. 'Poor you,' said Stella. 'You weren't hurt, were you?'

'No. It wasn't as bad as they're saying.'

'She's playing it down,' said her mother. 'She won't say, but apparently she was a real hero—broken glass

21

everywhere, and the fire, and she was cool as a cucumber, shepherding the young ones out.'

'Oh, *Mum* . . .'

'Now you've embarrassed her,' said her dad. As if that helped. He gave her that grin that grown-ups called *boyish*, for some reason, and went through to the kitchen.

'What did they do with him?' Clio said to Stella. 'That boy . . .'

'Charged him with wasting police time. He's in Moncrieff Road.'

'What's that—a prison?' said Clio.

'A kind of children's home—where they put the . . .'

'. . . the real tough nuts and losers.' Her dad poked his head round the door. 'They'll make mincemeat of him in that place.'

Stella winced. 'It's true. He's not a yob. He's kind of . . . nice.'

'That's awful,' said Clio. 'Can't they send him home?'

'That's just it—they can't. The address he gave—in Swindon—was a dead end. Dawn told me, at the police station. Nobody knows where he's from.'

'Don't you believe it,' said her father. 'No one's untraceable these days. All these surveillance cameras, Missing Persons, data bases, DNA. You're well out of it, Stella. More coffee?'

'Thanks. In fact . . . I did wonder, maybe, if I'd go and see him. Just to make sure he's OK.'

'Oh, Stella!' said Mum. 'You're impossible. Any lame duck, you'll be on the case!'

'It's *kind* of Stella,' Clio said firmly. 'If he hasn't got a family . . .' But her dad was making that noise with the espresso maker, so no one heard. Clio went up to her room. She hoped Stella would come up after her, so they could have a word alone. But the grown-ups stayed with their coffee, talking parent business.

Clio lay on her bed and clamped her headphones on. She turned up the volume and bass. Deep in her head a rapper launched into some serious attitude—not that Clio was exactly listening. She was in a place she liked to go to sometimes. Even her friends would think it was weird if she told them what it felt like . . . Peaceful. Calm. She turned the music up loud, loud, and she went down into it, under the storm on the surface, into a place like an underwater cave.

She pulled a pillow over her eyes, so it was dark. Yes, there were pictures of the other evening in her mind— not the kind her mum expected. Maybe these would have worried her more. What Clio saw was rather jolly, like a cartoon, and it made her smile: a naff plastic Santa with a big black cartoon BOMB in his hands. Behind him, riding pillion on the sleigh, was a young man in a long black coat. *Boom*: there was a sound like cheering. Everything went up in flames.

4

Changelings

S tella had a lot of time for Clio.

What a pity, she thought, that Clio was an only child, what with Mike and Jen being older than most parents—but Stella had been a kind of auntie to her, and Clio had practically adopted Toby as her baby brother. Stella liked her—for all the reasons grown-ups liked her, plus a few that other people rarely saw.

Clio had her moods—no shouting and stamping, more as if a thundercloud was passing by inside her eyes. Dark, with flickers of lightning. Then her eyebrows pulled together with that changeling look. Yes, Stella liked her spirit.

'What are you thinking?' Stella would ask her sometimes, and Clio would just smile. Stella liked that too. As for Toby . . . he thought Clio was wonderful. Children that age have an instinct. They know who they can trust.

So when the phone went, late one evening, and there was this hesitant voice—'Hello, it's me'—sort of faint and awkward, Stella was alert at once. She's in some kind of trouble, Stella thought. That didn't completely surprise her. It was a good family—Stella had seen enough of the other kind to know the difference. There couldn't be many adoptive parents who had worked as hard at it as Jen and Mike, and the girl had responded well—just a little too well, maybe. It would be almost a relief to have some proper teenage ructions.

'What is it, Clio, love?'

'I just thought . . . You know you were talking about that boy, at the police station . . . You said you were going to see him . . .'

'I did—I went this lunchtime. Is something the matter?'

'I just wondered . . . Was he all right?'

'He's fine.'

'Honestly? The way Dad was talking, I thought . . .'

'Well . . . To tell the truth, I *was* a bit concerned . . .'

To tell the truth, Stella had been more than a bit concerned. It might not be a prison, Moncrieff Road . . . but everyone behaved as if it was. The kids she had passed in the corridor didn't speak or meet her eyes. They could spot a social worker at a hundred paces. She could feel them watching her behind her back.

Max had been in the tiny library. *Out of harm's way*, the care worker said. *Search me why we've got him here. It's not as if he's, well, DONE anything, has he?*

At her first sight of him Stella felt her stomach sink. It was the way he whipped round to see who was behind him. This wasn't the self-assured young man of the other evening, but a slightly-built boy who could never have been one of the tough ones in his year at school. *Kung fu*, he'd said. She wasn't sure she believed that.

'This isn't an official visit,' Stella said when they were alone. 'Are you OK?'

Max shrugged. 'Well . . . there's the clothes they give you, for a start. Where do they *get* this stuff?'

'Be serious. Are they giving you a hard time?'

'The staff are OK.'

Enough said, thought Stella. 'I'm sorry,' she said.

'Look, tell me to mind my own business, but . . . why not just give the police a name and address, then they can let you out of here.'

'I *gave* them an address.'

'That's the other thing,' said Stella. 'The people in Swindon—Mr and Mrs Turner. They're not your parents, are they?'

He was watching her with his head on one side slightly, like a blackbird watching for a worm. 'Well . . . no. I *did* live there.'

'They were very upset, Max. You remember Dawn—the WPC. She contacted them. When Mrs Turner answered the phone, and Dawn said, *We've got Max Turner here* . . . the poor woman broke down in tears. You know why . . . ? I think you do. Max Turner . . . their Max . . . They said he died years ago, when he was little. Max Turner isn't your real name.'

'I didn't say it was. I said they were, well, *like* parents to me. The police misunderstood.'

For a moment she almost believed him. 'Anyway, it's not my fault,' he said. 'Mrs Turner got this thing about me, being the age her Max would have been, and the name . . .'

'So you *are* Max, at least.' Oh please, thought Stella, let *some* of it be true.

'Of course. Max . . . Tyler. Sounded similar, I suppose. That must be what started her off.'

'Mr Turner told Dawn you'd . . . strung them along . . . talked your way into his wife's affections.'

'He *would* say that. They never talked to *each other*. She kept giving me things. It seemed sort of cruel not to go along with it, when they'd been kind. I needed a place to stay.'

'And before that? The address you gave the Turners . . . the police say it doesn't exist.'

26

He shrugged. 'I moved around a bit. What were *you* like at my age?' he said. 'You weren't a good girl, were you?'

God, was it written on her face still, after twenty years? 'At least I was at school,' she said.

'School? I'm in a gap year,' he said. 'A gap year or two.'

She studied his face. 'You're not eighteen, are you? I know what you told the police but . . . come on.'

'Age doesn't matter.'

'Of course it does. Legally . . .'

'It doesn't matter to me. I just don't like being treated like a kid. Anyway, I've done A-levels. High flyer—did them early. Four As and a B.'

Somehow that B had made a difference. Besides, Stella felt suddenly weary. 'I *want* to believe you. What can we do about . . .' She had looked around the dingy institution room. '. . . all this?'

'Have you got a spare room?' he'd said, innocently.

Stella hadn't meant to tell Clio quite so much. It just came out. She realized with a jolt that they'd been half an hour on the phone.

'Did you say yes, then?' said Clio.

'No, no . . . But, well . . . I thought about it. Don't tell your mother. Anyway, the police wouldn't wear it. The terrorism man from London, he's coming down to talk to him again.'

'Poor Max,' said Clio softly, and Stella had an uneasy feeling.

'You don't *know* him, do you?' Stella said.

'N-no,' said Clio. 'Not exactly. I did talk to him that night.'

'At the Complex? You talked to *him*?'

'I talked to lots of people. It was that sort of evening—everybody asking you questions, all fake friendly, and not listening to the answers.' She paused. '*He* listened.'

'I see . . .'

'The thing is . . . Stella, I've heard everything you've said about him but I know, I just know somehow, he's *all right*. If he's told some lies, there's bound to be a reason. He might need help.'

'That's what I've been thinking,' Stella said. 'I suppose I hoped he'd trust me.'

'He won't,' said Clio. 'I mean, nothing personal. *I* trust you. But most people my age—specially if they've had bad things happen in their lives—they won't really talk to anybody over twenty.'

It was a moment before Stella saw where this was leading.

'If he could talk to someone more his own age . . .' said Clio, 'he might open up. And that would be a good thing, wouldn't it? That's what you've always told me.' A pause. 'What I mean is: if he talked to *somebody like me* . . . ?'

Apart from the first time she went to babysit, Clio had never felt nervous outside Stella's house before. She hoped Stella wouldn't ask her if she'd told her parents. She'd been about to, really, but they'd both been busy. She could tell them later—afterwards. When they couldn't say no.

The staff at the Home had agreed quite easily to Stella's proposal. The boy would only be out for an hour or two, and she *was* a professional. It wasn't quite regular, but nothing felt regular about this case. The kid was an enigma—to put it another way, he was a bloody liability. The police said they were following up leads in Swindon but it was dead end after dead end, and (the sergeant said, privately) what did it really matter any more?

'Oh, Clio, hi! This *is* a nice surprise.' Stella was in jeans and a sweatshirt, looking almost young, the way grown-ups try to at weekends. Sometimes Clio wished her parents, with their grey hairs, wouldn't try. Stella managed it better than most.

This is a nice surprise . . . Clio noticed that. So Stella hadn't told Max she was coming. Grown-ups can tell white lies too.

They went into the sitting room, and there were Max and Toby on the sofa, deep in a story. Max's hair fell forward, hiding his face. Toby looked spellbound.

'So there I was lying in my tent,' Max was saying, 'keeping very very still . . . because I could hear it outside . . . *breathing* . . .'

'What? What was it?'

'I didn't know. All I could do was lie there and hold my breath—like this. Are you holding your breath?'

Toby puffed out his cheeks and nodded.

'. . . and it went prowling round the tent . . . and round . . . and round . . .'

'Was it . . . a *tiger*?' Toby breathed out. 'A real tiger?'

'I wasn't going to poke my head out to see, was I? All I know is, when I looked out in the morning . . . Oh, hello!' He glanced up and caught sight of Clio. He flicked back his hair, and there was that grey-green gaze, like water. 'Hi,' he said, 'we've met before.' As if she could have forgotten.

It wasn't so much the face . . . He wasn't a boy-band pin-up, Clio thought, any more than she was a supermodel. It was what happened when he *looked* at you. And when he said 'Hi' in that voice, it felt as if no one else was in the room but you and him.

29

'Clio!' Toby leaped into her arms, cuddling fiercely. 'Max saw a *tiger*. Almost. It was in a tent. In India.'

'Oh, I think that was a story,' said Stella.

Max raised one eyebrow. 'It could have been a leopard,' he conceded. 'Tigers are quite rare.' Toby cupped Clio's ear in his hands.

'Max is nice!' he said in a deafening whisper.

It was not until Stella brought out the iced buns that she and Max got to talk. 'Are you OK?' she said.

'Me? Fine. Why? Nice cakes.'

'Stella said you were in a bit of trouble.'

'Aha. So it's not just a *nice surprise*, you dropping by!' He grinned. He had been listening. 'I knew we'd meet again.' He dropped to his knees by the coffee table, spreading out newspapers. 'Stella's been showing me these. We're big news.'

'That's not difficult,' Stella said drily. 'Small place, Milbourne.'

'*Why?*' said Clio, so abruptly that the others stared. She couldn't help it: it had been on her mind all day. 'Why did you do it?'

'Clio, love . . . he *didn't* do it,' Stella said.

'Yes, but he said he did. That's . . . weird.'

Stella made a nervous sound, but Max wasn't looking at her. Clio had his attention, every bit of it. 'I didn't start it,' he said. 'People think what they want to think, don't they? I just let them. Anyway, it *might* have been a bomb. I didn't know . . .'

'More bun,' said Toby in the background.

'That's the last piece now,' said Stella. 'No,' she said to Clio. 'I don't get it either.'

'Yes, you do,' said Max. Clio stared. That was the kind of thing that grown-ups get offended by. But Stella didn't seem to take offence. 'The whole thing was just brand names . . .' he went on. 'You said it yourself.'

'More bun, PLEASE!' said Toby.

'And all that glass . . .' Max turned to Clio. 'The lights . . . The place was asking for it—like saying *Come and get me*.'

'People got hurt,' said Clio.

'Like Kieran Scott? His grazed knee?'

'Ordinary people. Children. It said in the paper that a girl got burned.' It came out sharper than she'd meant . . . Max looked at Clio with a new respect.

'Sure,' he said, 'you're right . . . *You* weren't hurt, anyway. I'm glad about that.'

'What about *you*? You could have gone to jail *for life*.'

'Oh . . . life,' he said quietly, so quietly that Stella might have missed it. Clio didn't. She would think about it often, later on. 'That stuff,' he said, and he shrugged.

'More BUN!'

Stella scooped Toby up high and rubbed his nose with her nose, till he giggled. She was good like that. She whispered something in his ear. When she put him down, he sidled up to Clio. 'Mum says I've got *bunson-thebrain*,' he said, with an eye on the uneaten one on Clio's plate.

'We'll soon see about that,' Max said. His dark moment had passed and he launched into a ridiculous accent. 'I ham ze expert on zese things.' He bent alongside Toby, peering in his ear. He had the timing of a professional children's entertainer. 'Now . . .' He moved a hand on the other side of Toby's head. 'Ve just apply ze magic schnuffler.' *Puff*. As he blew in the ear, Toby jumped, and Max brought his other hand round with a bun in it. Toby hesitated, not sure whether to be worried, then he glanced down at Clio's plate—no bun—then back at the hand.

'He's magic,' said Clio, and Toby hooted with laughter.

'Max is *funny*,' he announced to the room.

They were a picture, the boy and the girl and Toby, laughing, easy and relaxed. Stella watched them from the kitchen door. For the first time, she realized what a striking young woman Clio was going to be. Those dark eyes and eyebrows, wide lips, pale-dark skin like someone built for living in a shady courtyard in a hotter climate . . . all the things people called *interesting* while they talked about her *personality* and *lovely hair* . . . People were going to get a surprise.

Why hadn't she seen it before? Maybe because it had only just happened—like the flick of a switch—in front of Stella's very eyes.

'All right, Toby. One last piece,' Stella said. She looked from Clio to this strange young man, as fair as she was dark, and she saw that they looked good together. Stella wondered what on earth she had begun.

5

Small Earthquake in China

A line of rain moved in from the Channel that night. It snuffed out the lights of container ships far out to sea. It crossed the ridge of Watchman's Down and moved along the Spit, the finger of sand and stones that sheltered Milbourne Harbour. The white and red lights on the masts of boats blurred and vanished. On the harbourside, plastic sheeting flapped on the damaged Complex, waiting for the lawsuits and insurance claims, as a gust of rain swabbed away the burnt smell.

Clio woke from a dream in which something clattered at the window, like a handful of grit, like someone trying to get her attention, outside in the dark. She sat up and parted the curtains. Of course, it was rain.

She never understood why people grumbled at the weather. She thought of the black clouds as living, travelling things, a whole caravan of them, nomads going somewhere across sea and land. She imagined them passing down the empty High Street, over trading estates and all-night service stations, straight through multi-storey car parks in the way they say ghosts walk through walls.

As for meeting Max at Stella's house, Clio hadn't made a *secret* of it. She just . . . didn't say. She hadn't wanted to worry them. *How was Stella?* Mum had asked casually, and Clio said *Oh, fine* and that was that. She thought round her school friends, one by one. She imagined them laughing, not unkindly: *Do you fancy him, then?* And she'd be saying, *No, no, that's not what I mean*, but they'd be turning to each other: *Hey, Clio's got a boyfriend. About time, too.*

But it wouldn't be true. She knew about fancying people . . . and this wasn't it. She was not even sure she *liked* Max. But the sound of the rain made her think of him now.

Out in the garden everything was dark and glittering. The line of rain had moved on. Was Max awake? Would he have heard it? What would he be thinking? She imagined him sitting on a hard bed in that prison place, looking out of a little barred window and suddenly, for no reason he could tell, remembering her.

Interviewer: *The remarkable thing about the Milbourne incident is the way the damage to the multi-million-pound leisure complex has been overshadowed by the media coverage of one young man—you. Does this surprise you?*

Max: *Not much. But it's ironic, isn't it? I understand the celebrities are pretty gutted, too.*

Interviewer: *We'll have shorter items about Cara Sanderton and Kieran Scott a little later in the programme. Max Tyler, the main controversy of the last few days has been whether you were an innocent bystander unsuccessfully framed by the police or—I have to ask this—an anarchist bomber released in an effort to cover up the nature of the incident. Can you put the record straight? Are you in fact a member of this . . . New Angry Brigade?*

Max: *Yes and no, definitely. This time last week the New Angry Brigade didn't exist. Now I'm sure there will be more attacks.*

34

Interviewer: *But—correct me—the police assure us that this wasn't a terrorist incident.*

Max: *You just don't get it, do you? This is an attack by the New Angries whether or not it really happened. The fact that there wasn't a bomb just shows how clever we are. We could strike anywhere, anytime . . .*

[Dear M . . . I can't make out your writing here — it's as if you were writing faster and faster, trying to get down the voices you were hearing in your mind. Then, later . . .]

Interviewer: *And you? You face a hefty sentence for Wasting Police Time.*

Max: *Wasting their time? I was very co-operative. I gave them everything they wanted. Anyway, I expect a public campaign to prove my innocence to be launched any day.*

Interviewer: *You mean: Free the Milbourne One?*

Max: *(modestly) You said it.*

Interviewer: *Mr Tyler, thank you for agreeing to talk to us tonight.*

'I don't like it,' said Stella. Clio knew when Stella was feeling edgy: she started tugging the ends of her hair. 'I don't like it, any of it,' Stella said, 'not the police, not Moncrieff Road, not this idea of yours, Clio. We both know what your parents would say.'

'They'd say we should try and help Max. They'd say what he was doing was a *cry for help*. They'd say putting him in some horrible Young Offenders' place would mess up his life for good. At least, that's what they'd say if they weren't getting worked up about *me* . . .' She leaned over and touched Stella's hand. 'I'm OK. *He's* the one with the problem. I just need to talk to him properly.'

35

Stella sighed. 'And if your dad knew you'd met him *here*?'

'Somewhere else, then. Moncrieff Road?' Clio saw the look on Stella's face. 'OK, silly idea. In a café, then. That one with gardens at the back—the Rockery—you know, I pass it coming home from school.' Stella still looked uneasy. She hadn't said *No*, right out, though, Clio noted. That tended to mean it would be a *Yes* in the end—just ask Toby.

'You saw how he was chilling out the other afternoon,' Clio pressed on. 'Half an hour of that and he'll be talking. That would be a good thing, wouldn't it?'

Stella nodded, cautiously.

'Well,' said Clio, 'I've got the last period off tomorrow—careers evening at school. So if you just happened to be in the café with him, about three . . . and I just happened to come by . . . ?'

Stella had that weary smile she wore when Toby was about to get his iced bun. 'Thanks,' said Clio and gave her a hug. 'You're a real friend. Sometimes I think that you're the only grown-up in the world who listens.'

Dear M,

I read about this place — I think it was in China — where there was an earthquake. Just a village in the country, getting on with country things. Then suddenly everything goes quiet. Like everything's stopped. People look at each other, saying, what's that sound? But it isn't a sound — it's silence. There's no wind. All the birds stop singing, they drop from the skies, hide in the bushes, very still. Next thing, all the animals go strange and restless — pigs barging at their pens, water buffalo trying to break free from their ploughs. All in this weird stillness.

A few minutes later, the earthquake . . .

I don't know if it's true — I read it in some rubbish magazine, in the doctor's waiting room. But I know what they meant, about that feeling. It was like that in the last few hours of school that afternoon before I met you. That hush in the air.

I couldn't have told anybody. They'd have given me a funny look: Clio, that's really <u>weird</u> . . .

I could have told you, if you'd been there. But you'd have probably told me how you'd been in an earthquake in Uzbekistan or somewhere, something massive on the Richter scale . . . and I'd have half believed you.

It doesn't matter. You <u>were</u> an earthquake, do you know that?

I think you did. I think you do.

'You came back,' said Max.

Clio had hoped he would sound a little more surprised. Around them, the Rockery gardens were empty and brownish with the wet leaves underfoot. In summer little kids would be swarming all over, playing at wild things round the bushes, on the little bridge, around the wishing fountain. It hadn't been easy to stop Toby following them out of the café even now, but a tray of Lego and a double-choc-banana sundae did the trick. Stella spread out her *Guardian*, ordered a café latte and settled herself for a nice calm half hour, as agreed.

Max and Clio sat under an awning, on a damp bench. He had a white silk scarf, knotted neatly, tucked inside the collar of his coat. No one else she knew wore things like that. It made him look older, or like a young man in a play about another age.

'I . . . I just happened to be passing,' she said. 'School's just up the road.' Max watched her, not exactly mocking—not as unkind as that. Some of the most provoking things he said, she was starting to find, were when he didn't speak at all.

'It must be good,' she said clumsily. 'A gap year. Was that India, where you saw the tiger? My friends all want to go to Thailand.'

'But not you,' he said. Clio bridled. She was used to grown-ups thinking they knew what went on inside her head. She didn't want it from him. Not even if he was right. 'Don't you ever want to travel?' he went on. 'I mean, just drop everything and *go*?'

'I've been plenty of places. Mum and Dad took me to Thailand, actually . . . Oh God, that sounded really snobby, didn't it?' She felt herself blush.

Without a word, he got up and walked slowly away from the café, not looking back to see if she would follow. Clio did. She came alongside him by the wishing fountain. It was switched off for the winter and in the fading afternoon the pond was dark and still. She leaned over, trying to see her reflection. 'Your parents,' she said. 'Shouldn't you . . . tell them?'

'What makes you think I've got parents? You're not the only orphan in the world.'

'Oh . . . I'm sorry,' said Clio, wrong-footed. 'How did you . . . ? Did Stella tell you that about me?'

'She talked about *a family she knew*—friends of hers who brought back a little girl from the other end of Europe. The way she said it, it had to be you.'

'Why?'

He just looked at her, and all the years of knowing she was somehow *different* rushed back over her. 'Sorry,' Max said, 'don't you like people knowing?'

'It's not a secret. And it's not a problem, either. Mum and Dad are my parents now. They're fine, and . . .

and it isn't the point. You must have, you know, next of kin . . .'

'You mean, in case I die or something.'

'No. Yes. Oh, come on, everyone has *someone*.'

'I'm not everyone,' he said. In the water, they were faceless silhouettes. 'Do you know what I wish?' he said.

She stiffened. Either this was going to be the tackiest chat-up line in the world, or . . .

'I'd like to get up and go,' he said. 'Right now.'

'Huh, nice idea,' she said, relieved and very slightly disappointed. 'Where to?'

'Abroad. Somewhere with a beach, a lot of sun. Free food, free drink. Music. Do what you like . . . and no one asking any questions.'

'Oh yeah?' Clio said. 'Dream on!'

'Can I trust you?' he said suddenly. The garden round them seemed very quiet.

She nodded.

'I'm serious, Clio. I can't take it. I've got to get out. Do you understand? I think you do. That's why you're here.'

'I was just . . . worried about you, that's all.'

'You should be. Let me show you something.' He waited till she nodded, then opened his coat a crack, peeled up a roll of his sweater, and on the skin between his waistband and his ribs she saw a long fresh bruise. 'That was just the first night,' he said.

'Who . . . ?'

He shrugged. 'Kids. At that place.'

'You should tell somebody. If the staff won't do anything . . .'

'Tell the police? Why do you think they had me put there? They're not allowed to beat me up, but if someone else wants to . . .'

'That's way out of order. We should tell the press.'

'The press! I phoned them from Stella's house. I

thought they'd like to talk to me. Guess what. No go. Someone leaned on them, someone like DI Wayland. News blackout, that's what it is.'

'They can't do that, can they?'

'It doesn't matter. I'm getting out. I mean it. Help me.'

'How?' Her heart was beating fast now and her mouth was dry.

'I left a bag in Stella's car. Back seat. Go in and ask her if you can get it. Say I want to show you something.' Clio looked round the empty garden and she couldn't move. 'You meant what you said, didn't you?' he said. 'You were worried about me.'

She nodded.

'Then do it,' he said. 'Please. It isn't much to ask.'

Inside the café, Stella barely looked up from the paper as she handed Clio the keys. Toby played on. Clio tiptoed out to the car park. She'd just opened the passenger door when she felt Max behind her.

'Get in,' he said.

'I can't see a bag . . .'

'Get *in*.' His hand was on her elbow, surprisingly tight. He steered her in, no argument, and shut the door. A moment later he was in the driver's seat. In a movement so smooth that she scarcely felt it happen, he lifted the keys from her hand.

Clunk, her door went. Central locking. The ignition fired. 'Hey,' she said, 'you can't . . .' but they were moving, slipping out between the parked cars to the road.

'Sorry,' said Max. He took a right, and they were on the road, going up through the gears. He had done this before. 'Don't worry.'

'Don't worry?' She found her voice. 'Stop. Now! Let me out!'

40

'Sorry,' he said again, but this time it wasn't an apology. 'This isn't about you. It's about me. My life, OK? Do up your seatbelt,' he said, oddly like her dad. 'I can't have you walking back into that café. You can see that, can't you?'

'You tricked me,' said Clio.

'You wanted to help. This is the only way, believe me.' They took a corner too fast. 'Let's not fight,' he said.

'What about Stella? She trusted you. She trusted *us*.'

'She'll understand. We've just borrowed this thing— half an hour, that's all. Anyway, it won't be your fault. I *made* you do it.'

'Did you?' It sounded dumb, but it was true: she didn't know.

'You've been kidnapped. Anything that happens from now on, you're *not responsible*. Think of it as a holiday.' She caught his eye again—the twinkle in it, so like Toby on a good day that she laughed. She didn't mean to; it slipped out. Max laughed, and Clio found she was giggling and she couldn't stop.

'You've never done anything like this?' he said when she'd got her breath back. 'Have you done *anything* wrong?'

'Of course!'

'Such as?'

'None of your business. Who says I *wanted* to, anyway?'

Max put his foot down and veered past a white van, which honked and gave them the finger. 'You don't know anything about me,' Clio said.

'Tell me, then.'

'No . . . You tell me about you. Then I'll tell you about me.'

He nodded, admiringly. 'You're no pushover, are you? Best kind of hostage.'

41

'Hostage? Like hell!' She unclicked her seatbelt and swung round towards him. 'I could scream if I wanted. I could grab that wheel. Put my hands over your eyes, so we'd crash and then we'd both be dead!' She reached out a hand; he flinched; the car swerved.

'You're mad!' They started laughing again, but quietly this time. 'That's settled, then. We're going for a ride,' he said. 'OK?'

'OK.' He took a roundabout with a squeal of tyres and she felt her mouth come open, just like Alton Towers. A man on a bike turned to glare at them, wobbled, and fell off on the verge. He raised his fist and Clio almost waved back. They were going for a ride. And she didn't ask where.

She knew Milbourne well enough, she thought, but they were in streets she didn't recognize—an industrial estate, all Cash and Carrys and car hire depots. Max went left, went right, went left and they were rattling over cobbles with old tram lines in them. 'Slow down!' she laughed, not meaning it, and he didn't, until they were round another corner. Then he pulled into the shadow of a wall and stopped. In front of them rose the grey side of a steel crane. Beyond that, the harbour. Only a low black chain between them and the drop.

Clio was very still. Dockside. Empty buildings. Wasteland. Everything in shades of grey, like an old film. Nobody in sight. Nobody to hear if she called. The laughter had gone and she was in a different story, the kind she had heard on the news—the kind that ended with floodlights on the harbour, and police divers . . . The scene of the crime.

She felt cold. Max was opening the door on his side, palming the keys as he went. Who was he? What did she know about him? What did he want? And what, oh, what in the world did *she* think she was doing here?

6

Short Cut Nowhere

'**Y**ou needn't look like that,' said Max.

'Like what?'

'A cornered rabbit. I thought we were having a good time?'

Her fingers felt for the door catch. He noticed.

'You want to go?' he said. 'Then go. I'm sorry you had to get mixed up in this. I was desperate. But I'm all right now.'

Just like that. A moment ago Clio had been scanning round inside the car: was there a wheel brace, an umbrella, anything she could use as a weapon? Now she felt silly. She could open the door, get out, walk away . . . and all this would be over. That was the sensible thing to do. But for some reason she hadn't moved. She looked at him. What was in that head, behind the blithe expression?

'Who says I want to go?'

There was a pause. He nodded slowly. 'Suit yourself,' he said. 'I've got some things to pick up. Stay in the car if you want to. Or get out and stretch your legs. Up to you.' He set off, walking quickly, his coat flaring out behind. Clio watched him go . . . then got out and followed.

Round the end of the building the cobbles sloped down to a slipway. Rowing boats were hauled up, covered with tarpaulin to keep out the rain. Others had been dragged under an arch beneath the warehouse. It was dark—an underground car park for boats, thought Clio as Max ducked inside.

Some things to pick up . . . Nobody lived here, except maybe tramps and homeless people. She could not grasp it—how someone as cool and clever as Max might know about places like this. Maybe he truly didn't have a home to go to?

She followed him to the archway. Inside, the dark was thick with smells of paint and creosote and damp, and for a moment Clio could not see Max at all. Well, came the strange detached thought, if he *is* a nutter and he wants to kill me, this is where it'll happen. This *was* mad. But she was doing what she wanted, like he'd said.

'There!' His voice was close, and she could just make out his shadow, reaching overhead for something tucked up almost out of reach. A shower of dirt and cobwebs came down with it. Back in the failing light outside he unwrapped the grubby plastic to reveal an ordinary canvas holdall.

'My worldly goods.'

'Truly? Is that really all?'

'You don't need much. Not when you're lucky. And I *am*.' He'd half-opened the zip and was feeling for something, urgently. Whatever it was, he found it and his face relaxed. 'OK,' he said. 'Let's go.' Back on the harbour's edge they stopped, to look across towards the Complex, patched with sheets of shabby plastic. 'Look,' he said. 'Our place! How sad is that?'

In the twilight, without neon, it looked like a cross between a warehouse and a greenhouse, with a bit of building site thrown in. Around the harbour, the first lights were coming on, which made the view, somehow, look dingier still. 'What a dump,' said Clio. 'Not just the Complex—Milbourne. *All* of it.'

'I thought you were happy,' he said. 'The perfect family.'

'Why does everyone keep *saying* that? You can stop sounding so sarcastic, too. My family's fine.'

'But . . . ?'

He left it at that. The *But . . . ?* stretched out over the harbour, Milbourne's almost landlocked sea. You couldn't even see the real sea, out beyond the dragon's-spine of beach huts on the Spit.

'But nothing,' said Clio. 'I don't get it. Why did you lie to the police? What was the point? And . . . why should *I* trust you?'

'Why? Because *I* trusted *you*? You could have gone straight in and told Stella.'

Stella . . . Clio gasped. 'Oh God,' she said. 'Stella! How long have we been?'

'Come on,' said Max. 'I'll drop you part way back. You can go and find Stella, or just go straight home.'

Find Stella . . . Clio imagined walking into the Rockery, to see the place in an uproar, Stella livid and panicky, phoning the police. More likely, she was gone already.

Or . . . Clio imagined going home. The news would have got there before her. Stella would have phoned. Even worse, Mum and Dad had come back to find a policeman on the doorstep, and the neighbours watching. She imagined walking in. Dad would go red, Mum very pale. But the worst thing wouldn't be the anger; it was the thought of the hours and hours they'd sit her down and talk and talk and try to *understand*.

All that would have to happen, no way out of it. But not just yet. For now—well, there was no undoing what had happened. The rush, the adrenalin tingle, hadn't faded. She might as well finish it, now that she'd begun.

45

'Who said I wanted to be un-kidnapped?' said Clio. 'What do we do next?'

Just beyond the industrial estate they hit the traffic. Rush hour. One way, it was solid, and no sooner had they joined the other line than it came to a standstill too. 'Where do you want to get to?' said Clio.

'Out. Out of this place. The bypass. What's the quickest way?' He was edgy again. 'Come on—you *live* here, don't you?'

Way up ahead were road works, with traffic lights. Red went to green for a moment, and the queue edged forwards. 'Oh come on,' he breathed. 'Come on *comeoncomeon . . .*'

'Next left,' she said, 'by the chippie.'

Green turned to red, to green again, and no one moved. Max revved. 'Shush,' she said. 'People will notice.' Green, red, green . . . and at last they were at the turning. Max swung in. 'You're sure about this?'

'It's a short cut.'

The street was narrow, parked on both sides, but the other end was in sight—another main road, where traffic seemed to be flowing. Max put his foot down. 'Careful,' Clio said.

'Damn!' He slammed the brakes on. Just before a small parade of shops were a chicane and a road sign. One Way. 'You said you were sure!'

'Sorry, OK? *I'm* not old enough to drive, remember? I've only walked it.'

Max glanced in his mirror: a dustcart had pulled in, blocking off the way behind. In front, the shops were closed, the road was empty, and the junction, just beyond, seemed very near. He put his foot down. 'No!' said Clio. 'It's a one—'

46

'Relax!' said Max and in that second, as he turned towards her, that was when the pizza delivery bike came out between the parked cars, looking carefully the other way. Their brakes bit, and they nearly missed him, but the bumper clipped the bike's back wheel. It lifted, twisting over, landing with a slow unnatural crunch.

'Shut up!' yelled Max, before Clio had even realized she was screaming. 'Just shut up. That's your fault.'

'It said One Way!'

'You brought us up it. If you hadn't shouted . . .' He jerked into reverse, then forwards, nudging past the buckled bike.

'Look, he's hurt!' said Clio. It was true. The boy was sprawled across the road in front of them, blocking their way.

'Quick!' Max killed the engine and leaped out. Clio was close behind him. On the pavement, several people watched them, non-committally.

The boy from the bike was groaning, struggling to pull himself up. It's OK, she thought, he isn't really hurt. He got nearly upright, then his leg gave way. 'My foot!' he yelled. 'Bastard! You've bust my foot.'

'We should get him to hospital,' Clio said.

'Where's that?'

'In town.' In other words, in the thick of the traffic.

Max shook his head. 'Ambulance. He needs an ambulance.' By now, they had a ring of faces watching, each of them hoping someone else would be the one to get involved. 'Somebody, call an ambulance,' said Max. 'Help me shift him off the road.'

The boy winced as he was levered upright. 'Bastards. My bike . . .' then he swayed and passed out. Clumsily, they dragged him to the doorway of a pub.

Mobiles were beeping round them. The pizza boy was propped up, looking very pale. His head lolled back, his eyelids at half mast, just the whites of his eyes showing, horribly. 'He's in shock,' said a man's voice in an *I'm-a-doctor* sort of tone. Max was stepping backwards, pulling Clio with him. 'Hey, where do you think you're going?' said the doctor voice. 'I've got your number,' it called as they made it to the car. They took off. As they reached the junction, a bus came looming round. Max jerked the wheel sideways; they squeaked past it, one wheel thumping hard against the kerb.

Thanks to the bus, there was an opening in the traffic, and Max cut round, into the stream. A nifty change of lanes, then a roundabout, and they slipped into the left lane, ready for the exit. Clio stiffened as the *nee-naw* of a police car pushed through the traffic, turning off the way they'd come. Then they were in a steady flow and heading out of the town.

'Do you think he'll be OK?' said Clio, almost in a whisper.

'Shut up,' Max said and they both stared straight ahead. 'Of course he will,' he said, much gentler. 'Shock, that's what the man said. It'll be a sprained ankle. Look,' he said, 'an ambulance was what he needed, not us.'

'Still . . .' said Clio. 'Shouldn't we . . . ?'

'What? Go back? Say sorry? If that's what you want, you can get out, right now . . .' He put his foot on the brake and the car behind them blared its horn.

'No!' she said. 'Don't stop . . . It was an accident, wasn't it? We didn't mean to.' She covered her face with her hands.

'We didn't mean to,' he said. 'But we did. Now . . . are you going to help us get out of this, or aren't you? Let's get real.' He looked as pale as when he'd told her about Moncrieff Road, when he'd shown her the bruises. 'Well?'

'I've got a choice, have I?'

48

'How many times have I got to say it? Yes. You can get out . . .'

'I know, I know . . . I can't just . . . leave you in a mess like this.' She stared at the road. They were coming up a small hill. They would be in open country soon.

'Was that a yes?' he said.

'I suppose so.' As they crested the rise, a hundred brake lights faced them. The road dipped, then the traffic was piled solid up a long straight stretch.

'No-o-o . . .' he said. 'How far's the bypass?'

'Over that next hill, and . . .'

'Right . . .' There was a bleat of horns behind as he cut into the slow lane without warning, then over the hatched lines into a slip road.

'It's Tesco,' said Clio. 'No way through.' He didn't answer. That was when she noticed the curious bumping from the left side of the car. Max pulled into the ranks of shoppers' parking and they looked to find the front left tyre—it must have been that crack against the kerb—was almost flat. The front right headlight was smashed in where the pizza bike had caught it, and a deep gash scored the paintwork all along the wing.

'Stella's car . . .' said Clio, bleakly.

'She'll have insurance.'

Then a phone rang.

The sound came suddenly, as if from another life: a wheezy tootling, an annoyingly familiar piece of tune. 'Oh, no . . .' gasped Clio, clutching under her waterproof.

'You've got a mobile! You didn't say . . . Switch it off,' he whispered, but Clio was already staring at the small green screen.

'It's Mum!' she said.

'Don't answer it. Not now.'

'I've got to. She knows I always have it on me. She'll

49

be worried sick if I don't.' Clio closed her eyes and put it to her ear. 'Mum,' she said faintly.

'Thank God,' came the far-off voice. 'Where are you? Are you all right? Clio?'

'Mum . . . Just listen, please. I'm fine. You mustn't worry.' She heard a muffled sound at the other end. Dad was there too. She could see them in the hallway, both trying to hear.

'I can't explain,' said Clio, 'not now. I'm in a bit of trouble, that's all.'

'We know. I told the police you wouldn't—*he* must have made you do it—he did, didn't he?'

'Mum . . . it's complicated. I . . .'

'We love you, whatever you've done. Just say where you are, we'll fetch you.'

'I can't. Just . . . can't.'

It was a moment before Mum spoke. 'Is *he* there . . . now?' she said, in a different voice. 'He is, isn't he? Is that what the matter is?'

'Yes. I mean no, he's here. It's not what you're thinking. I need a bit of time, that's all. I'll call you. Oh, and, Mum, tell Stella . . .'

'What about her?' Her mother's voice was sharp now.

'Tell her I'm really sorry.'

'*Sorry?* If it hadn't been for her stupid do-gooding . . .'

'It wasn't her fault, truly it wasn't . . .'

'Clio!' It was Dad's voice. 'Just come home. Do you know what you're doing to your mother? You should see the state she's in.'

'Dad! I can't, I just can't. Listen . . . Dad . . . Oh . . . look, I'll call you.' She clicked it off, at arm's length, and her hand was trembling.

'Better switch off,' Max said quietly. It rang again. That stupid tune. She switched it off and watched the screen go blank.

50

'Why won't he *ever* listen?' she said. 'He never does, once he starts. I just wanted to tell them . . . tell them . . .'

'Tell them what?'

'Don't know.' She stared at the ground. 'What am I doing?'

He laid his hand on hers, hiding the mobile. 'You need a bit of time, like you said. So do they. Give them a chance to cool down.'

'*Cool down!*'

'I mean it. Go back now, they'll be mad at you. Give it a bit longer, they'll be so glad to see you they'll forget to be angry, believe me. Phone them when they've slept on it.'

'You mean *tomorrow* . . .' Clio frowned, as if she hadn't really thought that far. Beyond the pink glare of the store and car park it was evening. I'm not going to go home tonight, she thought, is that it? It seemed it was. So? Some of her friends were always getting into scraps with their parents, staying out at parties. It wasn't the end of the world. Maybe now was the time?

7

In the Dark

'Are you all right?' said Max, as gently as she'd ever heard him speak. 'You're sure?'

She swallowed hard, and nodded. 'Where do you need to get to?' she said.

'Oh . . . anywhere. How about that beach? A few palm trees . . .'

'Be serious. *Where?* You must have a plan . . . haven't you?' He gave her such an innocent grin that it took her breath away. 'You don't! Look, shouldn't you be going *back* to somewhere? I don't mean Moncrieff Road. There must be somewhere . . . I won't tell, I promise.'

'Not you too!' he said. 'People always try to send me *back* to places. There's nowhere to go back to, can't you understand? Nowhere. I'd rather be dead.'

'Don't say that!' But Max had turned away, quite unconcerned, and was rooting around in the boot of the car.

'I go where I like,' he said over his shoulder. 'So could you.'

'Me?'

'What's stopping you?' He hauled out his holdall, then a crumpled jumper and some old jeans in a plastic bag.

'Those are Stella's,' said Clio.

'I know. Put them on.'

'You must be joking . . .'

'Sorry if they're not your style.' He dropped his voice, leaning close. 'Let's get this straight. If we're caught, I'm the one who's locked up. Not you. I'm the one who gets the bruises. I'm the one who's screwed for good if I don't make it out of here. This is my *life*, for God's sake. Is that clear?'

She glared back, stung.

'You're standing there in your school clothes, remember? That's the first thing they'll say when they put out our descriptions. Get out of that skirt and top—I mean, look, the school logo! Or start walking home.' They were eye to eye now, and it was all she could do not to look away first. She didn't. But she nodded.

'Good. And you'd better take this.' He tossed a thin scarf of Stella's at her. 'Do something with that hair of yours. It's the first thing people will notice.' He grinned. 'I did.'

She ignored that, or tried to. 'Where do I change?'

'Don't worry—I'll keep a look out.'

Back in the car, Clio swore to herself as she heaved the jeans up under her skirt, then wrestled the skirt off over them. The jumper was easier, but she kept on glancing to check Max was looking the other way. As she climbed out she zipped up her coat to hide Stella's horrible jumper, then bent down to the wing mirror, trying to loop the scarf round her hair. 'I need the loo,' she said.

'No prob. We're going shopping.' They wove in and out of the parked cars, up to the trolleys by the sliding doors. 'The loo's just inside. I'll meet you out here in a minute.' He put his hands on her shoulders. 'Thanks,' he said. 'I mean, really *thank you*. Sorry I was angry—I get jumpy. And you're really brave.' In the ladies', Clio locked herself into a cubicle, and let go of some stupid tears that had been building up behind her eyes. People came in and out, and Clio waited. At last the place sounded empty. Clio crept out and looked in the mirror. She screwed her face up in disgust, then set herself to making the best of Stella's jeans. They were shapeless round her hips, but with the belt tightened up they made her look like someone who got stuff from Oxfam, rather than a beggar or a girl in stolen clothes. She undid her hair and frisked it, then tied it in a tight bunch at the back of her head.

'Hi,' he said as she came out. 'Let's have a look . . . Not bad! You look twice your age, at least.' She wrinkled her nose, but he was steering her out already.

'What about the shopping?'

'Here.' He dug in his pockets and brought out a couple of pork pies, a couple of Mars bars . . . Clio stared at them. 'Eat,' he said. 'Get your blood sugar up.'

'I . . . I don't eat red meat.'

'Suit yourself. Have both the Mars bars.'

'Yuck . . .' She hesitated. 'Max . . . ? You did *buy* these?'

He grinned, and motioned just behind her. Through the automatic doors a very wide woman was pushing out a loaded trolley, nagging at a very wide small boy. 'It was for their own good,' Max whispered. 'Robin Hood, that's me. I rob the fat to feed the thin.' He planted the Mars bars in Clio's pocket, and she found she was giggling, though there was nothing much to laugh about.

When she stopped, she felt suddenly limp. 'They're going to catch us, aren't they?'

Very gently, he lifted her chin with a finger. 'That's the low blood sugar speaking,' he said. 'Trust me. They'll be watching the roads, not Tesco.'

'But what are we going to *do*?'

'Well . . . we can't leave your clothes in the car—dead giveaway. There's a bin over there.'

'Those are my school things!'

54

'OK, OK. Shove them in my bag. Then . . . you're going to eat a Mars bar. And me? I'm going to have a good idea. Quite soon.'

Crisp, brown, and crimped at the edges . . . she tried not to watch the pork pie as Max ate it. Even the thought of the Mars bars made her feel sick. He finished the pie, looked up and saw her watching.

'The pig was dead already,' he said. 'Can't bring it back.'

'I'm not hungry,' she said. 'Anyway I don't . . .'

'. . . eat red meat. I know.' He glanced round, dug in his pocket and showed her a glimpse of more pies and chocolate bars.

'Just in case,' he said. 'We've got a night to think of.'

'A night? Where can we stay?'

'Not here, that's for sure.' He looked around. Even in a busy car park it wouldn't be hard to spot a car with a flat tyre and a smashed-in wing. Stella must have raised the alarm by now. While Clio had been on the phone there'd been a siren in the distance. Now another one passed on the main road, nudging through the crawling cars. 'Let's get clear of this car,' Max said. On one side the lights of the car park lit a fringe of trees. Beyond them, darkness. That was where he headed, and a minute later he was back, smiling to himself like a man with a plan.

'Sorted,' he said. 'Now . . .' He looked at her hard. 'You can still go back, you know.'

'Stop saying that. If I want to go, I'll go, OK?'

'OK . . . So. Are you afraid of the dark?'

'I like it.' She grinned. 'Creature of the night, I am.'

'Lucky me. I've got the right accomplice.'

Clio nodded. *Accomplice* . . . Yes, she liked that word.

The shadows hid a wire fence, but in one place it was bent low. Someone had emptied a spill of rubbish into the bushes, where it dropped out of sight. Max reached a hand to help her, which she didn't take. Then he vanished. 'Careful,' his voice came from somewhere below. 'It's steep.' She was slithering too, grabbing at branches and stumps, then sliding on down till her feet hit level gravel. Max was there to steady her, and they both looked around.

It was as if the hillside had opened up, helpfully, to hide them. The cutting was quiet and dark. Some way back on a footbridge was a street lamp, and its orange glow picked out the glint of rails.

'We shouldn't be here,' Clio whispered.

'This is *perfect*,' Max said. 'Disused, too . . .' He squatted down to touch a rail. 'Look, rust. It hasn't been used for years. Didn't I say I was lucky?'

'I thought you said you'd planned it.'

'That too,' he said. 'Now, let's walk.'

The Blind Walk . . . It was a game Clio used to play with her friends on the way home from school. They would cut across Armistice Park, which was one of those flat old recreation grounds with a fringe of trees round the outside and, well, not much else at all. You could shut your eyes, and walk, and know there was nothing to bump into. You could *know* it . . . What your body *felt* was something else again.

Most of the girls never got ten paces before they started slowing. They'd be putting out their hands in front, like they say sleepwalkers do. Some of the girls just cheated. Clio never did—she would know, even if nobody else did. And she always won. Some afternoons, she walked home alone, without telling her mum. (Yes,

56

thinking back, she'd always had that kind of secret—not a lie exactly, just not-mentioning.) It was as if she'd been rehearsing for something. Practising. She did the Blind Walk on her own.

Now, the darkness of the tunnel closed around them. At first there was still the far-off street lamp, but it left an after-image dancing in her eyes. It was almost a relief when the walls curved slightly and the light was not there tempting her to look back.

The air was cold and very still. A drop fell. Splash. Did that mean there were puddles? Deep pools? Was the tunnel flooded? She was going slower now, listening for the sounds of Max's feet ahead. Her right foot was on clinker, her left slipped on greasy sleepers. Her right hand trailed along the brickwork, trying not to flinch at the touch of slime or cobweb. Once, she stubbed her foot on something hard.

'You OK?' Max called back. But she wasn't going to get all girly, no way.

'Of course,' she said. And they went on, one step at a time.

Then the side wall was gone. Her hand groped into emptiness. Max must have heard her stop because he whispered, 'It's OK. There's a kind of alcove.' A couple more steps and her knuckles hit brickwork again. She swore, out loud. This was his fault. He didn't know where they were going. For all he knew there could have been a rock fall in the tunnel; there was no way through. Or that 'alcove' could have been a fault line. Any moment, it could shift again.

'Clio . . .' said Max. 'I'm here.'

'I want to go back,' she said. Silence. Drip, splash. Drip.

'I'm here,' he said again. 'Clio? Say something.' His voice was just a little higher than before. 'Just talk,' he said.

So she was not the only one feeling frightened. Somehow that helped. 'Talk? What about?'

'Anything. What are you thinking?'

'Me? I'm thinking . . . it's dark. And it's wet. And . . . I never meant to be here. It's only because I was trying to be kind and I thought I could help you and that was really stupid of me and it's all your fault we're stuck here in this stupid . . .'

'. . . hole?' said Max.

'Don't try to be funny. I mean it.' But she couldn't keep it up, the anger. Now they were talking, nothing felt so bad.

'We can go back if you want to,' Max said, 'but . . . I think . . . yes . . . I can see a bit of light. Come here.'

She was already inching forward, one hand on the wall, the other reaching for him. Reaching. She took three steps, four, and he should have been there. 'Max?' she said, and when he spoke again his voice was just as close as ever . . . and not there.

'Max!' She stumbled, grating her knee on the gravel. 'Where are you?'

'Here,' he said. 'Stop. Let's calm down. Which side are you?'

'Right.'

'Same here. I mean left . . . I'm coming back towards you. It's weird acoustics in here—makes us both sound closer than we are. Just keep on coming . . . Trust me.'

Then she felt the warmth, she felt his breathing and— she couldn't help it—she just grabbed for him. As she clung on, it struck her he was clinging quite tight too.

'Now,' he said after a while. 'We're going to hold hands. Don't let go.'

'Were you afraid?' said Clio.

'Scared shitless. But you were so *cool* back there—I didn't dare say!' Then they both laughed a little and step by step, side by side, they found a pace together—very slow at first, then faster. She could see it now—a faint glistening far ahead on one wall. A few steps more and there was no doubt: she could see it glinting on the rails, she saw the shadows of the sleepers and when she glanced sideways she saw his face, very dimly, turned to look at her.

Just as they came out into the blessed half-light one of them—she couldn't tell which—let go the other's hand. Then they were out of the tunnel, in a cutting, with the street light in the sky above. 'We did it!' They threw their arms around each other, clapping each other on the back like team-mates who'd just scored the winning goal.

There was a curious shuddering in the air, like an aeroplane coming in to land.

Clio felt the draught on her face . . . cold . . . blowing out of the tunnel. Then the rails were alive, with a twanging whistling sound.

Max jumped and pushed her with him, as the shock wave threw them back, flat on the bank. The freight train slammed out of the tunnel—just a glimpse of the lit cab high above them, and the screech of engines, flashing wheels, then the thud and thud of wagons full of heaps of quarry stone. Thud. Thud.

It went on for ever, almost. Then as the sound and the smell of it faded she found herself up and kneeling over Max, lashing out with both hands. His arms went up in self defence but one blow caught him smack across the cheek and he doubled over, hands guarding his face, as she screamed at him—worse things than she'd ever said at school, things that weren't even words, or not in English. She didn't stop till every drop of strength and breath was used up, then she crumpled on the bank beside him, curled up just like he was, and began to cry.

8

Cloak of Night

'Go away. Leave me alone,' said Clio.

He was leaning over her. 'Clio, listen . . . please.'

'If we'd been a minute later . . .' she said. '*One minute!* And you *knew* all along. You knew it wasn't disused, didn't you?' No answer. 'There! I'm right. How could you? How? And *why?*'

'You know why. If I'd told you, you wouldn't have come.'

'Exactly!'

'Exactly nothing. Aren't you glad you did?'

She stared at him. In the dimness his face had an innocent look, like Toby had sometimes. His non-stick-saucepan look, Stella called it: you could tell him off all you liked, but not a word of it would stick.

'We could have been back in that car park,' he said. 'Cornered. Waiting for the police to catch up. Or we could be here—free! By the time anyone susses it out, we'll be a hundred miles away.'

'But . . . we could have been *killed*. Don't you *care?*'

She studied his face again. He frowned, as if it was a tricky question that would take some thought. She remembered him in Stella's front room, those words she'd not grasped at the time: '*Oh . . . life. That stuff.*' And that awful little shrug, as if to say, *Who cares?*

60

'You wouldn't have felt it,' he said. 'One bang and that's that. There's nothing to care about then, is there? Or have you got some religious thing about it? Well, then. We did what we wanted to, and it's OK.'

There must have been an argument against it, Clio thought. Dad would have had one, for certain, but her mind was blank. 'It can't be that simple,' she said. 'Can it?'

'Why not try it?' He grinned at her. 'Nothing to lose.' Then he was on his feet. 'My bag!' He ran back to the tunnel mouth, hunting around, and when she called out, 'Careful!' he didn't seem to hear. It was only a minute, then he had it. He came back cradling the bag in his arms like a lost child. He crouched on the bank and, like that time on the dockside, felt around inside. It was all right. Clio felt the wave of his relief.

'Fell between the rails,' he said. 'The train went right over it.'

'It's only a bag. You didn't care about *me*. Or yourself. What's so special?'

'Your precious school things?'

'Oh yes? What else?'

'Oh, just . . . stuff.'

'Let me see.' She moved quicker than he did, and the bag flopped open so that for a moment she glimpsed what his hand was resting on. A small box? No, a book.

'Private,' he said.

'Don't be so mysterious. What's the big deal?'

For a second he held it up: a fat leather-bound book with a clasp around it, and no title on the front—a book for writing in, thought Clio, not for reading. Then he stashed it away.

'What is it? The secret diary? The bestselling novel?'

'It's a trap. The last person who opened it without

permission—she vanished right inside it. She was never seen again.'

'Do I get permission?' said Clio.

'You? We hardly know each other yet.' He grinned, zipped up the bag and slung it on his shoulder. He was on his feet, looking up the steep bank of the cutting.

'Let's get on,' he said, 'while we're ahead.'

Dear M . . .

Was that it, do you think — in the tunnel? Was that the moment of no going back? Or was it earlier, getting into the car? At the café? The docks? Or Tesco? No, I think it was the tunnel, don't you? Must have been, or why didn't I just run off, run straight home, tell my parents that you tried to kill me?

It was somewhere down there in the dark. The point of no return.

They say I lost part of me — the good-girl bit, who'd never let herself be 'led astray'. Maybe part of me did turn back in the tunnel, when I said I was going to — turned back and made for the entrance, only she didn't quite make it back before the train came. Splat. Sometimes I think we both died in there, and the stuff that came after was a kind of dream.

That's crazy. Really what I think is that I didn't lose anything. I found a part of me, down there. When I screamed and tried to beat you to a pulp I meant it, you bet I did. I knew that from then on I was going to mean everything — no looking at the other person first, to see what they wanted. No holding back in case I wasn't it. I was mad at you all right, and I wanted to half kill you (just half) but all the time I was hitting you I felt sort

62

of great. ALIVE. I'd never ever felt so full of life.

Didn't I tell you that? I don't remember. I don't remember if I ever said it: Thank you.

Lying bastard.

I just thought you'd like to know.

They went up the side of the cutting on all fours, like animals. Once, Max turned round to offer a hand, but she scrambled past him. At the top she turned and grinned back. She felt wide awake now, although it was evening—as if she'd screamed all the tiredness out of her and if she wanted she could run all night.

'Right,' he said, when he reached her. 'Now . . . we're on a mission.' Over a dark field or two, on the ring road, headlights flickered through a line of trees. '*That's* what we need.' He pointed to a splash of light: the orange awning of a petrol station.

'What then?'

'Don't worry. Just do what I say.' He caught the flash in her eyes. 'I've done this before,' he said quickly. 'Trust me, OK?'

He parted the two strands of the barbed wire fence in front of them, treading one down and holding the other one up, like a bowstring, between careful fingers. Clio ducked through, trusting him, OK. She turned and held the wire for him, as he brought his long coat and his bag through safely, then without a word they were off across the field. She stumbled at first, among the ruts and clumps and thistles, but the more she kept her eyes down, the more she could see. Max was in front, moving as quick as a fox. As they came towards the petrol station he became a silhouette, a figure in a long cloak, like a highwayman, maybe.

63

'Hey . . .' whispered Clio, 'shouldn't we . . . keep out of sight?'

Light glinted on his teeth as he half turned and smiled. 'They can't see us,' he said. 'Look. They've got no idea . . .' In the light of the forecourt, cars pulled in, drivers got out, used the pumps and fumbled for their wallets, went to the kiosk with the all-night shop. It was almost unkind—they seemed so . . . helpless. It was like watching goldfish in a tank. Max raised his arms and waved towards the pumps. Clio caught her breath as one man seemed to look up from his petrol cap, straight at them . . . but he was looking at a wall of night. He clunked the pump back in its holster and stumped off to pay.

'See?' Max said. 'We're invisible.' Clio gave a little shudder. That magic gift she'd always wanted, in the stories Mum used to read to her, and that Clio read to Toby now: invisibility.

As they got closer, Max moved more slowly. Now the lights cast shadows and they side-stepped into one, tiptoeing down it till they were close enough now to hear voices, and the thump of someone's stereo. 'You wait here,' he said, peering round the automatic car wash. 'Watch me. Don't move till I give the sign.'

'Why can't I come too?'

'Because we might be on the news already. If we are, they'll be looking for a couple. If someone grabs me . . . well, it'll only be me. Watch the shop. When I put my arm up, like I'm scratching my head—like this . . . you come over. Don't run. You've just got out of your parents' car, you want a packet of crisps. Don't speak till I tell you. Right?'

She watched him cross the forecourt like a walking shadow. No one turned to stare. He hadn't waited for her answer to his *Right?* He'd even left his precious bag with her, he was so sure she wouldn't say no. She let her hand rest on it. She felt trainers, and soft shapes of clothes—*her* clothes, she thought with a small shock, all mixed up with *his*. And then she felt the book. Clio never kept a diary because she was so sure Mum would want to look. It was wrong, very wrong, to pry in someone else's diary. Still, she found herself easing the zip back a little. She could be looking for something she'd left in her skirt pocket—she almost persuaded herself she *was*—as her hand slipped inside.

The book felt oddly warm, like a live thing, and the leather felt as smooth as skin. She wasn't going to open it. All she wanted was to touch. She thought of her great-grandmother's Bible that Mum kept as a family heirloom. Like that Bible, Max's book had scraps of paper tucked between the pages, bookmarks, and as her fingers brushed it one came free. She flinched. She hadn't opened it, honestly. Still, she held the paper up to the forecourt's glow—too faint to read the newsprint, but she recognized the local-paper style. MI6 QUIZ HARBOUR BLAST MYSTERY.

So, he keeps his press cuttings, she thought, as she slipped it quickly back into the bag, back in between the pages. Was that weird, or was that normal? I mean, she'd saved hers when she had won the school verse-speaking competition, yes . . . but this?

This was no time to ask. She ran her hand across the holdall, as if she was soothing it, saying sorry, and settled down to watch the forecourt shop.

It was like watching a conjuror at work from backstage. Or watching it on TV with no sound. That way you don't hear the patter, which is what takes people's minds away from seeing what's happening. Isn't that how stage magicians do their tricks?

What she saw was this . . . Max in the shop—just a

coat, with his head down, between the shelves of travel snacks and maps and screen wash. The coat between the magazines and the coffee machine. The coat mingling with the half dozen other people always in there, though the others came and went and Max didn't. He kept moving, browsing, just enough that the girl at the till wouldn't notice him hanging around.

Everyone turned, though, when the father with the twin little girls came into the shop. They were older than Toby, and squabbling and whining—out past their bedtime and too tired for anything. The way the dad looked, he was just about to lose it too. *I want I want*, they'd be whingeing, and *She pushed me, Daddy, she pushed me* . . . He'd be offering sweets, crisps, anything that might just make them shut up for a minute. Clio saw this, framed in the lit window. She could tell that Max was watching too.

The man needed a coffee, fast. Max stepped aside, as if to let him go first. That was the first smart move. A minute later, the dad must have noticed that the girls were quiet. Without doing anything obvious, Max had caught their eye—first one, then the other. He must have given that twinkly smile, the way he did with Toby, because they lost interest in their quarrel, and one first, then the other, gave a cautious stare, then a smile, to the friendly man in the coat.

Max's arm went up. He made a stretch and a big scratch of it, so the girls nudged each other and began to giggle. Clio slipped from the shadows. Whatever the plan was, it was happening *now*.

By the time she got there, Max and the father were chatting, paper cups of coffee in their hands. The man must have been desperate for someone, anyone, to talk to. All Max had done was make sure that the someone was him. He caught Clio's eye: *Not yet*, his glance said,

66

and she studied the cans of soft drink, pretending to check out their ingredients in detail.

'Here she is,' Max said, loudly now, for her to hear. '*Helen*,' he said, 'this is Geoff . . . Poppy . . . Molly. Helen's a star with children. She could babysit for England.' Both the girls checked out this babysitter, who was young and new . . . and called Helen, apparently. Clio smiled.

'I'm Poppy,' said one of the girls. 'We've been skating. Daddy said I was the best.'

'Did not,' said the other.

'Did.'

'Only because you fell over and cried.'

'I always fall over,' said Clio, and next moment they were chatting happily. At least she didn't have to join in with Max and the father and say . . . whatever *Helen* was meant to say.

'What's *he* called?' said Poppy, or Molly, looking at Max.

'Uhh . . . why don't you ask him?'

'Don't want to.'

'Go on. He won't bite.'

Max rescued them. 'Joel,' he said, cheerily.

'Joel's been telling me,' the dad said, 'he's got two little sisters *just like you* at home.'

'Geoff's going to Farnton . . .' Max said to Clio.

'We're going to Mummy's,' Poppy piped up. 'She doesn't like ice skating.'

'. . . and maybe he could help us on our way home— just as far as the first service station.' Max was talking quickly. From the man's eyes, Clio wasn't sure he knew about this plan yet. 'As long as you don't mind squeezing in the back with the girls . . .'

'Oooh, yes please!' Molly and Poppy burst out together. 'Please, Daddy, can we *squeeze in*? Please?' Clio saw the struggle on the poor man's face. He should say no, of course. What would the twins' mother say if she knew he'd been picking up hitchhikers? Then again, she always told him he'd done it wrong anyway, so . . .

'Oh, why not?' he said. 'Good idea.'

By the time they reached the car he and Max were on to football. Clio climbed in the back and watched Max morph into an Arsenal supporter, since that's what Geoff seemed to be. You've got to give it to him, Clio thought, he's good at this. So good it was almost scary. But the car was moving. They were on their way.

9

Travelling by Word of Mouth

> *Belladora Belladora*
> *Princess of the midnight wood*
> *Belladora's gang will get you*
> *If you won't be good*

Clio knew the words by heart. One of her earliest memories of Mum was her reading the story from a big book
with bright pictures—and of herself thinking: *No, that's
not quite how it goes.* Mum only had to change a word
and young Clio would say: 'That's wrong.' Clio could
tell the story with her eyes shut, and she did so now,
as Molly and Poppy curled up as tight against her as
their seatbelts would allow.

> *Traveller, don't go near the woods*
> *Where Belladora dwells*
> *For fear you hear the icy sound*
> *Of gold and silver bells*
>
> *And if you hear the silver bells*
> *You'll follow where they lead*
> *In deep, in dark, in dreamlike paths*
> *And you'll be lost indeed.*

They swung down a slip road and under the motorway sign. After that it was the rhythmic strobing of headlights through the barrier as Clio whispered her story to the sleepy girls.

In the front, Max and the dad were chatting like old friends. 'It was meant to be a gap year,' Max was saying, 'but you know how it goes . . . I got this job on a sheep station on the way to Alice Springs . . .' She could have sworn there was a slight Australian twang in his voice, that she had never heard before.

The man sighed. 'That's what I should have done. When I was your age. When I had the chance . . .'

> *Then from the trees and shadows*
> *Belladora's robbers rise*
> *With gold and daggers in their teeth*
> *And murder in their eyes.*

Molly gave a little whimper. 'Shush, silly,' said Poppy, but gave Clio's hand a squeeze.

'No one gets hurt,' whispered Clio, just in case the dad had overheard. He hadn't. He had worries of his own.

'What with *them* . . .' said the father, '. . . and their mother on at me for money—the times I've wanted to, you know, get up and *go* . . .'

Max nodded as if yes, he understood. 'Go where?' he said.

'The States. The far west. Phoenix Arizona . . .' The father put his foot down, and they drove like outlaws on the open road.

> *They'll cut your purse and empty it*
> *Of every precious thing*
> *They'll build a pile of bracelet, necklace,*
> *Watch and wedding ring*

> *And then you'll hear the silver bells*
> *And every cut-throat thief*
> *Bows down: Hail, Belladora,*
> *Robber princess, bandit chief.*

'Is she beautiful?' whispered Molly. 'Is she scary?'

'Is she like you?' Poppy said.

'Oh yeah, Phoenix,' said Max in the front. (Was that a slight hint of American in his voice now?) 'It's got too big, Phoenix. You can't see the desert any more.'

'You've been to Phoenix?' said the father.

Max didn't answer. He stared into the night as if he had these memories: the desert sunsets, the coyotes, cactus trees . . .

People will believe anything, thought Clio . . . if they want to. Sometimes you don't even have to *tell* a lie.

'Good luck,' the man said as he dropped them by the service station. 'Hope you get home tonight.' Home for Joel and Helen was Crouch End in London, from what Clio had overheard.

As the car pulled out of sight Max turned to Clio. 'Ye-e-sss!' They did a palm-slap. 'We're a team. You did great.'

Clio couldn't help it: she was beaming too.

'Time for a coffee,' Max said.

'Coffee?' The rush of excitement faded suddenly, replaced by something colder. Worry. 'Shouldn't we be hitching?' she said.

'No! We don't hitch.'

'What, then?'

'We sit down and have a drink. Relax. OK?'

It didn't make sense. There they were, on the run,

and every second counted. Any time now, there would be descriptions of them flashed round every police car in a hundred miles. Max seemed in no hurry at all. They had time for a Diet Coke (for her) and a fierce black coffee (for him). With drinks in their hands, he leaned back and stretched. He kept chatting, vaguely, as if he was tuned in on some other wavelength. All the time his eyes were glancing round the room.

'Stop it!' said Clio. 'You're making me nervous. Like we're being followed or something . . . We aren't, are we?'

'Course not. I'd know. Years of practice. We're just waiting for our next lift.'

Whatever he meant by that, it hadn't turned up yet. After a while, he emptied his purse to get them both another drink.

'That stuff about Australia,' she said as he sat down again. 'You haven't been there, have you? *Or* to Arizona?'

'I've been all kinds of places. You'd be surprised.'

'What kind of answer is that . . . ?' said Clio. He was looking at her with that particular sly smile of his. *You* know what I mean, it seemed to say. Then he was leaning forward, very close.

'First time we met,' he said, 'I recognized you.'

'Oh yeah? Where from?'

'Nowhere. I just knew we were . . . the same species. Both people from nowhere.'

'Oh, come on. Just because Stella told you all about my family . . . which she shouldn't have—not that it's a secret or anything, but she was the social worker on the case, so it's a bit out of order . . . Anyway,' she took a breath, 'I don't think you even noticed me, at the Complex. You were just . . . working the room, weren't you?'

Then Max did something unexpected. Closed his eyes. Laid one hand lightly on the back of hers. For a moment he was motionless. 'There's five or six of you in the group,' he said. 'Five of you, plus a teacher.'

Clio had to think. 'Yes,' she said, 'there was me and Rachel . . . and Bethan . . . Jay, and . . . yes, Phoebe. Five. And Miss Travis.'

'This teacher, she keeps looking round at the younger girls behind you. So do you . . .'

'Pretty good,' said Clio.

'This is in long shot,' Max went on. 'Camera angled downwards slightly, could be from the balcony. You're framed between those potted palms and the big tree. Am I right?'

'I . . . I don't know.'

'Believe me. The thing is, all the others are moving around you, like you're the only one who's still. You know that trick with a telephoto lens, where you get someone coming towards you really far off, then it's blown up so it looks close, and they seem to be walking straight at you but they don't get any nearer? Then there's me, just the back view, coming your way—like I'm being pulled—like gravity.'

'What is this?' Clio tried to sound flippant but it wasn't easy. 'You've got the video, have you?'

'They'll have it all on their security cameras. They were everywhere—just like this place.' He glanced round. 'You saw the one as we came in from the car park.'

'No,' said Clio.

'That's why I let you go in first—so they didn't get the two of us together.'

Clio stared at him. 'Do you notice this stuff all the time?'

'Why not? *They're* watching *us* all the time. Fair's fair.'

Suddenly his eyes and ears were somewhere else again. 'Ssssh!'

'What?' At first she couldn't work out who he was spying on. He never stared—he was subtler than that. He nudged her.

'Don't turn round,' he said. 'Two tables back. Executive type. Middle aged—his hair's a bit too brown, because he dyes it. I said *don't* turn round, not yet. There's a woman with him—younger, pretty, blue jacket . . .'

'Go on, tell me her life story too.'

'Shush.' Max wasn't playing. 'You've got to be quick. She's getting up. If she goes to the Ladies', go in with her.'

'Me?' said Clio.

'Well, *I* can't, can I? Go in, wash your hands . . . whatever women do in there. And look upset.'

'Wha-a-at?'

'Cry a little. Not too loud—like you're heartbroken but you're being really brave. When she asks you what's the matter—she will, she's the kind sort . . .'

'Wait a minute!'

'We haven't got a minute,' he said. 'Listen. Don't say anything, OK? Let her be nice to you. Sniff a bit, look grateful . . . then bring her outside. I'll be waiting.'

'I can't just . . . I just *can't*!'

'Yes, you can. There she goes. Quick—it's our chance.'

Clio was on her feet, but couldn't move yet. 'What . . . I mean, why am I crying?'

'It's a runaway lovers thing. Romeo and Juliet or something. You just do the sobbing. Leave the rest to me.'

* * *

74

People will believe anything, thought Clio, in the Ladies', through her squeezed-out tears. It shouldn't have been so easy. The woman had noticed her in seconds, and her own blue eyes went damp with sympathy. We shouldn't be so predictable, we women, Clio thought. He shouldn't be *right*. But he was.

Max was waiting outside, ready to look surprised . . . concerned . . . then put his arm around her. (Clio stiffened slightly.) 'Thanks,' he said to the woman. 'We'll be all right.' He said it in such a soft shy voice that the woman could only say 'Really? Are you sure?'

'I think so. As long as we get home by midnight. Someone should be going that way . . .'

'You mean, you're on your own? At your age.'

Half the art was not to seem to *want* to tell the story. They had met on Corfu, he was saying, and everyone said *Forget it, it's just a holiday romance*, but they knew it was the real thing. Max looked at Clio, and she blushed for real.

'You're not . . . running away?' said the woman. Clio could see what she must be seeing: her and this boy with his fair hair and innocent face. Runaway lovers? Of *course*—the woman didn't doubt it for a moment. Maybe she liked the idea, secretly.

'No . . . I mean . . . well, Helen sort of ran away,' Max said. 'But we're going back to her parents now.'

'Do they know where you are? You've phoned them, haven't you?'

'Uh . . . yes, of course.' He's making it up as he goes along, thought Clio. This wasn't Romeo and Juliet. He was improvising, and he'd made a wrong move.

'If I was them I'd come and fetch you,' said the woman. 'I wouldn't let you hitch-hike in the middle of the night.'

'My dad would come,' said Clio, quickly. 'Only he

works away. With the car.' Back at the café table Clio caught sight of the man with dyed hair. Any moment now he was going to barge over and put a stop to this. 'We promised Mum we'd only take lifts with people we could *really* trust.'

The woman hesitated. 'Wait there,' she said and walked back quickly to the man.

'Thanks!' Max said. 'You were great.'

Clio shook herself free of his arm. 'Don't let this *runaway lovers* thing go to your head . . . Look. He's saying no.'

'He'll do it,' said Max. 'She can wrap him round her little finger.' Max gave that little *trust-me* smirk that made her want to kick him. Then the woman was beckoning. 'See? What did I say?'

The man had said yes, but he wasn't happy. When his eyes fell on Max, they didn't go warm and friendly like the woman's had. As they climbed into the back seat of the BMW an awkward silence settled, then the man clicked on the radio. Golden Oldies from the seventies, with a terrible local radio DJ . . . This one wasn't a pushover, not like Geoff and the twins. Still, they were moving. Max reached out and put his arm round Clio. *Hey* . . . he whispered right in her ear, *we're so-o-o-o in love, remember?* She hesitated, then snuggled up against him. Two could play at this game. Every now and then the woman glanced and saw them half asleep together, and seemed satisfied.

Lights flashed by, and a blue sign now and then. They were putting miles between themselves and Milbourne. Clio thought of the mobile, switched off in her pocket, and wondered how many urgent messages—WHERE R U? TXT ME—would be piled up, waiting. What would her friends be thinking? Rachel would think she's been murdered, naturally. Kareena

76

would reckon she'd run off with a secret boyfriend, which was what *she'd* always wanted to do. Did any of them know her, really? But the questions were too big, and the noise of the car was so steady, and the warmth of Max's arm around her made her think of family holidays years ago, when Mum would come in the back seat beside her, just to keep her company . . . and soon she was drifting into sleep.

Max stiffened. He was suddenly talking, quick and loud—she couldn't make out what about—someone else was talking at the same time. A newsreader's voice. The radio. The woman turned round; 'Pardon?' she was saying. 'Can't hear . . .' Max didn't stop babbling till the man switched down the volume. Max had heard a knocking in the engine, he was saying, and his dad's car made a noise like that before it broke down and . . .

'Oh, now it's stopped,' he said. 'Sorry.' Without a word, the man turned up the volume and they were back in the seventies. But Clio was wide awake. You know how you can be in a crowded room with everybody talking . . . and you always hear if someone says your name? She'd heard it. Her name. And the words *police* . . . and *Milbourne* . . . The rest had been drowned by Max's chatter, but Clio was prickling with fright. That was it then. They were on the news.

If the couple in the front had heard, they were playing it cool. Clio stared at the backs of their heads. The man just went on driving, like before. It was all right, wasn't it? He hadn't been listening. Nothing had changed.

Max's arm was tense against her. She could feel a pulse beating fast where his arm touched her neck, but whose it was she couldn't tell. She rested her hand against his arm, to keep it there. He felt that, and relaxed a little.

The lights flashed by. The moment had passed, for now. How often did news flashes come on this station? Clio found herself watching the car clock, wondering if Max would have to start babbling every fifteen minutes, on the quarter hour . . . and how long it would be before the driver twigged. But before the next bulletin came they dropped into the slow lane, and were pulling off left. The next services . . . The woman wasn't expecting it, either; she looked at the man. As he pulled up in the car park he muttered, 'Flowers. Forgot the flowers for your mother. You know.' There was something stiff about the way he said it. 'Come and help me choose,' the man said, pointedly.

'Shall we wait in the car?' said Max.

'Uhh . . .' The man glanced around, uneasy. Probably checking if there was anything they could steal.

'Actually,' Max said, 'we could do with a breath of air.'

They stood on the edge of the car park. Max was watching the retreating shapes of the couple. 'Damn . . .' he muttered to himself. Clio had never seen him so twitchy.

'What's wrong?'

'Me. I was wrong. I thought they weren't married. Didn't she look like his secretary or something? I thought they were having an affair.'

'What difference does that make?'

'*All* the difference. If it's a dirty weekend they won't be phoning the police now, will they? But . . . God, look!' He pointed to the service station. Just inside the automatic doors, where he thought he was out of sight, the man had stopped, like someone . . . using a mobile phone.

'Run,' said Max. 'No, wait a second.' He reached down into his bag. He found a pen and . . . Clio watched him

tear a page out of his precious book. *'Got another lift,'* it said. *'Save you going out of yr way. Thanks v. much. Joel &*
Helen.'

He tucked it under the windscreen wiper. 'Now,' he said. Just behind them was a bank with bushes. Shadows. He nodded towards them. 'Let's go.'

10

Dog's Breath

They crouched in the bushes till their knees began to ache. The BMW was still there in the car park and the couple had not reappeared. Cars pulled in, cars pulled out. No flashing lights, no police . . . not yet. Under them, the ground was damp and cold, and Clio felt it seeping through her jeans. The bush was prickly but leafless—not much cover. She was not sure whether to feel ridiculous or scared.

'Yes!' said Max, suddenly. 'Got it!'

'What?'

'The plan.'

'I thought you *had* a plan already,' Clio said.

'Yes, course, sort of. But this time I've *really* got it.' He gave her a small nudge, brother-to-sister-like, teasing. 'I think best on my feet.' He pulled her out into the open. 'Just act normal.'

Normal! But nobody looked. As they crossed the car park, cars came by, close enough to touch, but everybody in them stared straight forwards, shut in their little worlds.

'Come on,' said Max. They cut towards the filling station, into a no-man's-land of sleeping lorries, dodging in and out of wheels as high as themselves, with wheelnuts big as fists. When one had a light in its cab, Max steered Clio aside and pointed to the dark beyond the lorries. He ducked back the other way. A minute later he met up with her again.

'What happened?' Clio whispered.

'I'll explain later. Come on. Time we disappeared.'

There was no pretending now: they ran for it, towards the vague shapes of a hedge. A gate. By the time Clio got there, Max was waiting on the other side. 'Come on,' he said. 'What's the matter?'

'I don't know where we're going.'

'Trust me.'

Something flared up inside Clio. 'If you say that one more time I'll scream. Why should I trust you? Well? What do I even *know* about you except . . . except you're a bloody good liar?'

'You aren't bad yourself.' That stopped her for a moment. 'We've got to trust each other,' he said.

'OK. You first. Tell me. What's the plan?'

'We're going to the last place they'd think of looking . . . Back the way we came.'

'*Back?*'

He was watching her, really watching. He can see right through me, she thought, even in the dark. He could see the adrenalin glowing in her veins like neon. He could hear the disappointment in that *Back?* She might be bleary, cold, and scratchy, but the thought of going *back*—just going home and saying sorry . . . No!

'Not home,' he said. 'I know somewhere. Can't explain now, but I've got an . . . old friend. And I do trust you—got to: one word from you, I'm back in prison. So we need each other. Is that a deal?'

Before she could speak he put a finger to his lips, then to hers. It was only a touch, but minutes later, as they loped across the dark fields, she still felt it there.

* * *

The service station lights fell away behind, till there was just the sweep of headlights, too far off to touch them. They kept the road on their left. The fields seemed fast asleep, till a bird took fright and clattered off. In another field, there was a humming in the air, and they looked up to see the girders of a pylon. They went under the power lines quickly, keeping low, as if that humming electricity might strike, like lightning.

Another field, another gate . . . and there was a mass of shadows, breathing. The cows fidgeted, heavily, as they came close. One noise, thought Clio, they could stampede. Max motioned her on.

He was lucky again. There was bound to be a bridge across the motorway somewhere, but he couldn't have known it would be one mile, not twenty. The cow tracks led towards one corner of the field, a gate, and the steep ramp of a footbridge, splashed with cow pats, where the farmer drove his herd across the road.

They kept their heads down, by instinct. At the crest of the bridge, though, Max stopped and pressed his face against the railing. Beneath them rivers of lights flowed into the darkness—bright white one way, duller red the other. 'Be careful!' Clio whispered.

'They can't see us. *We* can see *them*. They haven't got a clue.'

'Come on,' said Clio. 'I'm getting cold.'

It had been a mistake to stop. She was tired and shivering. Max led on and they slogged through more fields.

'Hang on,' said Clio. 'Aren't we going the wrong way? If the road's on *that* side aren't we going *back* . . . to the service station?'

'Uh-huh. Can't hitch anywhere else.'

'What? Why didn't we cross the road *there*?'

'Not very observant, are you? There wasn't a bridge.

No one's going to be looking for us on the *other side* of the motorway. Smart, or what?'

It didn't feel smart to Clio. Ditches and hedges crowded round them and they couldn't find a gate. The ground was all over the place, uneven—she was stumbling, she was so worn out. Then her foot went out from under her and she lay there in the mud.

Max stood on tiptoe, gazing forwards, and for a panicky moment she thought he was going to leave her there. Then he was bending beside her. 'Easy,' he said. 'Slight setback, that's all. Good plan, small setback. We'll be there soon.'

'I can't. I just can't.' She bit her lip. She was not going to start crying. 'Too tired.'

'No, you aren't.' It was the tone she used to Toby when it was a bit too far for him, walking home.

In the crook of the hedge was an angular shape. It squeaked a little, as a pane of corrugated iron moved in the breeze. One end of the barn had fallen in, and if there had ever been doors they were gone. Inside there was a clutter of metal things, old tyres, plastic buckets . . . and the sweet-sour smell of hay. There were bales tumbled in the one good corner and they slumped among them, out of the draught. Max pulled some bales around them like a nest.

'I'm cold,' said Clio. 'Can I have my other top?' She reached for the bag.

'Your things aren't there.'

'Not there?'

'I left them in a safe place. At the service station.' He put his arm around her, shyly. 'We'll keep warm. Do you mind . . . ?'

Clio blinked. It wasn't what he'd said, it was the way he'd said it—kind of shy, as if he'd never asked a girl before. She should mind. She should mind that he'd dumped her clothes somewhere, and hadn't even asked her. But she was weary, weary, and his arm was warm. She let herself crumple against him, her head on his shoulder, and he pulled a scrap of old tarpaulin round them.

'We . . . we can't stop here, can we?' she murmured, but it was only a gesture, and she couldn't help herself: she fell asleep.

The hounds had her scent. They were closing on her—so close she could hear them snuffling. Panting. Once, Clio had watched an anti-hunting video with some of her friends who were into that sort of thing. She'd had bad dreams for months after—dreams in which the dogs were as much bigger than her as a foxhound is bigger than a fox. There was one of them right on her heels now, so close she could smell its breath.

She woke up. Dog's breath. Inches from her face, she saw a dog face, looking . . .

'*Max!*' He was fast asleep. She nudged him, hard.

'Uh? Oh . . .'

Even in the half light, she could see this was no foxhound. Nor was it a German shepherd or bloodhound or Rottweiler or whatever the police use nowadays. It was a patchy sort of mongrel, and way past its best-by date.

'No-o-o problem. There . . . No need to get excited . . .' It was a moment before she realized he was talking to the dog, not her. It cocked its head and listened. Max shifted an arm; the dog made a little rumble in its throat.

'OK, easy, easy . . .' Max said. 'Friends, friends . . .' He kept talking and the dog relaxed. It shuffled closer to their warmth.

'Where did it come from?' Clio whispered. 'Is it a stray?'

'Don't think so. Must be a farm somewhere. Poor old thing . . .' His voice went soft and purring. 'Have they left you outside in the cold? Won't have you in the house, because you're smelly and disgusting. There, there . . .'

That's his charm trick, Clio thought—like with the little girls in the shop. And before that with Toby, while his mum looked on.

Very gently, Max's hand went up to push the dog away. It growled. 'Uh-huh, I think it likes us,' Max said, and rubbed it behind the ears. The dog lay down, its head on Clio's lap. Moments later, it gave a little dog snore.

'So what now?'

'Two options,' Max said gently. 'Either I get my thumbs into his windpipe and hold on till he's dead . . . or we have an hour or two's more sleep. What do you reckon?'

'That isn't funny!' Clio shuddered.

The barn stirred slightly as the wind moved in and out of it, and corrugated iron creaked.

'You didn't mean it, did you?' Clio whispered. 'The windpipe thing . . . ?'

Max chuckled. The dog's breathing rose and fell.

'Not much like Ibiza, is it?' said Clio, after a minute or two.

'Ibiza?'

'You were going to a beach, remember? Sunshine and parties. It sounded like Ibiza.' Max was quiet. 'You don't remember, do you?' she said. 'You just make it up as you go along.'

'I didn't say Ibiza. No—better than that. My own place—somewhere no one knows about but me . . . And you,' he added quickly. 'It'll happen, trust me.'

'You're incredible. We're in a crummy filthy barn in a muddy field—we don't even know where—with a

85

smelly dog on top of us and you say *trust me!*'

'We get out of this, no problem,' Max said.

'How do you know?'

'Because it says so . . . in here.' He patted his bag.

'You mean the book?' said Clio.

Max nodded. 'Everything's in there. Everything.'

'Thanks! Got any more fairy stories?'

'How about this . . . ? *Belladora, Belladora, princess of the midnight wood . . .*'

'That's mine! You nosy bastard. You were earwigging from the front seat!'

'Just being observant,' Max said. 'So, what happens in the end? She slits everyone's throats?'

'Course not, it's for children. She lets them go. And she melts down their gold for her bells.'

'Oh yeah?'

'I suppose not. No one would ever fall for it again, would they? I think her men let her ride off with the gold and *then* they slit their throats.'

'Just what I thought. We *are* the same species, you and me.'

'You're so-o-o arrogant! You don't know me. *No one* knows me. Not Mum and Dad. No one.'

'Oh yeah? Tell you what . . . the first time I ran away from school, I lived with this Romany family—going round the fairgrounds, telling fortunes—and they taught me how to do *this* . . .' He picked up her hand and turned it palm upwards, then started to trace lines with his fingertip. There was just enough light to tell that he was gazing at her eyes. 'Shall I start with the life line, or the . . . ?'

'Stop it,' she said, so sharply that the dog stirred and snuffled.

He let her hand drop. 'Just a joke,' he said. 'What did you *think* I was going to tell you? Something about your family? Your real parents? You must wonder . . .'

'Leave it,' Clio said.

'They could still be alive . . .'

'*Stop* it. It's none of your business. Even if I did know. Which I don't. So that's that.'

'Your mum and dad—the ones here—*they* know.'

'No. There weren't any records. There was a war going on, for God's sake. Anyway, it doesn't matter now.'

There was a pause. Dog breathing . . .

'I was sleeping in this tent once in the Rocky Mountains, and I heard a sound outside—just like that. It was this grizzly . . .'

'I thought it was a tiger. That's what you told Toby.'

'Tigers? In the Rockies? What have they been teaching you at school?' He settled them both more snugly. One of his arms stayed draped round her shoulder, his hand resting on the dog's flank, soothing them both. The other found his bag, his precious bag, as if something inside was his comfort . . . and she knew what it would be.

In her mind, she could see the leather binding, worn shiny by touch. In the dark, his fingers were stroking the book, like a blind man reading Braille.

'We're going to get our beach,' he murmured. 'This friend of mine—he's got one. He'll let us stay there as long as we like.'

'Really? He's rich, is he?'

'Rich? Oh, beyond your wildest dreams.'

Just the word *dreams* was enough. Clio yawned. 'Don't stop,' she said. 'Tell me . . . about your parents. When did they . . . you know?'

'Never knew them. Anyway . . .' His voice was a gentle rumble. 'I had these really dull foster parents, and they didn't like me, and they sent me away to this weird old school, where I learned to do magic, and . . .'

'That's Harry Potter! I nearly believed you for a

87

moment.' She yawned a deeper yawn. 'Can you just say one thing I can believe? Just for a change?'

There was a long pause.

'I like you.'

'Pardon?'

'You heard. Believe me. Being here with you—it changes everything.'

There was a different light above her, and the scratch of hay beneath her cheek. Clio opened one eye. That was sky above her. Daylight . . .

'What time is it?' She sat up and looked round. 'Max? Where are you?'

'Calm down.' He was standing in the open doorway, as if he'd been watching over her. The dog was gone, leaving only the whiff of its smell to say that it had been there. With a small lurch, Clio remembered something Max had said last night, about the dog. But that had been a joke, and he gave her such an easy smile now, it couldn't be true.

'Hi. I didn't want to wake you. We'd better get moving.'

'I'm starving,' said Clio. 'Where's that last pork pie?'

'Inside the dog! We can pick up breakfast on the road!'

On the road . . . ? How could they? Wouldn't everyone be looking out for them by now? But she didn't ask. She knew he'd only give that small disarming grin of his. *Trust me*. And having come this far . . . well, what else was there to do?

11

Friends Like Us

Doing Invisible . . .

1. First thing: think invisible. If anybody looks at you, don't look at them, don't look away. Don't slow down, speed up, tense up. You can let their gaze pass through you without touching. Not many people know this.

2. 1. doesn't work with policemen, people who've fallen in love with you, people you owe money, guys with grudges, bullies etc. They've got radar. You can feel it. Best bet then is: create a diversion, and beat it.

3. Never walk through a door on your own. There's usually someone you can tag along with. Just a little to the side is good. Straight behind, they'll think they're being followed. Even ordinary people sometimes sense things too.

4. Security cameras. Bad invention. They don't pick and choose like people's eyes do. Never look at one direct. Let something else catch your attention, sort of naturally.

5. Or put on someone else's face. That often does the trick.

6. Shops are a problem. They've got staff on the lookout for shoplifters. See 2. Sometimes cameras, too. See 4. Avoid. (Even if they've got the morning papers. Even if you might be in them. Maybe even a picture, and you really want to see it. See if they've got your best side. One worth keeping for the book.)

The thing about Invisible is, once you've mastered it, you can spot someone else trying to do it—especially when they aren't as good as you. The two guys in the service station shop, by the magazines . . . they might as well have been wearing badges saying Men of Mystery. Max clocked them straight away. He hadn't taken his own advice about the shop, but this *was* an emergency.

Quite what his chat-up line was, Max didn't say. All Clio knew was that she was left waiting outside, till she started to get unsettling thoughts like: *How would I know if he's been arrested?* Or worse: *What if he just got a lift for himself and left me here?*

The thoughts disappeared as Max came back out to the car park. He looked pleased with himself. 'We've got our lift,' he said. 'Easy. All we have to do is . . . stay cool. Try not to worry, when you meet them.'

'Why?' said Clio. 'I mean, why not?'

'Nothing. They're just . . . two guys.'

'What kind of guys?'

'They've got some . . . unusual interests, that's all. We just keep nodding, whatever they say.'

'I'm not sure about this,' said Clio.

'You want to walk to Milbourne? Get a lift home in a nice police car? Is that what you want, after . . . everything? *Is* it?' He held out a hand, like goodbye.

'Don't be stupid,' said Clio. 'God knows where you think you're going, but I'm coming too.'

The van was black, matt black, with dark smoked windows. A man appeared from behind it, and looked

Clio up and down. He gave her a firm handshake. 'Franko. With a K. What do you think of the bus?'

'Uh . . . wow,' said Clio. 'It's really . . . black.'

'Stealth,' he said. 'Like the aircraft.' The other man stepped out behind them. 'Meet my Number Two,' said Franko.

She could see what he meant. With his close-cropped hair and shield-shaped patch of beard Psykes was like a photocopy of the first man, only slightly smaller, a bit grainy. He had a leaner face, more lined and stubbled, but their bomber jackets were identical, with the slight hint of a uniform. They both wore black trousers with a lot of straps and pockets, and serious black boots with, Clio couldn't help noticing, white socks underneath.

'Psykes,' the man said. 'With a P.'

'Hi, I'm Cli . . .' She bit the word off halfway. Wasn't she meant to be *Helen*? Franko was watching her with narrowed eyes.

'We know,' he said.

'You . . . know?'

'Didn't I tell you, Psykes?' said Franko. 'See?'

'We listen to the news,' said Psykes.

'We keep an eye on things,' said Franko. 'Proper little celebrities, you two.'

'Relax,' Psykes said. 'We're the best people you could have bumped into. Evasion of detection specialists!'

Franko gave a smile that might have been meant to be reassuring. 'My friend,' he said, 'in this world *everybody's* on the run. Only most of them don't know it. Join the club.'

It was a world of night-sight in the van. Everything outside looked strange and grey. Franko plonked a battered cowboy hat on his head and fired the ignition. 'No need for that,' he grinned as Clio fumbled for a seat-belt. 'This is the free zone, in here. Isn't that right, Psykes?'

'Sure is.' Psykes's face butted forward through a hatch from the back of the van. 'The government's writ does not run here. Let's go.'

Franko tilted the hat back. 'Yee-hah,' he said, and they pulled away.

Psykes's arm came through the hatch with two jumbo egg-and-bacon-burgers, fresh from the service station, in their polystyrene packs. 'Say *please*.'

They said it. Clio did not breathe a word about red meat.

'Smart equipment,' Max said, between mouthfuls. The dials and knobs on the dashboard looked like no in-car stereo Clio had seen.

'The listening station,' Franko said. 'Short wave—all the secret wavelengths.' He flicked it on, and there was a crackle of distorted voices. 'Police,' he said. 'So we're one step ahead.'

'We've got counter-measures,' Psykes cut in. 'So their infrared don't see us. To their spy satellites, we're just a patch of black.'

In the pause that followed, Clio's eyes fell on the magazines tucked under the dashboard. Bodybuilding. Paranormal stuff. And guns.

'You were telling us,' said Franko. 'Your . . . *experience*.'

'It was probably nothing,' said Max. 'It could have been a dream. I was only a kid at the time.'

'Very common,' Psykes chipped in. 'Cases involving children. Parents don't believe them. They tell them it was a dream. Criminal, that is.'

'They sent me to this lady doctor. She made me draw pictures.'

'Uh-huh,' Franko nodded. 'They'll have gone straight on to the secret files. The shrinks are all paid by the government. You're lucky she didn't wipe your mind with drugs right there and then.'

'Excuse me,' Clio said. 'What are you talking about?'

'Abduction,' Psykes said. 'Alien abduction. You mean he hasn't told you? Classic Type 2 incident, from what he's told us. No wonder the Authorities are after him. This boy is *evidence*.' She glanced at Max. *Leave this to me*, said his look. *Don't say a word*.

They came off the motorway at the first exit. 'Too many cameras,' Franko said. 'We need somewhere quiet. For a chat.' They turned down a back road, then a back road off that back road, finally pulling into an empty picnic spot. There was something about it Clio did not like. Her hand crept closer to the door catch.

'Relax,' said Psykes. 'I can see what you're thinking.'

'He's got X-ray eyes, Psykes has,' said Franko.

'What you got to remember,' said Psykes, 'is we're your *friends*. We've decided to trust you—seeing as how you need us. Am I right or am I right?' They nodded.

The back of the van smelt of socks and stale food, but it looked like an underground bunker. Piles of vague equipment were strapped to the roof and sides: aerials, satellite dishes, rolls of electrical wire, computer keyboards, things like heart-rate monitors and radar screens . . . As her eyes got used to the half-light, Clio made out charts plotted with a maze of points and lines. 'Sightings,' said Psykes. 'UFO hotspots. Take a look at this orientation. Significant, huh?'

Franko folded down a bunk: yes, there were living quarters crammed in somehow, too, with a tiny stove, a kind of a cupboard that might be a toilet and squeezed up next to it, an exercise machine. 'Oh, one thing . . .'

Psykes was very close behind her. 'Better give us your mobiles. Just for safe keeping.'

'I'd rather n—' Clio started. Max flashed her a warning frown. 'Sure,' she said. 'OK.'

'Good,' said Franko. 'Just a precaution. You know about NTAC, don't you—secret surveillance unit, MI6. They can trace mobiles, easy—bit of triangulation is all it takes. Most people don't know that.' He pocketed the mobiles. 'It's not as if you'll be giving Mum and Dad a call, is it? Now, Max, you just lie down here.'

Had Max ever passed out for no reason? Did he get flying dreams? Franko read the questions from a clipboard, tick-boxing the answers. Did he ever find himself somewhere, in broad daylight, and not know why he'd got there? The list of questions went on. *Hmmm*, said Franko to himself, when Max said *Yes*. When Franko said *Hmmm*, Max would talk on a little, filling in some details. It was like in the car with Geoff and the twins, when Max turned Australian. He was one step ahead of their new friends, telling them what they wanted . . . oh, but subtly. Were there places he felt *drawn back to*, mysteriously? Did he ever feel he'd had an hour or two of missing time? No, not exactly, Max said. Only . . . that time . . . years ago . . . he got home and everyone said, Where've you been all afternoon?

Psykes nodded to Clio as Franko folded his clipboard away. 'Classic abduction scenario. And you really never knew? You should think about it,' Psykes said. '*You* might start remembering, too.'

'Me? I've never . . .'

'Hmmm. You could be *in denial*. That's one of the signs. Abductees are drawn to each other. I mean, do

94

you know what brought you two together? Are you sure? How else would me and Franko have teamed up? We're such different people . . .'

Clio didn't reply. She was staring over Psykes's shoulder, to where Franko had opened the door of a neat fitted cupboard just behind the driver's seat. He'd slipped the clipboard in, that's all, but the moment was enough. Racked inside the door there was a rifle, a Rambo-style crossbow, wicked army knives . . .

Clio froze, for a moment too long, and Psykes turned round to see where she was looking. In that moment's hush Max looked, too, and finally Franko.

'Uh,' said Max to break the silence. 'You're well equipped.'

'Self defence,' said Franko. 'If the Authorities come knocking one day . . . they'll get a surprise.' He smiled at the thought. 'You're very honoured, you know. Not everyone gets to see inside our HQ. Nobody, in fact. Top secret.'

'Fine,' Max said. 'Fine, fine. We can do secrets, can't we, Clio? Last thing we want is anything to do with the Authorities. You just drop us off where we're going and we'll vanish, just like that. We haven't seen a thing. Total blank in our minds.'

But Franko was looking at Psykes, and Psykes back at Franko, and for a long while no one spoke.

'Good in theory,' Psykes said. 'But a bit naive. You gotta see, you put us in, like, an awkward position, asking for a lift and all.'

'Besides,' said Franko, 'we reckon you're our kind of people. We've got things in common. Why would you want to go hiding out on your own, when you could be with friends like us?'

'Is he right,' said Psykes, 'or is he right?'

* * *

'I need some air,' said Clio.

'Fine,' said Psykes. 'Stay in sight, won't you.' It wasn't a question.

They had parked in a quarry, with rock walls on three sides. The fourth was blocked by the van. Clio sat on a stone with her back to it. They would be watching, she could feel it. Maybe they'd got their listening equipment trained on her, trying to overhear her thoughts. Stop it, thought Clio, that's as paranoid as they are. Then there was a sound beside her. Max sat down.

'Max,' she said quietly, keeping her eyes straight ahead. 'I'm frightened. Those men . . .'

'They're big kids,' he said. 'Like train spotters. Bit of a joke.'

'Joke?' said Clio. 'They've got *weapons*. And there's you telling them all that . . . mad stuff.'

'That *mad stuff* is our ticket for this ride.'

'They've got our mobiles, Max. I don't even know where we are.' She snapped the seed-head off a dried weed. 'And if you say *Trust me*, I'll hit you, I really will. You talked us into this.'

'So I can talk us out of it.'

Clio glanced at him sideways. He looked pale and tired.

'It's all right,' she said. 'I'm not blaming you. But we're in a mess, aren't we? Why don't *you* trust *me*? I could *help*.'

'You *do* help me,' Max said. 'If it wasn't for you, I . . . I wouldn't be here. I don't just mean escaping. I mean . . .' Clio stared at him. For the first time ever, Max was lost for words.

Franko shouted. 'Over here, you two. Quick, you're on the news.'

'We're getting it on tape,' said Psykes, as they came

96

over. DI Wayland's voice was speaking for a moment, then it was the next item, other news. Psykes wound the cassette back. 'You're heading for London, apparently,' he grinned. 'Nice one.'

Click: the tape went on, in mid-item. *I know my daughter. She'd have never, never just run off like this. She must have been taken by force. If you're listening . . .*

'That's my dad!'

'They always do that. Family member. The emotional appeal. They'll have told him what to say.'

'If you're listening, Max, I appeal to you: come back now. You might not have meant this to happen. Just bring her back before any harm's done . . .'

Then there was the reporter's voice. Was that it? Clio thought. *I know my daughter*, Dad had told the nation. Did he? And his message had been addressed—from man to man—to Max, not her.

Max gave a small gasp, very sudden—'Yes!' He was staring at the middle distance.

'Don't take any notice,' Psykes said. 'These appeals are all the same.'

'No . . . not that.' Max pointed with a trembling finger. 'Clio, don't you recognize it?' All she could see was weeds and boulders. 'The shape of that stone . . .'

'Uh . . . What?' said Franko.

'A place you feel mysteriously drawn to . . .' Max said. 'I knew there was something, but I couldn't . . . couldn't . . . Clio, think of Milbourne—out across the harbour— what's it called?'

'Watchman's Down.' Now she looked at the stone, the one she'd sat on, she could see it, sort of: the familiar whale-back shape of Watchman's Down.

'It's all coming back,' said Max.

'Classic!' Franko whispered. 'That's how it happens.'

'Yeah,' said Psykes. 'All blanked out. Repressed. Then

something triggers it. Can you feel it now? The compulsion? Something telling you to *go there*?'

Franko had laid a hand on Max's shoulder. 'This is it. Contact. We've got to be there.'

'No . . .' said Max, weakly. 'Not the lights . . . the probes . . .'

'Don't worry, kid,' said Psykes. 'We'll be with you. Am I right?' He looked at Clio.

Max was staring at the boulder, like someone who's seen a vision. Clio thought what he'd said, minutes earlier: *that mad stuff . . . it's our ticket*. Watchman's Down must be where they had been going anyway.

Clio nodded. 'Oh yes. I think Mr Psykes is right.'

12

Nothing Like the Yukon

Milbourne had never quite made it as a seaside
town, though its suburbs straggled out in that
direction. The back of the harbour was where
it belonged. From the small quay at the harbour's mouth,
this fading afternoon, the town looked worlds away. The
van stopped near the concrete quayside with its shut
café, two shut shops, and a toilet, looking across the
narrow channel to the Spit and Watchman's Down
beyond. In summer a ferry plied to and fro; now, in late
November, you would have to drive miles round the
other way.

'We can't get there from here,' said Clio.

'I know, I know,' said Franko tetchily. 'This is recon-
naissance. Besides . . .' His face suddenly brightened in
a broad grin. 'My auntie brought me here when I was
a nipper. They did brilliant ice creams. Three flavours in
the same cone. Magic.'

Max tried the door handle. 'I need a pee.'

'Not so fast.' Franko scanned the car park, then
nodded. 'I'll come too,' he said. 'Sorry, but the way I
see it you're, like, *our responsibility*.'

Clio watched them go. The moment Max was out of
sight, all this started to seem crazy. Her picture on the
news. Her dad making statements. Everyone in school
would know by now. Then Max came back out, and it

all made sense again. Or it would, as soon as his clever plan kicked in and got them free of these creeps. Clio had no idea what the plan was and nor, she was starting to suspect, did he.

'Hey . . . it's OK, you know,' Psyches said without looking at her. 'You mustn't take all this too seriously.'

'Thanks,' Clio said, gazing bleakly at the sea.

'No, really. I mean, this is just what we do. Like Boy Scouts. If we were . . . birdwatchers or something, you wouldn't think twice about it, would you? I've seen them—they've got just as much kit as us. They're harmless, aren't they? Well.'

Clio was not sure she got the logic, but she nodded.

'You and Max,' said Psykes after a pause. 'You're, like, an item, are you?'

'No,' said Clio automatically. 'I mean . . . not exactly.'

'You don't seem very sure.'

'We're . . . friends.'

Psykes gave her a curious look. 'Hmmm,' he said. 'Good at making friends, isn't he?'

All the way from the quarry Max had been doing his charm thing on Franko, getting him talking, drawing him out. They had taken back roads off their back roads so Franko could show him where the most *significant* crop circle of the year had been. It had just been a field. But Max had been hard at work, getting the man to *like* him. Now a thought struck Clio, as clear as a light from the sky.

Poor Psykes was *jealous*.

Of course. For years now, he and Franko had been buddies, mates, with a hobby, doing what they did . . . which just happened to be being part-time superheroes, fighting to save the world. And now . . . She almost reached out a hand to reassure him, then she stopped herself. That's what she'd always done: tried to keep people happy. What would *Max* do?

'He's fitting in well,' said Clio. 'Just like one of the team.'

'Is he?' Psykes said sourly.

'Sure, you're a great team, you three. Shame this van is only big enough for two.'

Psykes's fingers had been busy with the dials in front of him. They froze. 'Anyway,' said Clio, 'you're the one with the know-how. All this technical stuff. You're indispensable. I mean, just because Max has done Computer Studies . . . He hasn't got your *experience*. That's what counts, isn't it?'

Clio waited a moment for all this to have an effect then, very deliberately, she began to cry.

Psykes turned with a look of alarm. Aliens and secret agents, that was one thing, but . . . a weeping girl was something else.

'I'm sorry,' she sobbed. 'Only . . . it wasn't true, what I said. We're more than *friends*, Max and me. It's . . . the real thing. But you guessed that, didn't you? Like Franko said, you've got X-ray eyes.' She took a breath. 'You've got to help me, Mr . . . Mr . . .'

'Call me Paul. That's the P in Psykes.'

'Paul, please . . . This UFO business, I know it's important, but . . . I don't want him to get mixed up in it.'

'But the Contact . . . If he's had a real Contact . . .'

'He hasn't! It's not true.'

Psykes looked at her sharply. A dangerous moment.

'He tells stories, he can't help it,' Clio said. 'It's just his way of making friends. But you saw through it, didn't you? With your X-ray eyes.' She paused. 'He'd be no good as Franko's Number Two. So . . . we'd be doing everyone a favour, wouldn't we, if me and Max just . . . slipped away?'

A gust of wind pushed at the van and the aerials jangled. 'Bugger,' Psykes said. 'Franko had his heart set on this. He'll go ballistic if he finds out he's been conned.' He looked at Clio gravely. 'He's got such a temper on him. I can't vouch for what he'll do.'

Dear M,

That was a kind of first time for us, Max, though you weren't there to see it. I told a lie about you —not just a little untrue thing like I did with Stella, or when I went along with being Helen in the other people's car, but a real cool deliberate whopper — and I watched someone believe it and I felt . . . I still don't quite know how to put this . . . that them believing it made it sort of true.

The good thing was (you'd have loved this, if you'd been listening) that it was true, the bit about you making up stories, only I told it like a lie, and I watched poor old Psykes be fooled — no, fool himself with it, isn't that what you'd say?

As for the rest of it, the bit about planning to run away together, being so-o-o in love . . . well, it was meant to be a lie, so it counts as one, doesn't it?

Anyway, it was a first. I think it brought us closer, Max. I suddenly knew what it must feel like, being you.

There was some disagreement about Clio's loo break. There was some disagreement all around them in the air. When Franko and Max came back, chatting and grinning, Psykes went sort of edgy and sharp.

'I suppose I'm meant to go in with her?' he said.

'Course not,' said Franko. 'Wait outside. What d'you think she's gonna do—flush herself down the pan?'

'This isn't a joke,' Psykes snapped.

'Ah, lighten up. There's got to be a good chippie some-where round here,' said Franko. 'How about it? Cod and chips all round.'

'I don't like cod. You *know* that.' Psykes turned away. 'I thought Provisions was Number Two's responsibility,' he said. 'Or is that changed now?'

'Can I go?' said Clio.

'In the back,' said Psykes.

'Let her use the proper toilets,' Max said. 'It's getting dark. No one will see.'

'Nothing wrong with our arrangements,' Psykes said. 'Aren't they good enough for you?'

'Oh, for God's sake,' Franko said to Clio. 'Just run over . . .'

'What's this?' Psykes said. 'I'm outvoted, am I? Since when has this unit been a frigging *democracy*?'

Clio missed the next few minutes. The toilet cubicle was cold and bleak. I could run for it, she thought . . . and the words seemed about as real as *I could fly*. Though, if Max was with her . . .

As she got back to the van she heard the voices. 'We're meant to be an effing team, aren't we? Just you and me.'

'You're not my bleeding *wife*, for Christ's sake!'

Pause. 'And what's *that* meant to mean?'

The door opened a crack, and there was Max's pale face. 'Now?' mouthed Clio. For a second he hesitated, then the door eased open just enough for him to slither out, clutching his bag.

'What started that?' he whispered.

'Me,' said Clio. There was a look in his eyes—pure admiration—that she would never forget. He clutched his bag to his chest, and they ran.

* * *

103

The light was going. Out at sea broken patches of it still hung there, steely, but a bank of dark clouds moved in on the wind. There was a jangling from the masts of a few sailboats hauled up on the slipway on the sheltered side of the quay. Already the Rip was the colour of slate, and along the Spit she saw a smudge of breakers in the gloom.

They crouched behind the padlocked, metal-shuttered cottages, listening. Now and then, they caught a muffled shouting: Franko and Psykes, building up to a fight. But all it would take, thought Clio, was one pause for breath . . .

Thud. A door slammed. 'Max? *Max!*' Franko spoke, then called, then shouted. 'Get your arse back here. Now! I'm not playing games.'

'We came the wrong way,' Clio whispered. 'That's the road out, over there.' They peered out at the car park just in time to see the van's lights come on, floodlighting the exit.

'There must be a back way,' Max said.

'No,' said Clio. 'That's it.'

'Ah,' said Max.

'So what was your plan?'

'My plan? This is *your* plan.'

'You got us here. What was meant to happen?'

'Don't know,' Max said. 'I knew something would turn up. That was pretty impressive, what you did.' In the middle of the car park, Franko came towards them, panning with a torch.

Max took her hand. She held on, as he towed her gently round behind the cottages, past the locked-up ice cream kiosk . . .

'Come out, yer tricksy little buggers.' That was Franko, coming round the houses.

'We're your friends, remember?' Psykes's voice was closer, coming round the other way.

104

There was a low wall now between them and the edge of the quay. Max let go her hand, sat on the edge, swung his legs over, and dropped.

There was no splash. She heard a little grunt as he landed. 'It's OK,' he whispered. 'Come on!'

It was only a few feet, but the sloping slipway threw her and she sprawled full length. Max was on his knees beside her. 'Look!' Among the hauled-up sailing boats was a small square-ended dinghy, with its stubby paddles in it. 'Easy . . .' Max said as they lifted it. And so it was: the dinghy felt as light as polystyrene, and as fragile, too. 'Sssh.' They kept close beneath the wall, as Franko's torch flickered overhead. From close to, the water had an even blacker look.

'Well?'

'Where are they?'

Psykes's voice and Franko's came together.

'You said they . . .'

'They went your way.'

Then they were bickering.

'Quick,' said Max. 'Now!' He waded in knee deep, steadying the dinghy for her. It gave a lurch as he dropped the bag in, and a worse one when he heaved himself in after it. He started fumbling with the paddles.

'Max . . . ?' Clio whispered. 'You do . . . *do* you know how to . . . ?'

'Easy. If I can do white-water rafting on the Yukon I can handle a rowing boat, for Christ's sake . . .' He tugged on the paddles. One caught, one splashed, and they lurched off sideways, in a slow spin. Clio held her breath. There was only a narrow channel between them and the safety of the sand spit on the other side.

Suddenly the boat swung on its axis, hard. Max dug with the oars but the water was flowing every which way, and the lights of Milbourne and the dark shapes

105

of the quay on one side, the Spit and the Down, had all started to spin. The eddy sucked them sideways, then helplessly backwards, faster and faster, into the narrowing throat of the Rip. Clio found herself lying on the boat's floor and didn't know quite how she had got there.

'No prob,' Max gasped, at her side. 'Don't move, that's all.' The quay loomed above them, as big as a bus. A warning light swung past, and a glimpse of an iron ladder, all bearded with weed. Then the harbour was gone and thump, they hit the first wave. Clio lifted her head for a second to see the water round them all rucked up in heaps of foam. 'There!' Max said. 'Nothing compared to the Yukon.'

'Liar!'

'*What* did you say?' She never had time to find out if he was really angry, because that was when the next wave hit them, side on, and this time they nearly went over. Afterwards she couldn't say whether she had been screaming out loud, or just quietly inside, but when she got her breath she found herself clutching him, him clutching her. Another wave threw them sideways, then the current gripped them, straightened them out so they reared up, almost vertical . . . and dropped, through the wave, and the next one, and the next, bucking less each time until the tumult settled to a slow swell. They seemed to be moving alongshore, down the sand spit on the current.

'What did you say just now? What did you call me?'

'Liar,' said Clio. 'You've never been on the Yukon. I bet you've never rowed a boat before.'

It was too dark now to see his expression, but she heard him laughing quietly. 'You know what?' he said. 'I'm really glad I'm doing this with you.'

'I suppose I'm meant to say the same thing, am I?'

'No need.'

Clio gave him a punch.

'Stop! You'll have us in the water.'

'You . . . You're so *arrogant*!' Then she was shuddering all over, as if she was suddenly cold. Max laid his arm around her.

'We . . . could have d—we nearly . . . Oh, God . . .' She raised her head to look round. In the darkness it was hard to tell what was waves, what was shore. All of it was lumpy, queasy, rocking as the dinghy rocked. Clio's hands ached with clutching the seat and she could not make them let go.

'It's OK,' Max said, so lightly that one crazy wish went through Clio's mind. She willed him to say that all this wasn't happening—it was a dream, it was one of his stories, but she could relax, because it wasn't true.

He did not say it. He just smiled to himself. 'It's OK.'

Toby yanked at Stella's sleeve.

They were in the supermarket, in the aisle between the freezer cabinets. The air was chill and buzzing, and she leaned in for a pack of frozen peas. 'Wait a minute, Toby Trouble,' she said wearily. They shouldn't be out this late, but she'd been jumpy and Toby was picking it up. He should be in bed now but there was no way he was going to sleep. 'OK,' she'd said in the end, 'let's go on a shopping adventure.' He knew what that meant. There would be an ice cream in it for him in the end.

'Look, Mum, look . . . it's Clio's mum and dad.'

Stella straightened up, and wished she hadn't. At the same time, Clio's mother caught sight of her, and flinched. A moment earlier, she could have turned back and pretended she hadn't seen her, but their eyes met.

'Jen . . .' said Stella. 'I . . .' They'd spoken once on

107

the phone since Clio and Max had disappeared. Jen had been stony, almost silent. Stella had managed to blurt out how she was sorry, I mean *really* sorry . . . how she'd never meant . . . she'd only wanted to . . . but . . . but . . . Then Jen had put the phone down, and when Stella dialled again, she got the answerphone.

Clio's father came down the aisle behind Jen with the trolley. Toby was quite still, his fingers locked in Stella's sleeve.

'How are you both?' Stella tried again. 'Are you OK?'

'What do you think?' said Clio's mother.

'Is there any news?'

Mike came alongside his wife. 'Look, Stella,' he said, 'leave it, will you? You've done enough harm already.'

'I just want to help.'

'I said *leave it*!' Mike's voice came out so loud that other shoppers turned to look. 'When they find her, when our daughter's back home safe and sound . . . then, just maybe, we'll have time for your excuses. Understood?'

They pushed past, and Stella was left standing motionless. Toby squeezed her hand cautiously. It was still cold from the frozen peas.

'It's OK,' Max said. 'Look, we're nearly there.' The dragon's back of beach huts was silhouetted on the dull glow of the lights of Milbourne in the sky. The way he said it, Clio thought, it could have been some kind of Promised Land.

'That's it, isn't it?' said Clio. 'That's where you've been taking us?' She tried to square that jagged outline—an abandoned fort, a palisade—with her memory of summer beach huts and ice creams and buckets and spades. 'You said you had a friend . . .'

108

'Sort of friend. Maybe. We'll find out.' Max fished for the paddles in the bottom of the boat, and they wobbled, scarily.

'Give me one,' said Clio. There was another lurch as they tried to shuffle side by side, then they each pawed at the water, uselessly. 'We've got to do it *together*,' she said. 'You don't know a thing about it, do you?'

'It's easier in the Yukon—downhill all the way!'

'Oh, shut up,' said Clio. 'Come on. *One*-two-*one*-two . . .' At last they took a little surge towards the shore, and another, till they came into the breakers. This time the waves were on their side. Each one lifted them and surfed them in. They came alongside a warning marker on the end of a groyne, a tide-breaking wall built straight out from the beach. Inside the groynes, the sea felt different, tamer.

'Max!' said Clio suddenly. 'I saw a light.'

'What?'

'A *light* . . . Look, there!' She was shouting now, over the sound of the surf, and that might have been what caught the attention of the figure with the light. For a moment it moved in front of the lantern, and seemed huge, then it had picked up the light and it came flashing their way.

'Row back!' yelled Clio, but it was no good. The sea would do just what it wanted with them now. 'It's them,' she said weakly.

Max stared. 'I don't think so.'

There was only one figure, it was true. As it came closer it was silhouetted by the sky behind. Now it was climbing along the groyne, flashing the beam their way, sometimes finding them, sometimes not. Then the dinghy grounded and the next wave nearly spilled them out. There was a splash as the figure forged into the surf and the boat was steady, suddenly, as a

109

fist clamped on the stern. 'Bloody hell. Kids. Kids in a toy boat.'

He did not reach a hand to help them. The face was just a patch of darkness, behind the dazzle of the light. Clio thought of stories she'd heard once on holiday in Cornwall—the wreckers who brought ships onto the rocks with false lights, who would strip a sailor of his valuables, cut the rings off his fingers, cut the fingers off if need be . . . then throw him back like a fish.

'Bloo-oody hell,' it said again, more slowly. 'It's *you*.'

'Hi,' said Max. 'We were on our way to see you.'

'Were you now? Bloody funny way to go about it.' For a moment the rough voice softened . . . Only for a moment. 'Well, you've seen me. Now you can sod off.'

'Help us,' said Max. 'We need a place to be.' The face came forward and Clio saw the narrow-creased eyes, the jaw like a stubbly potato, wisps of wild hair beneath the black wool hat. 'One night, that's all.'

'You're bad news, you know that? Bloody famous, you are.'

'Yeah, but we're in London, aren't we? Says so on the news.'

'Maybe. So this is your . . . little girlfriend.' He flashed the light full in her face. 'Very nice.' It didn't sound like any kind of compliment. With a jerk he tipped the boat, then reached out a hand to steady them as they stumbled through the shallows.

'Clio,' said Max. 'Oggie. He's not as bad as he sounds.'

It was a gamble. The man almost laughed. 'Don't bank on it.'

'One night,' Max said.

'Oh yeah? And if I don't . . . ? What's Plan B?'

'Plan B? This is Plan Z,' said Max. 'I'll tell you all about it.'

'I bet you will.' At last the man laughed out loud, one

short bark of it. 'You'll tell me nothing, OK? I don't want to know. You can have a hut. One night.' He turned to the dinghy and smashed in its bottom with the heel of one big boot. He pushed it back into the waves, which got hold of it like any other wreckage—flotsam and jetsam—and took it away.

'You'll keep your mouth shut. Lippy little bugger. You'll go in that hut and shut the door and you won't *breathe* till morning. Got me?'

'Don't worry,' Max said. 'We're not going anywhere.'

The man called Oggie nodded. 'Yeah. I'll see to that.'

13

Tea With the Ogre

The door of the hut closed firmly, shutting them in. There was a final extra *snick*. Max tried the handle but they knew already: it was locked. Oggie had told them as much himself.

'It's for your own good,' he had said, glancing out to sea. 'We'll talk about it in the morning.'

Inside, it was dark as a cellar, with a stale dank smell. Clio felt for a light switch, and she could hear Max fumbling round . . . then a crash beside her as he knocked something like a saucepan off a surface, and he swore. 'Do these places *have* electricity?' he said.

'Don't know.' She felt about for a bulb above their heads. 'Maybe they don't . . . Max, I'm cold. I'm sopping. Where are you?' She reached out till they found each other's hand. 'What are we going to do?'

'It'll be OK. People live here.'

'Only in the summer.'

'There must be candles, at least.'

Quite what use candles would be for her wet jeans, Clio was not sure. Still, just talking seemed to help. Now they were used to it, the pitch-black had softened. Just behind them, where her hand had found a window pane, Clio could make out small dim points of light—and remembered the metal storm-shutters that people would fix on these huts when they shut up for the winter—

112

some protection from the debris that the waves and the wind tossed about. The little holes were not enough to see by—just enough to show them where the windows were, quite big across the front wall of the hut, and smaller and dimmer at the other end. Clio found a window catch and rattled it, but the shutters had been screwed tight.

'Yes!' A match flared quickly . . . went out, and Max struck a second and a third before one stayed alight. As she blinked, Max's face grinned at her like a pumpkin, lit from underneath. Together they hunted through drawers, on shelves, in the little high-up cupboard on the wall—match after match—till . . . 'Here!' In an old-fashioned dresser in the corner, Clio found a box of candles. Once they had a couple lit, they could make some sense of where they were.

It was larger than a garden shed, though not much—maybe four metres long, not quite so wide. It looked like a lumber room at first glance, with old furniture in every nook, but half of that was the shadows cast by their candles, so the room seemed to shift itself around them as they moved. One corner by the door was a sort of kitchen—a cooker and a little sink with a bucket underneath. A rickety sort of dining table took up most of the rest of the floor space at that end. Along one wall a small hard sofa sat very upright, but there was nothing like a bed in sight.

'What did he mean: *our own good*? Why did you let him *do* that?' Clio said. 'I thought you were supposed to be his friend.' There was no answer. 'He could do anything,' she said. 'He could phone the police. They could be offering a reward for us, for all you know.'

'Uh-huh. Not the police. Oggie and the police . . . don't mix.'

'He could do *anything*,' she said again. 'He could kill us.'

'Nah. He likes me.'

'Likes you! Didn't look like it to me.'

'You should see him when he doesn't,' Max said. 'And he likes you too.'

All this might have been more reassuring, Clio thought, if she knew who or what this Oggie was. So far, she had barely glimpsed his face. As far as she was concerned, he was a big shape in the darkness—big across as well as tall—and a smell of sweat and old smoke, and a voice like something metal dragged on stone. She had felt the strength of his grip as he'd pulled her through the shallows. Whether it helped to be told 'he likes you', Clio wasn't sure.

'There's a kind of heater,' Max said. 'Looks like camping gas. And I think there are gas lamps. Ah . . . no cylinders . . .'

'Great!' Clio was shivering. 'What are we supposed to *do*?'

'Must be blankets or something somewhere . . .' He pulled open a small door. 'There . . . Oh, yuck.'

'What is it?'

'Chemical toilet, I think.'

'Good. I need to . . . you know.'

'I wouldn't advise it,' Max said. 'There's stuff growing in it. There's a bucket, though.'

Clio took one look. 'It's OK. I'll hang on.'

Max was still hunting. Under the seats there were storage boxes, but only beach things in them. 'Where do these people *sleep*?' he said. 'Of course!' Near the back wall was a steep sloping ladder, up to a hatch in the ceiling. 'There!' He pushed the trapdoor open. 'Bring that candle. Mind your head.'

The loft space was tall enough to crawl into on hands and knees. The eaves were crammed with cardboard boxes, just like any attic, but on the wooden floor were two thin mattresses, made of spongy, damp-feeling foam. Things did not feel so sandy up here, that was one thing. Best of all, one of the boxes held a pile of blankets— even if they were the kind you might keep in the car for the dog.

'Don't take this the wrong way,' Max said, 'but you've got to get out of those clothes.' Another cardboard box yielded some musty baggy sweaters and a pair of pink size 18 tracksuit bottoms.

'Yech,' said Clio.

'You'll be glad of them. Look, you're shivering now.' He held the blanket up for her, like a changing screen, as she wriggled out of her sodden things and into something dry. He didn't look. '*Thanks*,' she whispered. It was better in the loft space. They could keep close, for warmth, like they'd done in the barn.

It was so much easier to lie down than to try to kneel. Max was unpacking his bag intently, spreading damp things out to dry. Clio stretched out with a sigh.

'Are you OK?' he said.

'OK? You must be joking! God knows whose these clothes are. I don't like to think.'

'It'll be better in the morning, I just need to talk to Oggie.'

'I don't get it. Why should he help us? How can you be so sure?'

'I know a few things about him, that's why. Things he wouldn't like everyone to know.'

'Oh yes? He just told you, did he?'

'Actually,' Max said, 'yes. People do. Can't think why.'

At the front of the loft was a tiny window—shuttered, like all the windows downstairs, but the job hadn't been done quite so well. Max managed to open it a crack,

115

enough to press his cheek against the glass and squint out.

'What can you see?' said Clio.

'Nothing. Nothing much.' But he stayed there, trying this way and that for a better angle. 'You get some sleep,' he said.

'Uh . . . I think I'd better use that bucket.'

'No problem. I won't listen.'

She was almost too tired to care. It was all she could do to lower herself down the ladder and back up again before she fell asleep.

The ground was rumbling under her, like an oncoming train. No, it was a voice, a man's voice; someone buried but not dead was shouting, calling her, from underground. She opened her eyes in a tight dark space, as if it was her in the coffin . . . then remembered the beach hut, the loft . . . and it was Oggie's voice shaking the floorboards: 'Get down here *now*. You got some explaining to do.'

'OK, OK.' That was Max's voice, beside her. 'Coming,' he called through the hatch.

In daylight—or the greyish light that came in through the opened door—Oggie was as big as he had seemed in the dark. He nearly filled the space between the table and the sink. As Clio peered from the hatch the first thing she saw was his hair, the wild thinning straggle of it. There were traces of old copper-red among the grey. Down on a level with him, she saw that he wasn't that tall, but he had bulk—a lot of stomach, and a lot of muscle too. He made her think of those middle-aged bikers you get at the seaside, still in their same Hell's Angels denim and the same hair from the Sixties, and red in the face from the drink. The difference with Oggie,

116

as she'd find out soon enough, was that he wouldn't be a member of anyone's club.

'Right.' He was looking at Max, standing there with bare knees and some old-man's sweater hanging round him like a dress. 'Let's make this snappy. What the fagging hell did you think you were playing at?'

'Not *playing*,' Max said. 'Me and Clio . . .'

'I'm not talking about you and her.' Oggie glanced up and caught sight of Clio, halfway down the steps in her horrible tracksuit trousers. He narrowed his eyes, took her in. That was all. 'I'm talking about *you*,' he said to Max. 'That stunt at the Complex.'

'I thought you'd enjoy that,' Max said. Oggie gave him a look that Clio couldn't fathom. 'Anyway, it was a joke. Wasting police time. That can't be bad, can it?'

'Some people got hurt,' said Clio, from above. 'Burns, cuts, things like that.'

Oggie raised his brambly eyebrows. 'Got a mind of her own, that one,' he said. 'Not *so* much in lurv, then!' Clio felt herself blush. 'Don't mind me,' he called up to her. 'I'm a professional ogre. It's my job to scare the kids away.'

'Oggie's a kind of warden,' Max said. 'He watches the place in the winter.'

'Isn't it . . . lonely?' Clio said.

'Oh, *lonely*'s fine by me. Like music to my ears, is *lonely*. Like a drop of a bloody good malt whisky. You needn't think I want you or any bugger else to keep me company.'

'Ah,' smiled Max, 'but this is us. We're special.'

A wide grin opened in Oggie's battered face, showing a disastrous set of teeth. He came over and leaned on the ladder. 'He hasn't changed! Just let me tell you a few things about young Mark or Mick here.'

'Max,' said Clio.

'Max now, is it? Well, the last time I saw him he was

117

hitching up to London to work with a band—story was, he ran into their singer at a party and she said, *Drop by any time* . . . Did anything come of that?'

'They split up,' Max said.

'Sure they did. And that religious cult you were running away from—the one your parents gave all their money to . . . I guess that split up too. 'Cause I asked round a bit and no one had heard of any of it.' He gave a chuckle. 'You get the picture?' he said to Clio. 'I suppose he's told you all this? Say no more. Then of course there's the fifty quid I lent him—for a week or two!'

'I can pay it back,' said Max. 'We could help here. Odd jobs. We could . . . run errands. The occasional *delivery*.' There was something in the way he said it that made Oggie pause.

'What are you getting at?' said Oggie and for a moment he and Max were face to face. *I know a few things about him*: wasn't that what Max had said? Max kept the blandest expression—butter-wouldn't-melt—but his eyes didn't blink. 'Hah!' Oggie snorted. 'I knew I should have pushed you two back in the drink.'

'Don't worry,' Max said. 'We won't make any bother. We've got nowhere to go. No one we can trust not to turn us in.'

'And what makes you think I wouldn't?'

'Because you like us. And anyway, if we get picked up, the first cop who'll want to talk to me is DI Wayland.'

There was a hush; the grin went stiff on Oggie's face, and faded; a gust of rain swished on the shutters. Clio kept very quiet. Somewhere in the hut a leak began to drip.

'Well,' Oggie said. 'Detective Inspector now, is it? I don't expect he would remember me.' He grabbed Max by the collar. 'You didn't bloody mention me, did you?'

'No. Honest. Scout's honour. Cross my heart and hope to die.'

For a moment Oggie's grip trembled and his face was red, then a great laugh rumbled up from his belly. 'He's a cool bugger, isn't he?' he said to Clio.

'We can stay, then?' Max said. 'Just till the heat's off.'

'Who knows you're here?'

'Nobody.'

Oggie weighed him up. He looked at Clio, hard. 'Is that true? 'Cause if it isn't . . . I promise you this: I'll get you, good and proper, before they get me.'

Max did not blink. 'OK,' said Oggie, 'deal done. I reckon we should have a cup of tea to that. Get some clothes on, then follow me.'

What Oggie called tea came out of a filing cabinet in the small site office. The walls were plastered with tide tables, first aid posters, and a lot of adverts for happy summer things from years ago. Oggie got out three greasy tumblers, and poured a finger of what he called tea into each. He raised his.

Just the smell of the whisky burned Clio's throat, but Max nodded at her, and she took a sip, and choked.

'Did you see the explosion?' Max said.

'Matter of fact I did. A bit bloody spectacular, actually. Grandstand view from here.'

'Was it better than yours?' said Max, mysteriously.

Oggie smiled and poured himself another. 'You say that again, or anything like it, out loud, anywhere, ever, and I'll twist your fagging head off. Got that?'

'Sure, sure,' Max said. 'See?' he said to Clio. 'Me and Oggie—old friends. He's a good bloke, isn't he—as ogres go?'

* * *

119

There were conditions, of course. No wandering round in daylight, especially not together. They would keep a lookout—some idiots came for walks out here at weekends, even in November. Once in a blue moon a hut owner might come out to check it hadn't blown away in a storm . . . Oggie caught Clio's worried look. 'Don't worry. This one's not been used for years. Old couple, they were. Kept it on for the grandchildren, but they don't come here any more. Old folks have probably both gone gaga and forgotten all about it.'

Whatever he said, they just kept nodding. Any sign of strangers, and they'd lie low. They would live like mice, and be invisible. There was food in the shop behind the office, stuff left from last year; they could have anything past its best-by date, a big bottle of gas each for the fire and the stove, a canister each for the lamps— on condition the shutters stayed up. No open doors, no signs of habitation. Inside, he added with a smirk, they could do what they liked.

Clio nodded, nodded. She could still feel the burn of fire-water inside her and the bare bulb in Oggie's office seemed to shed an amber glow. Even the horrible clothes from the loft seemed like some sort of joke. Somewhere in the back of her mind, like the start of a toothache, were all kinds of questions with Mum and Dad and school and Stella in them somewhere, then she thought: you don't have to think about them. It felt like a little revelation. Just push them aside, and they fade. Why had nobody told her that before? Just let them go.

That seemed to be what Oggie did. He seemed to be a man who'd let a lot of things go, with a glimpse of belly hair showing through the frayed vest in the gap between his shirt and belt. In this light, even Oggie had his good side. He could have been handsome once, she saw that, and there was something grand about his squalor—no apologies and no embarrassment. In ancient history, he could have been a warrior. She didn't know what he'd been in real life—no doubt Max would have a story. She guessed that whisky would be part of it. Whatever, he was king of this small kingdom and, till now, its sole inhabitant.

And that was how it felt, as Clio and Max wove back between the beach huts to their own, with the keys in their hand. A small kingdom . . . It was theirs, too, and the mist had put a screen around it, magically erasing it from all maps in the world outside. They saw a line or two of foam in the mist-coloured sea, and no horizon, but there was a brightness further out as though the sun was shining somewhere and could break through any time.

They came between the huts, and saw the stiller waters of the harbour, fringed with reed-beds, where the wading birds ticked to and fro. Somewhere beyond must be a town called Milbourne, but it couldn't touch them. As Clio watched, a flock of grey geese appeared from the mist, flying low. They splashed down in the water and at once were busy and at peace. It was a *haven*. With that word, Clio had a vision: the thousands of miles they'd flown, from their cold distant places, knowing this was where they had to be.

When she turned back, Max was at the hut—their hut. He had unlocked the door, and she saw him inside, with a dustpan and brush, clearing sand. Their wet clothes from last night were hanging up to dry. He had lit a gas lamp and the hut was filled with its mild hissing glow. Clio smiled.

'Hey,' Max said over his shoulder. 'I've found the stop-cock. We've got water. Luxury!' Crouched, with his back bent and his hair flopped forward, he was not posed,

121

poised, and handsome, like he could be. He looked just like an ordinary person, who she'd known for ever. Now he looked up and smiled, as if he might be thinking the same about her, and here they both were, flown in out of nowhere, coming home.

14

Live Like Mice

It was a cross between a ghost town and a desert island. Two lines of huts straggled along the narrow Spit, like a backbone, so that half had the sea view, half the harbour. Some were lovingly painted, pink or sky-blue, and looked crisp and clean. Others were peeling, cracked, and blunt around the edges as if the salt and sand were wearing them away. All were locked and shuttered, with wire mesh or hardboard on the windows: empty—all, that is, except this one, with Max and Clio in it, and another at the end beneath the slope of Watchman's Down. That was the only way in from the land side and, as if guarding it, there was the Ogre's den. Clio and Max were not invited, and it seemed not worth the risk to pry.

'He's a bit moody.' Max sat on their porch, picking at the salt-parched decking. 'When he's in a downer . . . well, you wouldn't want to know!'

'You two go back a long way, do you?'

Max laughed. 'He gave me a lift once. We got talking.'

'You're a quick worker,' Clio said.

'I've got to be.' There was something in his voice that made her look again. Most of the time he seemed ten years older than he looked—and not in a bad way. Compared to him, the boys she knew at school were

123

just pretending, always glancing at each other to check they were doing it right. Not Max. He was sure.

Then suddenly you'd catch him off guard, looking . . . sort of young. It made her think of Toby when he hadn't been found out yet but knew there would be trouble when he was. Whatever they say about him, Clio thought, deep down Max is OK.

Who was he, deep down, truly? She wanted to know.

'Max,' she started. 'Tell me . . .' But he'd already moved on—he was up, ready for action. He did a dance move, clicked his heels then took her by the hand and tugged her to her feet. 'Come on,' he said. 'Old Oggie's done his rounds. He won't be around for hours. Let's explore.'

A desert island . . . And it nearly *was* an island. All that joined the sand spit to the mainland was the bulge of Watchman's Down. That fell away in steep cliffs on its seaward side, but on the other a thicket of thorns and rhododendrons crouched low between it and the harbour. A track wound through it but they hadn't seen anyone yet. Who would come there? The Spit was a dead end. It might be a resort in summer, but in the winter it felt like an accident. A freak of the tides kept dragging the sand off other beaches and dumping it here, in the lee of the headland. Then the wind blew and piled up dunes, against the groynes, against the beach huts, against anything that stood still. You could tell the huts that had not been used for a while, because the sand had crept up to their doors, looking for cracks. Even the beach huts were a kind of driftwood. All it needed was a small tsunami, Clio thought—that, and a bit of global warming. Milbourne could wake up one morning, blink, and all this would be gone.

* * *

Oggie banged on their door. 'Hi,' said Max cheerily, but the big man wasn't there to chat. He was off for a few days. Bit of business. They'd better keep their heads down. And if he came back and found the slightest sign they'd interfered with anything . . .

'Message understood,' said Max. 'Like mice.'

'Messy buggers, mice,' Oggie said. 'I kills 'em. You'll want something to read.' He dropped a newspaper on the table—one of the tabloids, open at an inside page. In a moment they heard the cough and clatter as he kicked his old van into life. They listened as it puttered off and faded. A wading bird made its *wheep-wheep* in the reed beds. They were on their own.

'What does he do?' said Clio.

'I don't think he'd like me to tell you,' Max said, 'even if I knew. Which I don't. Still . . . it makes sense of last night. Why he was so edgy . . . Why he packed us out of sight like that . . . Why he was watching out for someone, but it wasn't us. And what he meant by *for our own good*. I don't imagine they'd have been too pleased to see us here . . . whoever they were.'

'But it's all right now,' said Clio. 'Isn't it?'

Max looked around the dingy beach hut, as if this was their five-star hotel. 'Oh yes,' he said. 'Very all right. I'd say we've got a really sweet arrangement.'

'Oh yeah? Cold water? No drains? Every time I want a pee I've got to use the toilet block? The *men's* end, 'cause the women's is locked up for the winter!'

'What's wrong with that? No one's around.'

'What's wrong with that? It stinks, that's what. Or don't men notice?'

'There's always the bucket.'

She ignored that. '*And* no electricity? Sand in everything. And damp. We can't even see out of the windows, for God's sake. You want me to go on?'

125

'People pay money for this,' Max grinned. 'It's called *getting away from it all*. And . . .' he said softly, serious again, 'that's what you wanted, wasn't it?'

Clio tried to think. Was it? Then she caught the glint in Max's eyes. 'What do you fancy for supper?' he said. 'Let's go raid the village store.'

It was as she was opening a can of baked beans—the cheapest, not the sort they had at home—that she happened to glance at the paper.

'Max!' she said. 'We're in here. It's us.'

'I know. Not front page, but at least we're national.'

Clio stared at the page. 'They're holding someone. In Birmingham. They think I've been murdered or something! That's so horrible.'

'You haven't, have you? They found your clothes, that's all.'

Clio looked from him to the paper and back again, and it fell into place. 'What did you *do* with my school things? You said you'd left them somewhere safe.'

'I did. In the cab of a lorry. Someone was bound to find them.'

'But . . . the poor driver. And . . . oh, God, my mum and dad!'

He came and stood beside her and for once he didn't speak. Clio was grateful for that.

'You don't know what Mum's like—even when there's nothing real to worry about. And Dad . . . when she gets anxious, he gets angry. They're not good together in a crisis, without . . .'

'Without you? Poor Clio.'

She stared at him. The cheek . . . That was the kind of thing Stella said, her and her textbook psychology.

126

'Max, they think I've been raped and killed or something! How *could* you?'

'What shall we do?' he said, reasonably. 'Phone them?'

'*Phone* them?' She thought of the last time. She couldn't face Dad's voice like that again. 'I could text them,' she said, 'if those weirdoes hadn't nicked our mobiles.'

'Anyone could text them. It's got to be your voice . . . Hold it,' he said. 'Don't phone them. The police will be expecting that—probably ready to trace it. Phone somebody else who knows your voice.'

'Rachel? Kareena?'

'Someone adult. They'll believe them better . . . How about Stella? Do you know her number?'

Clio nodded. 'Uh . . . what do I say?'

'What do you *want* to say?'

She stared into the can of baked beans as if she'd been asked for the meaning of life.

'*One*,' said Max: 'are you OK? Healthy?'

'I suppose so. Bit cold.'

'Say that. Not the bit about the cold. *Two*: are you with me? They'll want to know.'

She looked at him: 'Am I?'

'Oh yes. You bet. *Three*: am I holding you at knife-point? No? Am I brainwashing you . . .' He swam his face inches from hers, his eyes wide, '. . . with my mes-mer-iz-ing powers?'

'No chance!' She pushed him away from her, laughing.

'Good. Four: are you coming home? Like, tomorrow?'

'No . . .' Her laughter vanished. 'Not yet . . . Max, all I want to say is . . . well, *I want some time.*'

'That's it then. Say that. Then ring off. Forty seconds, tops—one twenty-p piece. Oh,' he added casually, 'and we're in Liverpool. Keep them on their toes.'

127

'I'm not sure I can do this,' she said, when they reached the phone box. It looked disused—the old red kind, salt-rusted, in behind the toilet block. She almost hoped it wouldn't work.

'Yes, you can.' He squeezed in beside her. 'Don't worry. I'll be right here all the time.'

And she could. Her heart raced and her breath went short, as if she'd just run up a hill, but she punched in the *number-withheld* code, then Stella's number, and it rang, and then . . . Anticlimax. The answerphone. Clio nearly slammed it down, but Max nodded: *Go on*. She said the words, like reading from a script. 'And . . .' She reached the end. 'And I'm really sorry, Stella. It wasn't your fault, honest. It wasn't anyone's fault.' It came out in one breath. Max nodded. She put down the phone.

'That was good, at the end,' he said, opening the door. 'And they've got it on the answerphone.' He stepped out into the breeze, leaving her still trembling, keyed up, as if somehow there should have been *more*.

'What would you have done,' she said, 'if I'd shouted *Help! I'm on the Spit, in a beach hut, get the police*?'

He held the door wide open, and gave her his most glittering, childlike, guileless liar's smile. 'It never crossed my mind.'

'You're impossible!' It was the kind of thing you heard adults saying, usually to children. Or to other adults who they were really fond of—like her mum to Stella. She'd never quite known what it meant, when she was little. It was true, he was *impossible* . . . but so was all this: we two, on our desert island. And he grinned as if he understood completely: she was *impossible* too.

And now they'd settled that, it was time for baked beans. Ravioli. Little cubes of stuff they called Fruit

Cocktail. And a couple of bags of kiddies' sweets, as if this was a holiday.

Toby was quiet, coming home from school. It wasn't like him. Most days, he would be babbling, skipping as they walked, but today he was quiet and pressed himself against her when they stopped to cross the road.

Oh, Toby Trouble, Stella thought. Only this was her trouble, and it was the real thing, not a game. Stella wished she could tell him that Clio was playing Hide and Seek . . . that any moment now she would appear from the bushes and everyone—Stella, Mike and Jen, the police, Stella's boss—would burst out laughing.

As she turned in to her street Stella knew that it was going to get harder. Something was different—more cars than usual, and more movement than there should be on a working day. Old Mrs Effingham at number 12 was on her doorstep talking to a young man. It was the way they stopped and turned as she and Toby passed that made Stella uneasy. The old lady did not smile or wave.

The man who stood on Stella's front path must have been waiting for some time. 'Miss Horton?' he said. 'You're the social worker in the Clio Palmer case.' She was about to say something when she noticed the mini-disk recorder in his hand. She shook her head. A car door clunked behind her, and she turned to catch a camera's flicker-flash.

'You've been suspended,' said the first reporter. 'Pending disciplinary action, am I right?' Flicker-flash. Stella pushed past the man on her path, pulling Toby as close as she could.

'Wouldn't you like to give us your side of the story?' one of them called out. Stella fumbled with her keys.

Inside the house, the phone was ringing. 'There are plenty of people who've got things to say about you. Have you read the papers?' Stella wrenched open the door, and pushed Toby in. As she glanced back, the man from Mrs Effingham's doorstep was right there, in the garden. He had stepped over the low fence, onto the grass.

'Get out,' yelled Stella. 'Just leave us alone.' Flash-flicker, went the cameras again.

After she had slammed the door behind her Stella leant against it for a minute, eyes shut, panting. 'Mu-um?' said Toby faintly. He was standing in the hallway, stopped just where she'd pushed him, and as she looked at him the tears rose to his eyes. It was some time before she had cuddled him and calmed them both enough to remember the phone.

One message on the answerphone . . . Stella got Toby settled at the TV, then pressed Play. At the first words, she froze.

The voice was halting, choked up and a long, long way away . . . but Stella knew from the first breath it was Clio. The floor seemed to sway beneath her feet. She'd been on the doorstep. If she hadn't turned round to shout at the reporter, she could have been talking to her now.

Stella punched in 1471. A moment's silence. 'Please,' whispered Stella, 'please . . .' Then the soulless automatic voice cut in: *You were called at 4.15. The caller withheld their number.*

It was too much. A terrible numb weariness came over Stella as she wondered whom to call—Clio's parents or the police—to tell them she had messed things up again.

* * *

'That reminds me . . . something . . . oh God, yes!' Max was rolling the green sweet round on his tongue. It had more of a smell than a taste. 'I use to work in this bubblegum factory . . .'

'You? In a factory!'

'Sure. I've done all kinds of things. You'd be surprised.'

'But a *bubblegum* factory . . . !'

'Don't laugh. It's a dangerous job . . .' Max had unfolded a deckchair and lounged with his back to the door of the hut. With the light behind him, Clio couldn't see the expression on his face.

'It's the fumes,' he said. 'Imagine *this* . . .' He leaned forward, breathing the sickly sweetness at her, '. . . magnified a thousand times. Huge open vat of it, boiling away like lava. And we had to lean in and unclog the stirrer—great mechanical thing, with blades—every time it got stuck.'

'Gross,' said Clio.

'Grosser than you think. You know what I found in there one day?'

'Don't tell me,' Clio said, meaning *do!*

'Dave.'

'What?'

'Dave. The foreman. Grumpy old bloke, always shouting at me. But he had these dizzy turns. He must have gone in to check the vat, and leaned over . . .'

'No!' cringed Clio. She was sitting on the floor now, almost at his feet, and clutching the arm of his chair.

'Yup. Dead. Think about it—mega-gallons of the stuff, all gooey and bubbling. He must have tried to hold on to the stirrer—that's what clogged it up—but the stuff sucked him under. And . . . you know what?' He paused, stretching out the moment. 'He must have shouted something, 'cause he'd blown this great enormous bubble round his head, and it had set like that.'

131

'That's horrible!' Clio clamped her hands over her ears, as if she could still keep the thought out, but she'd started laughing, and Max had started laughing, watching her. They laughed till it hurt. 'The question is . . .' said Max, gasping for breath, 'do you think—when they opened it—just for a micro-second—it was still in there?'

'What?'

'The thing he shouted. The last word he said.'

'Oh, Max . . .' said Clio, shaking her head. 'Did anybody ever tell you that you're weird?' Then they were off again. Five minutes later they finally managed to stop, more from exhaustion than anything, and they were limp, with tears in their eyes. Quite why it had seemed so funny, Clio couldn't recall.

Dear M,

What do you think you're playing at? That's what Oggie said, wasn't it? And you said: Not playing! That's what Toby would say when he's deep in a game, so it's like real to him. Or maybe not — maybe he'd look up at you in a way that's like: You can see what I'm playing at — what game are YOU playing?

He'd have understood what we were doing, no prob.

Remember you told him that story with the tiger and the tent? After that, he kept on draping a bedspread over a couple of chairs and sitting in there — sitting very tight, with his knees tucked up and his eyes all big and wide . . . listening for the tiger.

Stella told him that you'd made it up — but did that make any difference? No way. He knew better.

I can understand that, can't you? Sometimes you

132

just huddled closer. Maybe you could hear the tiger padding round the beach hut. Pad, pad. And its breathing, like the sound of the wind and the waves breaking. I'm surprised we didn't find the paw prints in the morning in the sand.

15

Secret Sharers

'What's that?' said Max suddenly.

'What?'

'That noise. It's a car.'

'Oggie?'

'No, that's not his.'

Then they panicked. 'Shut the door!' Max struggled up in the deckchair, and it folded under him. Clio went scrambling over him, towards the open door.

'No!' he hissed, and grabbed her arm. 'Keep down. They'll see you.' Side by side, they crept on hands and knees towards the threshold, and peered out.

The sound of the car had stopped, as if they'd both imagined it. From the porch, all they could see was the beach towards the sea. The track ran past the other row of huts, behind them, out of sight. Max first, then Clio, they crept to the decking outside, and peered again.

There it was, its white snout pulled in between two huts. 'Police car!' Clio whispered. 'Shall we run?'

'No—back inside.'

'What if they've got dogs?'

'Then we've had it anyway. Come on.' They pulled the door to very carefully, but the click of the latch was as loud as a stick being snapped. Max turned the key and they stood there, face to face in the gloom.

134

'Better get upstairs—just in case.' Once they'd climbed into the loft they pulled the ladder up behind them. It wasn't easy, and for a horrible moment it got wedged in the hatch . . . then a bit of careful angling and a sharp tug got it through. Clio closed the hatch beneath them, and pulled a mattress over on top. They were back in the dark. Max had his face pressed up to the crack in the tiny window.

'What can you see?'

'Nothing. They must be round the other side.' For several minutes neither of them spoke. 'Like Anne Frank, isn't it?' Max said. 'Hiding in the attic. Soldiers searching for her . . .' He kept his face pressed to the glass, and went on, just like idle conversation. 'You know about that, don't you?'

'What? We read it at school.'

'No, I mean really. Where you came from. There was a war?'

'Everyone knows that. I don't remember. I was very small.'

'Your mum and dad . . . I mean the ones in England . . . did they . . . pay money for you?'

Clio stiffened. 'They wanted to give me a good home. They couldn't have babies of their own.'

'Are they old? Is that why they couldn't adopt the usual way?'

'Why should that matter? It was a *good* thing they did. You make it sound horrible.'

'Sure, sure.' Max did not move from the window, just shifted his awkward crouch from time to time. 'You must wonder, though.'

'There's nothing to wonder. I didn't have anybody. My . . . other parents . . . well . . . It was an orphanage, for God's sake.'

'Ssssh!' said Max. 'Keep your voice down . . . So, I

was right,' he whispered. 'We both come from nowhere.'

'It wasn't nowhere. It's got a name. And you don't come from nowhere either. No one does.'

If that was a question, Max didn't answer. 'Sorry,' he said. 'It *was* a good thing they did. If they hadn't, you wouldn't be here now . . . And I'm really glad you are.' He still didn't turn, but Clio felt his fingers find her shoulder, and rest there in a way he had not done before. She drew back.

'Max, one thing . . . That story about runaway lovers, you know, what we told the people in the car . . . it *is* just a story, isn't it? We made it up for that lift.' It was very quiet in the darkness. 'And I *do* want to be here. I really like . . . this. It matters. We just mustn't get it mixed up with the boyfriend-girlfriend stuff, that's all.'

'*What* matters?' Max said. 'Tell me.'

'Just being with you. It's like the first time I've ever felt . . . *all there*. You know, like *real*. Even if you do tell lies.'

'Lies? *Me?*' His eyes went so wide and innocent that for a moment she was lost for words.

'You know . . . like—everything!'

'Sssh!' Max was squinting at the window. 'There he is.' Then inexplicably he started laughing. 'There—he—is!'

'What's the matter? Are you going crazy?'

'No! He's got his toolkit with him. He's a workman. Yes—he's just come out of the toilet block, that's all.'

As quiet as mice: they held it for a few more minutes, while the man walked onto the beach, lit up a cigarette, and stood there for a quiet moment, gazing out to sea. 'What's he doing now?' said Clio.

'Just checking the sea. In case it's got a leak or something.'

The man finished his smoke and ground the stub into the sand, then he climbed back in his van and drove away.

'They should concrete this place over,' Max said.

'What?' Clio sat on the groyne, eyes closed, listening to waves on the shingle. In spite of the shivery wind, it made a holiday sound. 'You're cracked,' she said.

'Not cracked—practical. Look.'

Between the edge of the shingle and the huts, she saw a double row of footprints. The sand on the Spit was the finest Clio had ever played in as a child: barefoot, you could feel it like warm silk between your toes. Now, in the cool and the damp, it held a perfect print of every gull that landed. The council workman's tracks were still there from hours before. Max held up his trainer next to the print it had made. You could almost read the brand name in the sand.

They retraced their steps, doing their best to scuff the prints away behind them. They had to *think*. From now on there would be danger zones—the sand that would betray them as clear as signing their names . . . the warning crunch of shingle . . . Safe ground was the clumps of wiry beach grass, and tarmac and hard standing. In between the huts was safer than the open, and the side towards the sea was safer than the harbour side. Anywhere within sight of the quay, with its coin-in-the-slot tourist telescope, would have to be out of bounds. Any place with a view was a place where someone else could see them. Safest, of course, would be to crouch in the loft of the beach hut, waiting to be found, like Sardines at a children's party, but who could stand that? No, this was their place now, and they had to live in it. But they would have to be on lookout, all

137

the time. Clio thought of the little birds you see in town—always one peck and look up for danger, peck, peck and look up again.

Yes, it was their place—theirs and the ghosts of a thousand other people's holidays. DOG DAYS, said the nameplate on the scruffy hut next door, with a cute little painted paw print. The much too neat one on the other side was EVENTIDE. THE LAST RESORT . . . HANGIN' LOOSE . . . Everyone had to think up a naff name, it seemed, like an advertisement for what sort of people they were. She stared at the plaque on their own hut: BILMAR.

'What language is that?'

'It'll be names. Bill and Mary or Marjorie or something. Don't you just hate married couples?'

'Oh, I don't know,' said Clio. 'Hey, you know what that makes us?'

'CLIMAX,' they both said together. 'Boom-boom.'

Inside, they made themselves at home. In daylight, the hut was as cunningly put together as a toy house or ship's galley. Thirty years ago the melamine table and the sliding cupboard on the wall would have even looked smart. The benches, doubling as storage boxes, in an L-shape round the dining table, must have seemed a neat idea. They could never have been exactly comfortable, but this was where Clio unearthed the clues to long-gone holidays, like archaeology. She found sunglasses—big and round, in coloured plastic frames—and a tube of ancient sun cream, all crusted with sand. She found flip-flop sandals and two pairs of green wellingtons, a rubber face mask and a snorkel . . . one flipper, and a picture book that Clio vaguely remembered from when she was small. That gave her a twinge of sadness: even the grandchildren must have grown up and lost interest in the place by now.

She wished she could open the windows wide, to blow away the smell of age. When they found a local paper in the waste bin it was years old and yellowing. Small beachcombings littered the shelves of the old dresser—a crab claw, shells, and a bottle of cloudy thick glass—alongside the china pot in the shape of a donkey, with a straw hat that lifted off for a lid, and a set of glass animals, and a huge spiny conch shell from some more exotic beach than this. Max found a couple of paperbacks—a book about historic naval battles that had to be Bill's, and for Mary . . . ? By the bookmark, she seemed to have left her heroine, lovelorn, on a Cornish cliff on page 173. Yes, the hut felt sad. Maybe it needs us, Clio thought: wasn't it better to be squatted than abandoned? Bill could be lying in a nursing home, and Mary sitting by his bed, for all she knew.

Max found a couple of waterproofs—shapeless cagoules that would do for anybody, any size, plus scarves, some rumpled woolly socks, and an umbrella. He turned out all the boxes in the loft, in hope of some proper clothes. 'Somebody's bound to see us one day,' he said. 'We just don't want them to think: *Hey, aren't those the kids on the news?*'

'I'm staying indoors then. You needn't think I'm going out in this stuff!'

Max pondered. 'Time for a bit of dressing-up, I reckon. Now, who are you going to be?'

'Who are you going to be?' I loved the way you said that — like you were opening up a box of magic — like I could be anything I wanted, the way you could be. All I had to do was choose.

I remember I looked in the mirror — that silly little mirror in its plastic frame above the sink.

139

There were both our faces — you were just behind
me, looking over my shoulder, like my good angel. Or
the other kind — I don't remember which shoulder it
was, and anyway it was backwards in the mirror,
so . . . Oh, I don't know.

There was nothing wrong in asking. It was a
good question. Yes: 'Who are we going to be?'

Max crept up behind her, and flicked a scarf around her
head and chin.

'Hey . . .' he said. A stranger looked back from the
mirror, a bit like her friend Kareena in her headscarf.
Dark eyes and an olive complexion looked twice as
intense, framed like this. 'Dramatic, or what?' said Max.

'Dramatic? It's supposed to be *disguise*!'

Max shrugged. 'Pity.' He wrapped the scarf around
his own face and grimaced at the mirror. 'That's it!' he
said. 'It's the hair.' Now he was rummaging in the
drawer. 'Aren't there any *scissors* in this place?'

'You can't use those!' He had pulled out a pair with
blades speckled with rust. He set to work, trying to angle
them towards his own reflection.

'I can't stand this,' Clio said. 'Here, let me have a go.'

At first she wasn't any better than he'd been. She
kept pinching strands of hair between the blunt blades,
and Max would wince. Then she got the grip right, and
with a *snick* a lock of hair dropped at her feet. It was so
fine and fair, lying there, it looked almost white.

'More. I want it *short*.' He leaned his head into her
hands. She felt the warmth and weight of it, and she
noticed the fine stubble starting on his cheek and chin,
where a wispy beard could be. 'Go on,' he said. 'Don't
be nervous.' She tried not to think of that time Toby
had a go at his long-haired teddy with his mother's nail

140

scissors. At first, she went at it cautiously, going over the same patch again and again. She got the knack of lining the hair up, lifting just enough, so the longer bits came even with the short. At last Max ran his hand round the back of his head and nodded. 'That's brilliant. Now, what about you?'

'Me?!'

'I know, it's beautiful. Everyone's always told you, *Clio, you've got lovely hair*. Am I right, or . . . ?'

Clio blushed.

'Well, then?' he said.

Clio did not answer, or speak. She went back to the mirror, leaning close until it only held her face: a dark-eyed robber princess, with her glossy tangled Belladora hair.

What would you do? Clio asked her. *Me?* said the face in the mirror. *I'm an outlaw, remember? I do whatever it takes.*

'OK,' said Clio. 'You know how Stella has her hair— sort of bobbed . . . ?'

'*No prob-a-lem,*' said Max. 'I shared a flat once with this Italian guy Vincenzo. He . . .'

'Don't. Don't tell me, or I'll think it isn't true. Just cut it.'

Dear M,

Let me tell you a secret. Don't breathe a word to anyone.

I was scared, on the beach. Not scared of being caught, of being dragged home, locked up, stared at. Not scared of Franko and Psykes, or of Oggie — not even of you.

No, I was scared you'd find me out. Scared you'd look up one day and blink and see that really I

141

was ordinary, nothing special. All that Belladora stuff, that was kids' games, like a little girl with Dressing Up. Even the things about the war, the orphanage, and the adoption — that was all about my parents, really. I couldn't be sure the things I thought I remembered were true, because I'd heard them telling people so often. Sometimes I wished they'd just forget it and let me be ordinary. That was before I met you.

Then everything was different. Every time I caught you looking at me, I felt my breath stop. I wanted to know: What can he see? What did I look like, in among all your fantastic stories? Maybe you were just imagining I was someone special, when really . . . ?

No. I was sure of one thing. Whatever you thought you were seeing when you looked at me . . . that's what I wanted to be.

16

Shopping

At first Max was hesitant with the scissors, then he got a rhythm going, lifting the hair up with the little comb he always seemed to have in a pocket so he could give his hair a flick. She started to wonder if it might be true about Vincenzo, till he started whistling that ice-cream advert, so she wasn't sure.

On the floor, on her lap, on her shoulders, the beautiful curls were piling up. 'Careful,' she said now and then. 'Not too much.'

'Don't worry. Just even this bit up and . . . now, look.' He propped up the mirror in front of her, and stood behind with a biscuit tin lid inside out, so she could check the back, the way real hairdressers do. She could not see much. She didn't need to. For a moment she was speechless.

'What have you done?' she shrieked. Her hair, what was left of it, stood up in frizzy spikes. Whichever way she ran her fingers, it bounced up again. 'You've ruined it.'

'It's Retro,' Max said. 'A bit Punk.'

'You idiot!' She plucked at the ends. 'I can't go out like this!'

'Like what?' He grinned. 'Not like *Clio*. That's the main thing, isn't it?'

'Yes, but . . .'

143

'So nobody's going to turn round in the street and say, *Look at that beautiful hair* . . . You're going to miss that, aren't you?'

'Now you're making out I'm *vain* or something. This is just a rubbish haircut.'

Suddenly he grinned—that guileless Toby smile. 'I'll tell you what you look like. Like a changeling. You know: when the fairies came and swapped a baby in its cot.'

'Fairies! This is meant to be a fairy story?'

'Not the kind of fairies you're thinking of—not pretty little things with lacy wings. No, the real ones, I mean the ones in the really old stories, they're almost as big as us, and sort of powerful and wild. The fair folk. They can do *anything they want*.' He paused. 'A bit like us.'

'How do you know all this stuff?'

'Been there, of course.' He swivelled her back to face the mirror. 'Shape-shifters. We can be anyone. Maybe Franko had it right—we're aliens, swapped for ordinary people. What do you reckon to that?'

'I reckon you're crazy.'

'Good kind of crazy, though, isn't it?' He kicked her tangled hair into the corner by the swing bin. 'We can go anywhere. Time for a mission, don't you think?'

'We can go *anywhere* . . .' Max said it again.

'I want to stay here.'

'I don't mean far. A bit of shopping, that's all.'

'That's mad. I mean . . . why? Why risk it?'

'Because we'll have to, one day. We need clothes, for a start. The longer we wait, the more scary it'll get. Let's do it now . . . Oh, never mind. Stay here, if you like.'

'No way. If you're going I'm coming too. If you think I'm trusting *you* to buy my clothes for me . . .'

'They aren't Clio clothes, remember. You're not you.'

144

'Who am I, then?'

He looked her up and down. He narrowed his eyes, as if he could see right through her. 'You're a plain-clothes supermodel,' he said, 'doing your best to look a mess—just can't quite manage it.' Clio was not sure whether to blush or punch him. 'Don't worry,' he said. 'You can still be you when you come home.'

Clio gave herself a secret smile. He'd said it. *Home*. He had called this place *home*.

'I can't keep up with you,' she said. He tossed a smelly crumpled cagoule towards her, and the shopping trip was under way.

They were glad of the rain, for once. It moved over the harbour in soft gusts, blurring everything. They put their hoods up and their heads down and set off, taking the anglers' footpath near the water's edge. It was a good short cut. To drive to Watchman's Down from Milbourne meant miles of bungalows, and you still had an expanse of windswept grass to cross before you reached the shelter of the trees. On foot, you could duck between the tall reeds and if there was any trouble you could scuttle out of sight like rabbits. But no one was out, and no wonder. Clio began to be glad of the horrid cagoule. Only the birds in the shallows seemed unbothered by the cold and damp, scooting to and fro with clockwork legs and squeaks.

After a mile or so they reached houses. The sandy shoreline ran out and the footpath went inland, between gardens, with a wire fence either side. 'Let's go back,' said Clio. 'I'm scared.'

'Too late. Somebody's coming.'

An angler with his bag and rod was trudging down the path towards them. 'Act natural,' Max said. Clio tried to remember how.

145

Then the man was in front of them. They stepped aside. '*Artnun*,' he grunted, and was past, shuffling on with his eyes on his feet.

'There!' Max whispered. 'You fooled him.'

'He didn't look.'

'Exactly. People don't. Did I ever tell you how to be invisible?'

The footpath turned into an alley, and they stepped into the shopping street so suddenly that Clio did not have a chance for stage-fright. There were crowds—that was a good thing—with kids going home from school, kids from a school where she didn't know anybody on this side of town.

She checked her reflection in a window. It was true: she hardly knew herself. Without the hair, even the shape of her face seemed different. She angled her head this way and that, then frowned. 'What's wrong?' Max said over her shoulder.

'The eyes.'

'You've got nice eyes.'

'They're still *my* eyes. Can't I wear dark glasses?'

'Oh yeah, and a fake moustache, and a big badge saying *Secret Agent*! Besides, it's the middle of winter. Trust me: you're just great.'

At the door of the charity shop, she hesitated. Yes, the charity shop! The kind of place Mum said: *When I was your age, I got everything at Oxfam, none of this silly fashion stuff* . . . Clio winced.

'You're fine,' said Max, behind her.

'I know.'

'Sure you don't want me to come in? I could help.' She gave him a shove. 'OK, OK,' he said. 'I'll see you by the fountain, half an hour.'

* * *

146

Just remember, you're not Clio. That was all she had to remember. Most of the stuff in the shop had Last Year written all over it. That would matter to Clio, not to her. Find something neutral. Plain-clothes . . . It was another way of doing Invisible, that was all.

She walked into the shop and nothing happened. No one raised the alarm. Nobody even looked. The woman at the counter went on flicking through a magazine, and four or five people picked their way around the racks. None of them looked at her, or at each other either. She began to relax.

She found some chain-store jeans, and a baggy top. She was so sensible—Mum would have been proud. Clio thought of the cold in the hut, and took a sheep-coloured fleece with a hood. Things like that.

In the furthest corner, almost hidden by a rail of dresses, was a full-length mirror. Clio held the things she'd picked against her. They would have to do. Then she noticed the bin of random hats and scarves. She glanced round—no one looking—and threw a fake leopard-skin stole round her shoulders. She plopped a purple floppy French-style artist's beret on her head. For the first time, the young woman in the mirror smiled.

Another scarf was rainbow tie-dye, hippy colours like a few of Mum and Dad's friends still wore. But Clio had fished out a black and purple drape of some kind. It had tassels and dark sequin-pattern stars on it, and Clio folded it round her like wings. She wrapped it round her face and hunched a little, with a witchy look. Changeling! Then the black hat caught her eye.

This was no witch's hat. It might have been posh once—at least as far as funeral clothes go. She slipped it on her head and put on a tragic look. She was a widow, a Black Widow from some Mafia feud, eyes flashing with

147

plans for revenge. She whipped out a black net veil and draped it round the brim. The world went shadowy.

'Hey!' A dark shape stepped up behind her shoulder. 'Whose funeral is it?' said the voice, in the same instant that she jumped and spun round.

'Max!'

Their eyes met, and he wasn't laughing. He gave a little shudder. 'Got your stuff?' he said.

'Yes. I haven't paid yet.'

'Half this stuff comes from dead people,' he said. 'Pay up. Let's get out of here.'

Outside on the pavement he relaxed. He was wearing a new padded jacket. 'Hey—smart!' she said, as they walked on. 'Where did that come from?' It was sort of casual-cool but chunky too, a bit military, as if the Men in Black had used designer labels for a change.

'Oh, another charity shop.'

'Good bargain, then.' It looked brand new.

He reached in his pocket and dropped something on her head. She looked into the nearest window to see herself wearing the beret from the charity shop. 'Hey, I didn't pay for that . . .' But his look stopped her.

'No one else would have bought it,' he said. 'It was meant for you. It *was* yours, I think, in another life.'

They were nearly back to the alley, when she thought: *knickers!* She'd been in and out of the shop without a glance at underwear. Did they *have* underwear, in charity shops? Were some people so poor that they had to get theirs second-hand? The honest answer was: she didn't know. And anyway, she wasn't going back in there.

'No problem,' Max said. 'There's an Under-a-Pound shop.'

Clio felt through her pockets. In her palm, the loose change made a very small pile. 'What am I meant to do,' she said, 'ask for half a knicker?'

He shrugged.

'I've *got* to have some.'

'No problem.' He led the way to the shop. 'Find what you want. I'll give you a minute, then I'll go and chat up the girls at the counter. Don't worry. They'll love me.' He gave that little smirk of his. 'Once they're laughing, pick up what you want and go . . . Oh, come on. You *would* pay, if you had the money. And all this stuff's rubbish anyway. It serves them right for selling it.' He held her gaze until she had to smile.

Keep calm, thought Clio, as they walked in. Be rational. Half the girls she knew had taken something when they were younger—not real *shoplifting*, everyone knew that was wrong—just a packet of crisps, for a dare. She had never done that, so . . . maybe she was owed one. Just one. She could even come back and leave a pound on the counter one day.

Still, her heart was beating so hard she could scarcely think. She fumbled with the packets on the rack, and almost at once there was Max at the counter, going into his little routine. Like clockwork, the women at the till were smiling, then creased up with laughter. Now, thought Clio, with her heart stuck in her windpipe. She slipped a packet of five pairs underneath her sweater, tucked them in her waistband and sauntered . . . calmly now, take a look at that rack of dirt-cheap CDs, as if there was all the time in the world . . . out of the door.

Max joined her round the corner, minutes later. It was so hard waiting, standing still, when everything inside her was still racing. 'Easy,' he said. 'You've done it before.'

'I haven't!'

'You've missed out on a great career, then. You were great.'

'I'm not doing that again. Never . . . Why are you

149

looking at me like that?' Then she realized: she still had the stolen beret on her head. As her hand went up to whip it off, he stopped her. With his other hand he slipped a pair of glasses on her nose.

'Hey . . . I don't wear . . .' But the world around her looked no different.

'*And this elegant design, madame . . .*' Max purred, '*these are the glasses you may wear to Cannes the year your first film wins the Grand Prize.* No,' he said in his own voice, 'no, I'm the film director. You'll have to be something else.'

'Like an undercover reporter,' she said. 'Like I'm doing a documentary on the lives of *totally deranged* people on the run . . . Where did you get these?'

'Big optician in the precinct. You were worried about your eyes, weren't you? They've got all these frames with blank glass, to try on. It's just disguise. Smart, though.'

'You're . . . impossible.' She slipped them off. 'They've still got the price tag on them.' She tore it off quickly. 'Max! These are over a hundred pounds.'

'Sure, and they cost about a quid to make. Everyone knows those places are a con. Besides . . .' Suddenly he wasn't laughing. 'I did it for you. Not me—you. And you'd do the same for me.' He gave her another kiss, not a joke one, but so quick and light it scarcely brushed her forehead, and before she could think what to say, he was running. 'Come on,' he called. 'Race you home.'

By the time she caught up they were on the footpath and went ducking, laughing, swinging their carrier bags, through the trees. In a while they saw a spray haze drifting over the Spit, whitish in the twilight, and they heard the thrill of big waves on the shore.

Back in the hut, Max lit the heater and the stove, and

turned the gas lamps up high. 'Blow the expense,' he said. 'Oggie'll give us more gas.' Quickly the hut filled with a cosy, steamy heat. He pulled the curtains; even with the shutters, not a chink had to show through the holes. He emptied his carrier bag, and a great slew of newspapers spilled out on the table, overflowing onto the benches and the floor.

'Now . . .' he said. 'Get ready to find out what it feels like to be a *celebrity*!'

17

Being News

Stella had never had much time for daytime TV, or for people who watched it. What kind of sad and empty lives must they have, she used to say.

That was before Max and Clio . . . Before her manager had called her in to his office, sat her down and talked for ten minutes trying to avoid the word *suspension* . . . Before her old colleagues started sounding awkward and backing away. It was before there'd been reporters baying on the doorstep and, even worse now, disappearing, leaving her with the vague feeling of still being watched, maybe by telephoto lenses, out of sight.

She had the TV on most days now—the more mindless the better, so she could blank out and not think, not remember. That ruled out all news, national or local: the Clio and Max story could crop up anywhere. Old black and white films were good, or quizzes about sport. Chat shows could be dangerous, because they could stray into *issues*, like Post Traumatic Stress. One had actually mentioned Milbourne. Apparently there were teams of counsellors going round the schools helping kids who'd been at the Complex cope with terrors more long-lasting than their bruises, cuts, and burns.

I could be doing that, helping, Stella thought. But the last person anyone would trust now would be her. She'd have been better off counselling Clio when she'd had the chance. Poor kid, maybe that's why she'd run off—flipped, with that trauma building up inside her while she'd looked so calm outside.

Time was when Stella would have plunged into a serious novel, something big and Russian that she'd always meant to read, or written long letters, or got herself a project and spent her hours surfing the net. Not now. She felt stunned, listless. She used to think it would be easy, being a couch potato, but she couldn't do it. No sooner was the TV on than she got up and paced. Now, she went to the sitting room window and eased the curtains apart, just a crack.

The street looked empty. Everybody was out at work, except a few old ladies. The windows of the houses opposite stared, blank. At the corner of the street there was a car she had not seen before. In an instant she went from listless to panic-mode. She could not breathe. Stella sat down quickly, in the half-dark, with the TV flicker and the thumping of her heart.

She took several deep breaths before she dared to look again. The car had gone . . . if it had ever been there. She could not be sure. I'm starting to imagine things, she thought—a shadow in the alley, on the way to school, or a footstep just behind them . . . and when she turned it was gone. *You've got to stop this, Stella*, she thought. Get a grip. She had to think of Toby. The last thing he needed was a nervous wreck for a mother. Even if that *was* someone watching them, some reporter snooping on their way to school, she had to act as if it wasn't, for Toby's sake. Stay calm. Deep breaths. *One . . . two . . .*

The phone rang, and she jumped to answer it. Clio, please let it be Clio! She could not forget that faint voice on the answerphone. If only I'd been there, thought Stella, she'd have talked to me.

'Stella,' said a man's voice. 'We need to talk.'

Her heart sank. Toby's father. 'Oh, it's you,' she said.

'You sound in a bad way.'

'Pretty bloody, yes.'

'I'm sorry,' he said, but he didn't sound like it. He had on his lawyer voice, like always when he tried to put her in the wrong. 'I just thought,' he said, 'we ought to consider Toby's needs in all this. It can't be doing him any good, this trouble you've got yourself in.'

'Oh, he's all right, you know him.'

'What I mean is: wouldn't it be best if Toby spent more time with me?'

'Thanks, no. We're OK.'

'I'm not sure the Family Court would see it that way. You're plainly under stress. Not coping . . .'

She slammed down the phone. It took all her strength of mind to do that, just *before* she screamed and swore. She screamed and swore, and that felt better. It was a minute before she looked down and saw that the phone had missed the handset. He would have heard her screeching like a crazy woman, every word. She replaced the receiver carefully, put her face in her hands, and cried.

Max fanned out papers and magazines round them on the floor. He scanned the latest *Hello*, and threw it down. He seemed genuinely surprised not to find himself in there. Next to it lay the Milbourne Advertiser. Max glanced at it, then gave a huff of contempt.

'What's that?' said Clio.

'Oh, you know the kind of thing.' He tossed it her way. 'Every cheap local paper in England, they have a story like this every week.'

Clio stared at the headline. BRAVE JADE BATTLES TRAGIC TERROR BURNS.

'Max,' she said, 'that's *our* story. That was the girl from the Complex. She's in a bad way. Scarred for life, it says.'

'I know. And there'll be a picture of her family standing round her bed. And her mum or dad or brother saying she's a brave girl and how she was going to be a ballet dancer and they're starting an appeal to raise money for some special treatment, and . . .'

'Max, don't be horrid.'

'I'm not being horrid. Am I right? Well, am I?'

'Well, yes . . . more or less. Actress.'

'There you are. And they have a story like that every week . . . Oh, come on . . .' He touched the back of her hand, not laughing, and his clear eyes held her with a gentle look. 'There's nothing we can do,' he said. 'Don't worry. I don't like to see you sad.' He left his hand there, and she left hers, and they read on from paper to paper, side by side.

'Hey,' he said after a while, 'we're in Liverpool!'

'Stella told the police about my message, then.'

'Better than that. There's been a sighting, it says here.'

'In Liverpool?'

'Sure . . . And one in Manchester, and one in Hull. What did I tell you? People see what they want to.'

'Why should they want to see us in Hull?' asked Clio.

'Well, they need a *bit* of excitement . . . Don't you see—deep down, they *all* want to be doing what we're doing? We're stars.'

One of the tabloids had them on an inside page—the *teenage-lovers* angle. 'Hey, look,' Max said. '*Melanie Bailey, schoolfriend of the missing girl . . .*'

'Schoolfriend? *Her?* She hates me.'

'Everybody's going to be your friend now. *Schoolfriend of the missing girl, says that she was alongside Clio on the night of the fire, and saw the young man single her out.*

"It was like he knew her from the way they talked. Like they knew each other really well."'

'She's making it up.'

'Yeah, but that's what it felt like, didn't it . . . ?'

Then Clio caught her breath. She had turned over the page and found herself staring at a photograph she hadn't recognized at first.

'Poor Stella!'

Max crouched down beside her. 'That's a stinker of a picture,' he said. 'The Madwoman in the Attic, or what. And she's quite pretty, really—for her age. They've really got it in for her.' His finger traced the sub-headline: *Social Worker—Gullible or Negligent?*

A statement from Milbourne Social Services said: While we are at pains to stress that Ms Horton was not acting in a professional capacity in this case, there are grounds to suspect that there has been a serious error of judgement . . .

'Poor Stella,' said Clio again. 'Poor Toby.'

'Don't let it get to you.' Max reached out a hand to touch her shoulder, but she pulled away. 'Hey, tell you what,' he said. 'I picked up some beer. Let's drink to Stella. Wish her luck.'

When he came back from the sink, with two glasses and an opened bottle, Clio did not look up. She pushed a page towards him—a social-work supplement, the bit of the paper only Stella would usually read. 'Max,' she said, in a small voice, 'look at this . . .'

LOVING YOUR JAILER: THE STOCKHOLM SYNDROME
On 15 April 1974, viewers in America were shocked by a closed-circuit video of a bank being robbed in San Francisco, broadcast on peak-time TV news. It wasn't the robbery that caused the sensation, but the sight of one of the robbers

standing guard behind the others with a submachine gun in her hand. It was Patty Hearst, 19-year-old heiress, who had been kidnapped two months earlier by an unknown revolutionary group calling themselves the Symbionese Liberation Army. A wave of public sympathy had gone out to the family when the group threatened to kill her if her millionaire father did not meet their impossible demands and give away his fortune to the poor. And now here she was, with a gun in her hand, on national TV. Shortly afterwards a tape was received with her voice angrily denouncing everything her father stood for and declaring that from now on she was 'Tania', a fighting member of the SLA. This tape would be played later, at her trial, when Patty was sentenced to thirty-five years in jail.

What the court might not have known was that just a year earlier four hostages had been taken in a bank robbery five thousand miles away in Stockholm. When the police broke in, to their amazement the hostages defended the hostage-takers and refused to testify against them in court. From this and similar cases, psychiatrists began to piece together a picture of what they called the Stockholm Syndrome—victims captured and imprisoned, beaten and threatened with death, who begin to make friends, even fall in love with their captors—an effect that persists even after they have been released. Today, scientists see this as a form of brainwashing, using isolation, fear, and threats of violence interspersed with moments of 'kindness' and relief, which produces a 'conversion' experience like that cults use to entrap new members.

Experts on the Stockholm Syndrome have been called in to advise police investigating the disappearance of Milbourne schoolgirl Clio Palmer . . .

'Great picture,' Max said. The blurry newsprint photo showed not Clio but a thin and stern-faced girl with a 1970s hairdo, perfect teeth, and a gun. 'Mind if I snip that one out for the book? Have you noticed—cover up her hair, she looks a bit like you?'

Clio turned away, but he went on. 'Hey, we could make a ransom video. Mail it to the press. Demand a million pounds. Then we could really go somewhere brilliant—where do you fancy?'

'Max,' she said. 'Stop it.'

'Sorry? Hey, what's the matter?'

'Nothing. Just . . . stop it.' Clio stood up amid the scattered papers, and went to the door. She looked out at the night.

'Careful,' said Max. 'The light . . .'

Without a word, she slipped outside, shutting the door, and leaned back on it, staring at the sea. Max's voice came through the door behind her.

'Clio?' He tried the handle. 'Clio! I thought you were . . . feeling happy?'

'Well, I would be, wouldn't I? I mean, if I was going crazy, if that Stockholm thing is true.'

'That's stupid. I never even asked you to be here. I kept on telling you to go home . . .'

'Is that what you wanted—to get rid of me?'

'No! But *you* didn't know that, did you? That Stockholm stuff, that'll be something your dad put them on to. You saw what he said: *she might need psychiatric help when she comes home*. He's the one who thinks you're crazy. Look, I know he cares and all that, but . . . He just can't believe you're doing what you want to. You *are* doing what you want to, aren't you?'

A gust of wind curled round the hut, making the shutters whine. 'Oh . . . how do I know?' But she let the door open a little, just enough to make him struggle as he wriggled through.

'It's cold,' he said. 'Come back in.'

As they shut the door, locking the cold outside, she

shivered. 'I'm tired,' she said. 'So tired.' He slipped his long coat from the hook by the door where it had hung since he'd had the new jacket. They'd agreed that he shouldn't go out in it—too recognizable—but he kept it hanging there, with the white scarf draped around it, like the ghost of his old self. Now he wrapped it around her like a blanket, and she leaned her weight against him. His lips touched the top of her head. She shook it.

'I need some sleep. You do understand, don't you?'

'Sure, sure.' He helped her up the ladder, then climbed down again. When he was gone, she propped up the little mirror she'd found in the loft, and leaned into the light from the hatch, slipping the stolen glasses on again. With a shock, she realized: they were really good. They were just right for her face . . . and yet she hadn't been there. Somehow he'd picked out exactly the pair she'd have chosen: he must have looked at her—not like boys normally do, but really *looked*. He'd walked into that optician's with a perfect picture of her in his mind.

Suddenly she wanted to say sorry for being so edgy, for doubting him. She waited, curled under his coat, with the scarf like a comforter against her cheek. But half an hour later he was still downstairs with his book out, sifting through the papers, snipping bits out for the story of his life.

18

The Dream Time

That was the start of the dream time.

She must have fallen asleep, and when she woke with wind moaning round the roof she could not be certain if she'd slept at all. She must have, because she remembered climbing downstairs and the door was banging open. When she went to close it, there was the sea, almost up to the doorstep, throwing up flotsam and jetsam, piles of it, like a barricade. She had to try and shift it, but every time she heaved a plank or tree stump back into the water something larger washed up—a huge ship's figurehead, grinning . . . two skeletons of sea snakes, twisted round each other . . . And there was something smaller in the tide wrack, like a wet sack, only when she looked she saw that it was Toby. That was when she woke up, trying to scream but she could not make a sound.

There was daylight at the little window. Max's face appeared at the hatch. 'You OK?' he said. 'You were moaning.'

'What time is it?'

'Who cares?' He grinned. 'It's *our* time. Rule one from now on: no watches, no clocks. Whatever time it feels like, that's what time it is.' He laid his hand on the side of her head, very gently, and it felt warm, and her head was too heavy to move it away.

This time she slept deeply, with no horrors. When she woke up Max was crouching beside her with a mug that smelt good. He had salvaged a tin of old ground coffee and heated up some long-life milk. It didn't taste great, but he had been working at it down there, just for her. 'Thanks,' she said. 'Can it be any *day* we like, too?'

'Why not? How about Thursday?'

'No, thanks. It's rubbish TV on Thursdays.'

'No TV, remember? It could be *Maxday*. *Clioday* tomorrow. What about the year?'

'All that stuff downstairs, it's like a time capsule. Some time in the 1970s, I think.'

'Lucky we don't have to have the music, then!' They laughed till Clio slopped her coffee. He propped her up, putting an arm around her.

'Don't,' she said. 'I'm all sweaty and revolting.'

'You can't shock me. I've heard you snoring.'

'Beast! I don't snore . . . do I? Thanks, though. You've been looking after me.'

'The least I could do, considering. Have you still got that Stockholm Syndrome thing?'

'Oh, that. I hope so. I never got coffee in bed before I had it!'

And quite soon it was night again, and somehow time went on.

A dog. There was a dog!

Clio had been dozing, but she was down the ladder in an instant. 'Max!' He was bent over the sink with his head half in the sudsy water—washing his hair . . . *again*. He straightened up. 'Ta-da!' he said. 'How's that?' His hair was dark. He had dyed it as dark as hers.

'*Max*, there's a dog outside!'

They listened, motionless.

161

'Police dogs don't bark like that,' Max said. 'It sounds titchy.' Very carefully they slipped outside, ducking between the huts until they had a view. An old man had come down the track beneath the Head and was calling a squat dog . . . which ignored him, plunging about in the shallows, wrestling with a lump of wood. The man walked on, while the dog heaved the sodden log out of the shallows, whining and snarling at it, wagging its stump of a tail.

'Better get back in,' Max said. 'It might smell us . . . It might *like* us. Think how gross that could be.' It took half an hour for the man to get to the end of the Spit and back, vanishing at last between the trees.

'This is going to happen, isn't it?' said Clio. 'We'd better keep watch.'

'What, all the time?'

'We can take turns. I'll go next. You have a break.'

In fact, Clio liked being lookout. She liked the still world of the harbour, with its bird flocks sweeping to and fro, like swishing a scarf. Milbourne, in the haze, looked like a faded painting of itself. Sometimes just the church spire and the gasholders showed through—other times, nothing. Once a pair of swans came beating low across the water, and the air was so still she could hear the whistle of their wings. They made straight for the Rip and through it, out to sea.

Dear M,

Nothing.

No message. Just being in touch.

Just remembering that the best times, the best times of all, were when we weren't doing anything, not even talking. (Yes, even you stopped talking sometimes. No more stories.)

162

Nothing.

The eye of the storm, remember? Like that first night at the Complex, when all the crowds and babble round us seemed to stop, in freeze-frame . . . and the fire and the explosion waited in their cylinder, and the glass in the windows waited to shatter, and the ambulances waited at the hospital, and we said a word or two about nothing that we could remember afterwards, and everything was very patient, very calm and still . . .

School . . . The thought came to her suddenly, with a lurch of the gut, and she realized that it hadn't crossed her mind for days.

'What's up?' said Max. He did that all the time now—seemed to sense what she was thinking—even though she hadn't said a word.

'Am I taking a gap year?' she said. 'Not a year, of course,' she added quickly. 'Gap . . . week? Month?' She paused. 'I can catch up. I'm ahead of most of the others anyway. I can go back any time I want.'

'Any time—if you want. If you can't think of anything better to do.'

'I've got GCSEs coming up, then AS, then A levels . . . Everybody's got to.'

'Not me.'

'I thought you'd done that. That's what Stella said.'

Max smiled. 'Maybe I had smarter things to do than school.'

Clio stared at him. He was wrong, of course, he must be. Then again . . . She thought of the plans she'd worked out with her parents for ten years ahead—A levels, then uni. Good plans, but had it ever occurred to her that she could *not* do all that? That she could choose?

163

Not for a moment. How smart is *that*? thought Clio, wryly.

Max watched her patiently as if, of course, he knew.

One day, without warning, he was sick. He rushed out to the toilet block and did not quite make it. He came back, cold water dripping from his sweater where he had tried to rinse it clean. His skin felt hot, but he looked pale. Clio helped him upstairs into bed.

'I think it was that haggis,' he said faintly. The night before, he had been proud of his latest scavenging from the beach shop: a McWhittle's tinned haggis. He had laughed at her flinch of disgust.

'Serves you right for eating stuff out of a cow's stomach. Sorry!' she said quickly, as he retched again. 'We've got to stop eating stuff that's past its sell-by date.'

Max groaned. 'No food. Don't even mention it.'

She brought him drinks, up the ladder, every hour or two. Mostly he dozed, and she liked it when she crept up to the loft and found him sleeping. Then, his face had that guileless look again, like Toby's. It was hard to believe that he could ever tell a lie. Next morning, she was watching him sleeping when he woke up with a little start, saw it was her, and smiled.

'Do you fancy eating something—I mean, very small?' she asked carefully. 'Something really plain? When I'm poorly, I like warm rice pudding with a blob of strawberry jam on top.'

'Nothing out of a can, please!'

'What, then?'

'Oh, something special . . . ice cream!'

'Dream on!' She laid her hand on his forehead. It was cooler. 'The next ice cream van should be out here . . . oh, about June.'

'OK. I *will* dream on.' He closed his eyes and fell asleep.

Clio ransacked the shop. First she stocked up on basics. Toilet paper, washing-up liquid . . . Oh, and tampons. So . . . She smiled to herself. So I'm thinking of being here a couple of weeks longer, am I? It seemed she was.

It had been mean of Oggie to give them the out-of-date stuff. She read all the labels and took most of it back to the beach store, swapping it for the in-date stock. No one would notice until next year, long after they'd gone. Then they would bring them back and complain, which would serve Oggie right.

She stared at the empty, switched-off freezer, with all the sorts of ices advertised above it. She knew what she wanted to do.

The thought came with a little thrill, a prickly feeling on her skin. Their shopping trip had been OK—good fun, in fact. But then, Max had been with her. This time she would do it on her own. He would get his ice cream.

Insulation—that was the challenge. Clio took a fold of ancient aluminium foil from the bottom of the cooker, and stuffed an old woolly sock in her pocket. For the first time, she was pleased that the weather felt cold. It wasn't that far to get back from the shops by the footpath—she would simply have to run.

It was the thought of Max lying pale on his mattress, in their loft, that got her past the gardens and the garages, into the final alley and into the street. She slipped on the glasses, and made for the ice cream parlour. That was the first setback. The sign on the door said Closed, though it was full of little children—someone's birthday party had it to themselves. Clio gazed through the glass for a moment, like the one child who had not been asked.

She tried the nearest sweet shop, the newsagent's . . . They were not selling ice cream at this time of year—

only the odd lolly and the kind of fancy gateau families might have for tea. Max wanted ice cream, plain and simple. Nothing else would do.

In the Eight-till-Late shop she found it—plain and white, though in a posh make, all organic and free range and . . . She felt for the change in her pocket, and her stomach dropped. That was the second setback: forty-five pence. No way would it have been enough, not even for a simple cone. How stupid is that, thought Clio. But she wasn't going home without it. No.

Everything seemed very still and clear. Her heart beat faster. She felt good. She glanced round for the CCTV camera. Thanks to Max, she had an instinct these days: she saw any street like a film set, and the passers-by were actors caught first on one camera—there, my best profile!—then another, in long-shot or close up. She had seen how he would cross a street or turn his face at an angle when he sensed a camera near. In a shop like this, there would be a split screen of six or eight little images. On one would be a blurry figure, with short hair, in bad clothes, wearing glasses. Clio put the ice cream in her shopping basket, just like anyone.

As she turned away from the camera, she reached up to the top shelf, as if for one last thing. She tipped one plastic bottle over, and it fell into the one behind it, which— quite slowly, as she walked down the aisle—fell into the next and crash, there was a satisfying landslide on the shelf behind. As everybody turned to look, she came round the end of the aisle, put down the basket, slipped the carton inside her cagoule and walked through the door.

When Max woke up and found her crouching by him, he showed no surprise. He opened his mouth for a spoon of half-melted Vanilla, and said *Mmmm*. Then he said, 'You're lovely, you know that?'

'Mmmm,' said Clio. 'More?'

19

Dragon Birds

It was on her watch that Oggie came back. Clio heard the beat-up Escort coming down the track, and the sight of the big man heaving himself out of the small car made her want to hide. But they would have to face him. The thought of this moment had been in their minds for days, though neither had said so. She took a deep breath and stepped out of cover.

'Oi, you!' Oggie shouted. 'What d'you think you're—Oh, it's you.'

'You see?' said Clio, quickly. 'No one's going to recognize us. Max has given himself a makeover too. We're being really careful.'

He looked her up and down. 'Shame about your hair,' he said. 'I liked it.' He leaned closer and a waft of sour drink hit her. 'Get out of here, for your own good,' he said. 'Tell him you want to move on.'

'We need to stay. Please! You won't know we're here.'

'Oh, I will. I will.' He was staring at her as if he could not quite focus. 'But you're lucky—caught me on a good day—feeling mellow. You get, like, a stay of execution.' His voice dropped. 'And another thing. Anything he's told you about me, it's lies. Forget it, wipe it. Got me?'

Clio nodded. As she turned to go he grabbed her arm. 'You be careful,' he said. 'Your tricky Mickey—Mack or Max or Mick or whatever he's calling himself—he *steals*

167

bits of people. You know what I mean? Think about it.' He let go. 'Now beat it. Before I come to my senses.' He lurched towards his hut and she walked back fast, trying not to run.

The hut smelt of cooking. Max had got back his appetite. The tale he'd told her about working as some TV chef's assistant didn't seem likely, but he knew his way around a kitchen. He liked to do things well. Just that morning he'd talked her through a fantasy breakfast, with a little lecture on how to make an omelette *properly*—something her mum had never achieved. It was theory, of course: to make it for real they would need eggs. Still, her mouth had watered at the thought.

Max did not hear her walk in. Seeing him leaning at the sink made her pause. Just why had he dyed his hair a couple of days ago to the same colour as hers? Why had he cut hers as short as his own?

He steals bits of people . . . Oggie had said. But Oggie was just a sad old bloke, and drunk. What did he know about Max, or her? Max had *given* her parts of herself, parts that she hadn't even known existed. Now he looked up with a twinkle. The moment of worry was gone.

After the meal, they took a breath of air. 'I knew it would be OK,' Max said. 'The Ogre likes us.'

'I like *this*,' said Clio, gazing over the reed beds. But Max gave a little shiver.

'Gives me the creeps,' he said. 'Dead water. Stagnant. Probably full of dead things, down there in the mud.' He towed her by the hand, between the huts, on to the bare and windy seaward shore. 'This is our side,' he said. 'You don't want to be looking back at Milbourne all the time, do you? *Do* you?'

'Course not. I just like the birds.'

'We've got birds this side. Look.' He pointed out along the nearest groyne . . . then the next one, and the next. On the end of each was a post, and on the post a red warning marker. On the top of each, a lean bird squatted, staring out to sea. 'Dragon birds!' said Max.

'They're cormorants,' said Clio.

He gave her a pained look. 'I *know*. I can give you the Latin name if you like. Would you rather have that, or dragons?' As they watched, one of the birds dived and vanished. For a minute or more they stared at the sea—do they ever *drown*? thought Clio—till its dragon head popped up again, impossibly far out.

'I saw a dolphin this morning,' Max said.

'Oh yes, and a sea serpent yesterday. You don't get dolphins round here.'

'That's what you think. These things happen all the time, with me.' As if to prove his point, the grey cloud cover broke for the first time that day. Right overhead, they looked into a narrow chasm with the gold of sunset in its upper reaches, and a glimpse of implausible kingfisher blue. Five minutes later, it was night.

'I've been thinking,' Max said, as they came back to the hut. 'Princess Bella-whatsit's father . . .'

'He isn't in the story.'

'She must have had one. So, the father, he's this bandit king, back there, in the place you came from.'

'It isn't a fairytale,' said Clio. 'Pretty bloody, really. Anyway, it's history.'

'Clio!'

'What?'

'Your name. Of course, that's you: the Muse of History.'

Clio frowned. 'How come you know all this stuff?' she said.

'Oh, you'd be surprised . . . This bandit king—some kind of warlord—he'll have friends in the government.

And one day he gets to see a British paper and there . . . there's his beautiful daughter.'

'That's a silly story. Save it for your book.'

'Oh, it's in there already. So are you.'

Clio forced out a laugh, but inside her heart was thumping. 'Show me,' she said.

'Not now. When I'm famous! When it's a bestseller you can be on the chat shows with me. I'll write a clause in the film deal saying no one else can play the part of you but you.'

'I'm going to look,' said Clio. 'I know where it is.' She moved towards the ladder, and he grabbed her. They tussled like boys in a play-fight, till their legs gave way and they crumpled between the ladder and the sofa.

'Never, never touch that book,' Max said. 'I'm not joking. You know what it's made of?' She stopped pretending to struggle.

'What?'

'Well, the man in the junk shop said it came from a house clearance—old German guy who'd been in Poland in the war. You know what the Nazis made lampshades out of?'

'No! That's sick, that's gross!'

'Sor-ry! You'd rather have a fairy story?'

'Oh, not that again.'

'This is another one.' Max rolled on his back and looked up at the ceiling. 'There's this robber king's daughter, she's in exile in another country, and she's sort of happy . . . except that she's not. Because nobody, not her foster parents, *nobody*, sees who she is. Until one day . . .' As if by accident, his arm had settled round her shoulder, just like she would do with Toby. As innocent as that . . . but it was hard for her to keep her mind on the story, with the warmth of it there, and the tips of his fingers lying just along her collarbone.

'You want me to stop?' said Max.

She shook her head.

'Until . . . until one day she meets this *shape-shifter*—don't ask me how he got to be that way, it's what he is . . . and he's sick of it.'

'Why? It sounds good, shape-shifting.'

'You don't know what it feels like. Imagine. He can fool anyone, easy, like taking sweets from kiddies. He wants something at school? He just schmoozes the teachers till he gets it. He bunks off—makes up some story—they believe him! He can be anything—fool anyone except . . .' His gaze was in the middle distance now, and frowning, as if he was watching a film he didn't like. 'Except the ones who matter, the ones in the *famous* club, the ones you read about in magazines.'

'Like Maylene? Like that footballer bloke?'

'Shush. It's a *story*. So . . . they laugh at him, they throw him out, and he's so angry, he could burn the place down just by looking. Go *boom* and take all of them with him. And then . . . then something strange happens. He meets someone. Someone special.'

'Special?'

'Oh, yes, in lots of ways. But the main one is: she can *see* him. I mean: see the real him. You'd think he'd run away, but he doesn't. No, he does a dangerous thing.'

Max got up. He walked to the dresser, with his back to her. 'He takes his real self and he puts it in a bottle—like a genie. And gives it to her.' Max turned and tossed something in Clio's direction. She had caught it before she saw what it was: the cloudy-grey glass bottle. Inside it, he had pushed a double-folded curl of paper. Clio laughed and poked a finger through the narrow neck, but the paper had unfurled tight to the sides; she could not hook it out.

'Don't look,' he said. 'Just keep it safe for me.'

Then neither of them was laughing. The slight dark-haired boy Max had shape-shifted into looked so young and small, there was nothing for Clio to do but put her arms around him. He was awkward for a moment, but she held him tighter, and his lips touched first her shoulder, then her cheek. This time she did not pull away.

He leaned his weight against her, and they stumbled. 'Careful,' Clio said. They came to rest against the sloping ladder.

'You OK?' he murmured.

'Mm.' It was going to happen. She had always known, deep down, that it would, just like in the stories and films. She moved her face against his till their lips touched, clumsily at first, then they found the angle and it was a proper kiss.

Lips. Tongue tips. Not too quick, now.

It was gentle, that was what surprised her. It was like a question. She had expected him to be so sure, the way he was about everything. He must have done this so often, he would be bound to notice what *her* experience added up to: letting some boy or other she didn't really fancy snog a bit at parties, so they could talk about it later to their friends. This was different. She hardly dared move, in case she lost it. Bit by bit their lips relaxed against each other, and they felt each other's breathing, and the single heartbeat she'd felt that time with him in the car.

His hand moved up behind her head to cushion it against the ladder. That was sweet. He stroked her hair. 'I like that,' he said.

'There's nothing there. I used to have nice hair.'

'You feel like a cat,' he said and trilled a deep purr that she felt inside her. The stroking was surer now, down to the nape of her neck, letting his fingers play

172

inside the back of her T-shirt. Then he was pressing against her and his breathing had changed.

'Slowly . . .' she said, and he pulled back a little. 'No, it's OK,' she said quickly. 'Don't stop. Just . . . slowly . . .'

'Sure, sure . . . Catwoman . . .' His other hand stroked down her back, right to the spot where a tail ought to be. 'I can be Superman,' he whispered. 'Who would you like me to be?'

'No one. I mean, just *you*.' Suddenly she wished that she could see his eyes. But they were too close, out of focus.

'Spoilsport. I can be anyone . . . Hey, I'm going to be a film star,' he whispered. 'Cara Sanderton told me she'd get me a part. The lead, with her. But I'll tell her I'd rather have you.' His hand had found the stud at the front of her jeans. She felt the waistband go slack. 'Wanna come to LA with me?'

'Don't,' said Clio. 'Not here.'

Neither of them wanted to stop touching, even as they climbed the ladder. Each rung she climbed, he would be there right behind her, nuzzling the back of her neck or her ear until she craned her face round for the kiss. Her neck was stiff before they reached the hatch, but every inch of her he had touched was glowing.

She spilled into the near darkness of the loft. In the moment it took him to climb in beside her, she had unhooked her bra, so they wouldn't have to fumble. In the films, nobody fumbles. She just wanted it to be all right.

He found her by touch, nudging against her, and rested his head on her midriff a moment, tracing a circle, getting wider, with his tongue, as he eased her T-shirt up and waistband down. She caught hold of his head and gently pulled him up towards her. 'Kiss me.'

173

'That film part. I lied. It's going to be a dirty movie.'

'Sssh . . .' she said. 'Kiss me again. That was nice.'

'. . . and this is the screen test. They've got infra-red cameras up here filming *everything* . . . so it had better be hot.'

'Max, no. Please. No stories. Not now.'

'What do you want, then?' He pulled back, and there was an edge to his voice.

'I want *you*,' she said, 'just you.' She reached out for him and her hand touched his waist, so she loosened the stud there, as he had with hers. It was not quite what she had meant, but it was happening, and he had sounded so urgent, maybe this was what she was supposed to do. She wished she could see his face. He was too quiet, suddenly.

'Max? Say something.'

'You told me to shut up.'

'I didn't. I said no more *stories*. We don't have to play games.' But Max was very still now. It was going wrong. 'Max, please . . .' He pulled away, and as she clutched for him, her hand slipped down inside his waistband. It was only for a second, but he flinched away as if he had been stung.

'It's OK,' she said, desperately. Maybe he hadn't been ready, or she'd spoiled it somehow. 'I'm sorry. There's plenty of time.'

He was sitting upright now, pulling his clothes back together. 'Why do you have to spoil things?' he said, coldly. 'What's your problem? Why can't you just pretend, like everybody does?'

'I'm sorry, sorry . . . Max! All I said was: I want *you*.' She reached out, but he pushed her hand away. Then he was scrambling down the ladder.

'You were right in the first place,' he called. 'You said we weren't going to do the love stuff. You're the one

174

who changed your mind. I can't breathe in here. I'm going for a walk. Leave me alone!' For a moment the sound of the wind and waves rushed in, then the door slammed, and Clio stayed lying there, like the sole survivor of a shipwreck, in the darkness of the loft.

20

The Emptiest Place on Earth

For a long time she lay without moving. In a moment he would walk back in, all this would have been a mistake, none of it would have happened . . . if she just kept still, and did not think.

Max did not walk in. Outside, the wind and waves had never sounded nearer. One big wave, thought Clio, that's all it would take to sweep us away. Now would be a good time. But nothing happened. She got up and went to the door.

He was nowhere in sight. It was night, though the glow of the town across the harbour meant it was never quite dark. Out to sea, the foam gave off a whiteness of its own. With a sudden uneasy feeling, Clio stepped back into the hut. She glanced at the hook near the door. The long black coat and white silk scarf were gone. She ran out on to the shingle, calling '*Max!*'—not caring now if anyone could hear.

The rain came and went, and already she could feel it seeping through her clothes. He could not have gone far. He would have to find shelter. She tried the toilet block, still calling, then searched in among the huts, rattling any door that was not padlocked. Everywhere was empty, cold and dead.

A bad thought struck her. *Oggie.* Had Max gone down to his hut? He was always talking about how much the

Ogre liked him—though it didn't look like that to her. Would he let Max in? And if he did . . . ? All she knew was that Oggie would not mind if Max disappeared.

There was a light in the warden's window, and the faded curtains did not meet. Between them Clio could see Oggie in his one chair, slumped, with bottles around him and a tiny portable TV. He didn't look as if he'd moved all evening, but she steeled herself and knocked. He lifted up his big face with a scowl.

'It's Max,' she said as the door opened. 'Have you seen him?'

'Gone, has he?' A lopsided smile appeared among the stubble. 'Good riddance. So he's left you on your own.'

'No! I mean, he's somewhere. He just . . . got upset. I'm worried.'

The smile became a slow grin. 'Well, if I was going to top myself, I'd do it down by the Rip. Current'd take the body miles out. They wouldn't find you for months. Hey . . .' he called after her. 'If you're lonely, you can always knock on Uncle Oggie's door.'

Clio ran. The Rip . . . Now nothing mattered—not the wet slap of rain in her face, not the cold—nothing but getting there. Just in case . . . Or just in time . . .

She came out past the last huts and paused, panting and sobbing. The sea was a haze, the waves a constant crash and backwash. Clots of greyish foam blew tumbling towards her. There was no one on the beach.

Ever since they had been there, the end of the Spit had been out of bounds—too exposed, only a stone's throw from the car park on the quay. Just the thought of the Rip had made her queasy since that night in the boat. Now the water was black and dull, as if even the light would be dragged under and washed out to sea.

177

At the narrowest point, the Rip was edged with concrete walls—a sheer drop, with a chain between low bollards and a sign warning parents to keep their children well back. People strolled here in summer, with ice creams. Now it was the emptiest place on earth.

One of the bollards shifted slightly. Clio looked again. Max sat, in his black coat, hunched up, rocking slightly back and forwards. His arms were hugged around himself, his legs out of sight. He was beyond the warning chain, sitting right on the edge of the drop.

Holding her breath, Clio moved towards him. Don't call out, she thought. He was balanced so precariously, staring down. Just startling him could tip him over. And all the time he was rocking, like disturbed kids do for comfort. Or was he testing . . . how close could he get to the point of balance before he just tipped over and was gone?

Don't creep up. Don't startle him. She kept to the edge, or as near as she dared, inching towards him. Not yet, not yet . . . Only when she was close did she clear her throat, as softly as she could.

'Max?' she said. 'It was my fault. I'm so sorry.'

'Piss off.' His face half-turned her way, as if he could not keep his eyes off the water beneath. Just looking made her head spin. 'Go back,' he said, in a cold voice. 'Go home. Tell them I brainwashed you.'

'You didn't.'

'I never wanted you here.'

'That's not true.'

'How do you know? I'm a liar, remember?'

'Max . . . I know.' She took a step closer. '*I know you.*' She reached to touch his shoulder.

'No!' He flinched, and they both stiffened. 'Don't *dare* touch me—unless you want to come in too!'

'Don't say that. Max, I said I'm sorry. What . . .

178

happened just now—it was just an accident. We need to talk, that's all.'

'Talk! What else have we ever done? That's all I'm good for, isn't it? You've been wasting your time. I was right that night at the Complex: there's *no point*. I should have walked off the edge of the harbour and been done with it. I thought of it, you know.'

'Don't do this, Max. You're just being horrible. You're saying this stuff to hurt me.'

'Don't flatter yourself. You're nothing in this, nothing. You've never had the slightest idea!'

'Max, stop it!' Clio touched, and held, his shoulder.

'Let go.'

'No. Not even if you jump.' He pulled away, and for a moment they were braced against each other. Then her foot slipped and they both fell sideways. Max's hand flung out and grabbed the chain behind him and held on.

'There,' he said, bitterly, as he pulled them both back from the edge. 'See? I can't do anything. Not even that.' In the dim light his face was wild and cold. 'Now you know,' he said. 'I'm useless. No good to you. Just run off home.'

'And what about you?'

'Doesn't matter.'

'It does. It matters.'

'Not to me.'

'To *me*, then.'

'You'll get over it. I'm . . . *nothing*, don't you understand?'

Very cautiously she laid her hand on his. 'Max, that's one of your stories. Like you're different from everybody else on earth.'

'You don't get it. No one gets it. I can just imagine Stella: *Oh, poor thing. It was a cry for help* . . . Like hell it was. *Oh, poor thing, all he needs is therapy* . . .'

179

'Well,' Clio said, 'maybe . . .'

'See? You're just like the rest of them. You're so naive. Yeah, it's one of my stories. Like everything. I've been laughing at you all the time. Everything I've said, it's been a lie.'

'Then so's this!' Clio said, and for a second Max looked uncertain. 'I can tell when you mean what you say.'

'So what? I *always* believe what I say. Don't you see? *Anything* I say feels like it really happened. Now . . .' His voice was almost pleading. 'Will you let me go?'

Clio closed her eyes. She could not argue. All those hateful words . . . they hurt but they didn't mean anything. Sticks and stones. She dug her fingers into his coat sleeve. He pulled away fiercely, she held on, and together they rolled on the hard ground. Then he was struggling free. He got to his feet, wriggling out of the long coat, and stood there in his thin clothes, in the cold rain, laughing.

'There! You've got it.' He whipped the silk scarf from round his neck and tossed it at her. 'All the costume. That's all there is to it. That's me!'

Clio was numb now. As the coat slipped from her fingers, he snatched it up—held it, dangling, with the scarf around it, like a headless ventriloquist's dummy, and in one sweep launched it over the edge. For a moment it hung in the air, its arms out like a skydiver, then crumpled and fell, swallowed up in the water, black on black.

'Now,' Max said, 'run away. Have I got to chase you off? What have I got to say? That it's my fault? OK, it's my fault. I let myself start thinking something stupid, that's all.'

'What?' said Clio.

'That you could help me. How stupid is that?'

'I can,' she said. 'I can help you.'

'Stupid,' he said again. 'Like you, for believing me.' His voice was taunting but his eyes said something else. *Help me*. This is the last chance, she thought. If she did not answer, he'd be gone for good.

'OK, so you're right,' said Clio. 'You're nothing. Fine. So? So you've got nothing to lose. What are you afraid of? Trust me.'

A pause. Two drenched kids, shivering in the dark and rain. 'So what's the magic answer, then? What do you think *you* can do?'

'I don't know . . . yet. You'll have to show me your book.'

21

Last Best Chance

*I**nterviewer:** Tonight our special guest comes straight from the Cannes Film Festival, where his entry* The Complex *has caused a sensation. Please welcome Matt Taylor. Congratulations, Matt. This is the first time a one-man home-produced movie has walked off with the coveted Palme d'Or. Word on the street at Cannes is that you're the hottest new thing to emerge since Steven Spielberg.*

Matt: *Yeah, that's what Steven said to me. Then again, he would, wouldn't he?*

Interviewer: *That sounds like an offer. Can we take it you'll be on the next flight to Los Angeles?*

Matt: *I guess I should try to fit it in. My agent handles most of these things. There's no hurry—Hollywood needs me more than I need Hollywood. I don't see it affecting my creative direction.*

Interviewer: *You're referring to your pseudo-reality-plus technique without scripts . . . or actors? I was going to ask you about that.*

Matt: *What is there to say? We've had Reality TV. I've just taken it one step further. Everybody's life is a movie, whether you like it or not. They're being made all the time.*

Interviewer: *So it could have been anyone's movie,* The Complex*? Surely not?*

Matt: *Of course not. Most people's lives are just one movie. Mine's as many movies as you like. And quite a few you won't like.*

Interviewer: I see. Can I ask you a personal question? You made this movie without actors or production costs—indeed, I'm told you don't even own a camera. Can I take it that this box office success is going to make you very rich? Will it change your life at all?

Matt: Not at all. I've always lived as if I'm very rich . . . and now I am. Any more questions?

Interviewer: I don't think so. Thank you. And now, let's talk to one celebrity who is said to have been seen with Matt Taylor in a most exclusive club at Cannes. Please welcome Cara Sanderton . . .

She hardly dared touch it at first. It had always been there. Even in their secret moments, whispering in the dark, the book had been with them. Now Max pointed to it in its hiding place. She felt for it gingerly, as if it was a live thing, a strange pet of his, that might bite.

Coming back from the Rip he had been silent, looking stunned or lost. He had reached the hut shivering and Clio had waited until he was wrapped in blankets, with a hot drink in his hand, before she had mentioned the book. 'Take it,' he'd said dully. 'Doesn't matter any more.' Now he was propped up on the sofa. She sat on the floor and read.

'Hey, this is clever,' she said, surprised. 'This interview, it's funny. You should do comedy. I mean it.' He did not smile, or look pleased, or offended, or anything. It scared her. It was as though he'd gone, run off, and left his body sitting there.

There seemed to be no order in the book. The first page had to be recent, because it talked about the Complex. Some pieces further in had to be older. Some were neatly printed, others done with loops or in a spiky scrawl—as if several different people had been writing.

183

Sometimes she could see it change from one to another in mid sentence. He could change his writing like he mimicked voices. He could forge for England, Clio thought.

There were blank pages too, as if he opened it at random every time. She found a long entry about a boy in Swindon, and whether he was Max or the dead boy whose family he had lived with, Clio could not tell.

'It's true, what Oggie said. You steal bits of people. That stuff you told the police, the Angry Brigade, that was Oggie, wasn't it? Oh God, I must be in here somewhere . . .'

It was eerie, the way everything he'd written in there seemed to be told from the outside—always 'he', not 'I'—as if the storyteller was somewhere in the distance, watching . . . even when the person in the story *had* to be Max himself. It made Clio think about the tales of near death experiences, when people find themselves looking down on their body on the operating table, seeing things they could not possibly have seen. It was the view surveillance cameras saw.

She handled the book with care, trying not to dislodge the torn strips of newsprint slipped between the pages. The clippings she glanced at were odd—one about abandoned children, one about a baby left in a recycling bin, or a toddler in a house where he'd survived by eating packets of cornflakes. Car crashes, disasters, someone drowned in a school swimming pool . . . then a suicide bombing, and freakish things, like the Most Tattooed Man in Britain, or some millionaire who was going to be deep-frozen when he died. This was the kind of thing she glanced at in the papers, like everyone did—glanced and moved on. What did this stuff mean to him?

184

'Police have surrounded a building in which the young urban terrorist Marcus Tatler is staging a desperate last stand. Tatler is known to be accompanied by his one-time hostage turned accomplice, Clio Palmer, who has issued a defiant statement saying that she intends to fight to the death for Tatler and his principles . . .'

Oh, really, Max! thought Clio. But she smiled. He must have been writing it, secretly, in the last few days. Everything they had talked about seemed to be there, melted down into one of his stories.

'Ms Palmer's adoptive parents have refused to comment on the speculation that Tatler demanded, and has been paid, a large ransom from the Eastern European criminal gang whose leader may have been the girl's true father.'

Oh, Max, *really*! Clio thought again.

'A cordon has been thrown around the area to hold back crowds of sightseers—among them a number of well-wishers who have turned up with flowers and placards in support of the couple inside. Police admit that they are baffled as to Tatler's true identity, and have appealed to members of the public who think they might have encountered him to come forward . . .'

Clio glanced at Max. He was locked up inside himself, miles away. But he wanted her to find him. Suddenly it seemed so clear. Every lie he had told, every tale in his book, was laced with clues. It made her think of the trail of breadcrumbs Hansel and Gretel had left in the wood. Every time he had talked about people he'd conned, or the teachers at school who never spotted that he'd cheated, she heard that edge in his voice, sort of angry, sort of disappointed: *and the idiots believed me!* He wanted someone to find him, and they'd let him down, every time. Until now.

'It's never happened before,' Max said out of the blue.

'Pardon? What hasn't?'

'You know—what happened, with you, earlier . . . I've been with loads of girls. You'll find some of them in there.'

'Don't worry about it,' Clio said. She was not going to look for them. 'It doesn't matter.'

He looked blankly at her. 'It should.'

'Let's forget it.'

But he wouldn't. 'If you hadn't started arguing . . .'

'Me? I . . . Oh, whatever! All I said was, let's be real, that's all . . . Max, please, can't we leave it?' She shuffled up against the sofa and laid her head on his arm. 'I was worried about you. I thought . . . I thought you'd . . .'

'Gone for a swim?'

'I don't even want to say it. I'm glad you're OK.'

'Am I?' There was a silence. 'You said you could help.'

'Give me time. There's a *clue* in here, somewhere.'

'What are you after—the big secret? I was abused as a kid or something? That's what Stella would say, isn't it? Well . . . what if it's worse than that?'

'*Worse?*'

'Yeah. What if there *isn't* a secret?'

Clio looked at him, puzzled.

'Think about it,' Max said. 'What if there's *nothing*? No trauma? No secret? Nothing to make sense of anything? Isn't that worse than the worst thing you can think of?' He leaned back, limp as a dropped puppet. 'Like you said: it doesn't matter.' He closed his eyes and tucked his knees up like a baby in the womb.

The next page was all jagged writing, hardly in lines, as if he'd thrown it down there in a rage.

*Saw this rubbish film. Same tired old shit about the homeless.
Long shot of one outside Marks and Spencers, this kid in the
ripped khaki clothes. Close up on the broken glass and dog shit,
then his bit of cardboard for the money, then his face, looking
down, pathetic, muttering Spare-some-change-please . . .
Honest-I-just-need-my-train-fare-home . . .*

*Well, here's the next shot. He looks up, straight at you, and
he sort of smiles. What does he mean by that? You've got no
idea, have you? Don't you know he's been watching you, day
after day? He knows all about you, he knows where you live.
And you—you haven't got a clue. For all you know he's a kid
from the best school in town, who bunks off, sneaks down to
the station where he keeps his homeless clothes. He spends the
day on the street, practising his hungry look, for you. You can't
explain him. You'll never know how, come five o'clock, he
gathers up your change and goes into the poshest shop in town
and blows it on something stupidly expensive, something no
one needs.*

*Close up again. Can't you glimpse the silk scarf, just a tassel,
under the combat jacket? And he's smiling. Why? Because he
knows, whatever they do to him back at school, they can't touch
him. Whatever they do, he'll feel the silk against his neck and
he'll smile, like a slap in their face—because they won't know
why.*

'That's you, isn't it?' said Clio. 'That's your scarf! Is
it true?' He slumped there, with his back towards her.
'Max! You're doing it again. Every time we get
anywhere near to stuff that *matters*, you go blank—or
you start telling stories. Any time I mention anything
about school . . . Don't look like that. You must have
gone to school.'

'Sure I did. Plenty.'

'And you ran away or something?'

'Now and then. I got bored. It isn't worth talking about.'

'That can't be all—there's something you're not saying. Look: *whatever they do to him*. What does that mean? And wasn't there a cutting . . . about some school . . . a swimming pool?'

'Leave it!' Max said sharply.

So—touched a nerve there, Clio thought. She was riffling through the notebook as she spoke. She was not being careful now. She picked up the book and shook it, until cuttings showered out like autumn leaves.

Then she stared. Among the scraps of newsprint were bank notes—tens and twenties. She was looking at hundreds of pounds on the floor. Max sat up and looked at it, too, as if he had forgotten what the stuff was.

'You've got money!' she said. 'I spent *all* mine in that charity shop on those crap clothes. And you went off and bought brand new. You did, didn't you?' She scraped up the notes in her hands . . . and flung the crumpled pile at him. 'You had this all the time!'

'It's not mine. It's from Oggie.'

'Oggie? Oggie gave you money?'

'He'd just done some business. He was feeling generous.'

'Generous? Him?' She wasn't going to ask about the *business*. 'Don't tell me it's because he *likes* you. What is it: blackmail? Is that what you do: get people's secrets out of them and . . . ?'

'It isn't like that. He gave me that . . . so we'd go away.'

'What about *me*?' said Clio. 'Don't I get consulted?'

'He was drunk. I thought if I just agreed he'd probably forget. I didn't say *when* we'd be going. And it *is* for both of us,' Max added. He slumped back again. 'Don't be angry with me.'

Clio sighed. There was no point. The cocky, smart-arse Max was gone—the one who was cooler and more confident than any boy she'd met, so that when he'd said *We're members of the same species* it had made her feel like the most special thing on earth. In his place was a thin boy huddled in a blanket. And he had given her his most private possession: his book.

'It's not about the money,' Clio said. 'It's . . . You made me steal that stuff!'

Max turned round. 'Me?' he said. 'I *made* you?'

'I'm not a thief. I don't *do* things like that. I don't tell lies . . .' She faltered in mid sentence, as the catalogue of all she had done reeled back in her mind. 'How did all this happen?' she whispered.

'I couldn't *make* you do anything . . . not if you didn't want to—deep down. Clio . . . don't give up on me.'

She couldn't help herself: she put her arms around him. 'That was my last chance,' he said. 'At the Complex . . . Why couldn't they have given me a proper trial? I'd have been more famous than Cara-stupid-Sanderton and Kieran-stupid-Scott then, wouldn't I?'

'Maybe . . .' said Clio, very carefully, 'maybe you *could* do with some help?'

'You mean, like, therapy? Social workers, psychologists, all that? They'd put me away.'

'They wouldn't. Even if they did . . . I'd visit you, I swear!'

'Do you think they'd let *you* see me? After all this?' He sounded weary. 'They wouldn't be satisfied until they'd made me sensible and stupid and . . . *not me*. I'd rather be dead.'

'Don't say that!'

'Why not? I thought you wanted me to be honest?'

'All right,' she said slowly. 'If you don't want help . . . you'll have to do it by yourself—with me, I mean. Will you try?'

189

She found the cutting she had been looking for. 'Listen: *Police investigating the suspicious death of a boy in the swimming pool at an exclusive boarding school say pupils have been giving evidence of a catastrophic breakdown of discipline, involving alcohol and drug abuse and unchecked bullying. Officers were called to Ardley Hall, near Culverton, last week, following the theft of the headmaster's car* . . . Why did you keep that?'

'I don't know.'

'There you are. That proves it.'

'What?'

If only Stella was here, thought Clio. She could have explained it. 'You've blanked it out. You're *in denial*. People do that when something feels too bad to face.' She grabbed his hands. 'But it *isn't*—whatever it is. I'm with you.'

'What am I meant to do?'

'Close your eyes. Don't try to do anything. Now . . . what do you see when I say *swimming pool*?'

For a moment he was still, then his fingers tightened. 'Yes,' she said. 'What can you see?'

'Bubbles . . . coming up. And the water's dark all round. It's weird—a splash, then . . . nothing . . . And then the bubbles, kind of silver.'

'What happened? Someone fell in?'

'Not *someone*—the car—old Samuels . . .'

'Who's he?'

'Teacher. Smooth git. He's got this old Jaguar, really shiny and black—like the water . . . Except the lights in the car are still on underwater. Everybody's laughing, till . . . they stop.'

'Well? Go on.'

'I can't. I don't know . . .'

'Try!'

He shook his head, as if to shake the pictures

190

out. Then Clio had her idea. 'We've got to go there,' she said. 'Find the school. If you can see the place, and face it . . .'

'Then?'

'Then . . . you'll be better. Everything will make sense. You won't *be in denial* any more. Max, will you do it . . . for me?'

He looked back at her, warily. This is the danger point, she was thinking. One doubt now, I've lost him. So she did a chancy thing: she laughed.

'Or have you got another plan?' she said. 'Apart from jumping in the sea, that is? Just give this a try. You can jump in the harbour *after*, if you've got to.'

It was OK. Max smiled. 'You started this. I was all right.'

'No, you weren't!' But she knew what he meant. She'd started something. Like it or not, she was the only person in the world he would trust. *The only one.* The thought sent a tingle through her bones. His last best hope. How much more special can you be?

'Thanks,' he whispered. 'Thanks for coming after me.'

'I always will,' said Clio.

'Promise?'

'Promise.' He laid his head on her shoulder, and for a long time neither of them said a word.

22

A Gap in the Wall

Oggie was singing, more or less.

> *'Goin' up Camborne 'ill comin' down*
> *Goin' up Camborne 'ill comin' down . . .'*

He turned round at the driving wheel and grinned at the two of them in the back, with all his bad teeth. 'Old Cornish rugby song. You don't have a problem with it, do you?'

Clio shook her head. Max had that same shell-shocked look he'd had all day. For the first time in their hitch-hiking together, Max had not gone for the front seat, up there with the driver, and Clio had no wish to be right next to Oggie, so they sat in the back, like kids.

'Good,' said Oggie. 'It always comes into my head when I'm happy. Must be because I'm getting rid of you two.'

'We're really grateful for the lift,' said Clio.

'Don't be. I'm not your bleeding fairy godmother.' He smiled, more to himself than Max or Clio. 'Thing is,' he said, 'I'm a creature of habit. Nasty habits, some might say, but that's their lookout. Having you two hanging round . . . disturbs things. Best for us all if you're gone.' And that was as close to friendly as they could hope for, Clio thought. Except when he was drunk, that is—and then . . . she didn't like to think how friendly he might get. Now they were leaving, it was easier to see him as

192

a sad old loner with a guilty past—not mean, really, just afraid.

'Understood?' said Oggie.

'Understood,' said Clio. She just wished he would not keep on turning round when they were doing forty through a winding country lane, with hedges coming at them from all angles.

They had not asked for a lift. When Oggie had come across them in the site office, rooting around to find a map, she had thought: *That's it, we're in for it now.* But once she had explained, the old ogre had nodded. 'Culverton . . . Yeah, that'll do,' he'd said, as if somewhere in Central Asia would have been better, and he was getting the car out quicker than she and Max could pack their bags.

As they veered through the lanes, Max stared out of the window. Sometimes he closed his eyes and she knew he was back in the dark of his mind.

'He's quiet,' said Oggie. 'Sickening for something, is he?'

'Just tired,' Clio said. 'He didn't get much sleep.'

Oggie gave a short laugh. 'You two made it up, then,' he said. She ignored that. Maybe if she didn't reply he would shut up. She wanted to be inside Max's head with him, hunting through piles of stories, trying to find a true memory buried underneath. The drowned car . . . and the swimming pool . . . She squeezed his hand, and he squeezed back. Yes, she *was* on the right track. She was going to do what no one had done—not schools, not social services, not the police or prison. She was going to help Max find *himself*. Maybe afterwards they would go home and tell everyone. She imagined it— Mum, and Dad, and Stella—how their faces would gradually change as they realized what a brilliant thing she had done.

'The 'orses stood sti-i-i-ill,' boomed Oggie. *'The wheels went arou-ou-ound, Go-o-o-in' up Camborne 'ill comin' down.'*

Culverton . . . Then a sign said Ardley. They drove through a scrap of a village, passing a primary school . . . and next moment they seemed to be out the other side. Oggie did a bad-tempered three-point turn.

Back in the village he pulled over. The only moving figure in the street was a man coming slowly towards them with a round red face. 'Ask the village idiot,' Oggie said. 'I'm fed up with this game.'

At the words *Ardley Hall*, the man's eyes went, then he nodded. 'Ah,' he said. 'Such goings on . . . *Where* . . . ? Oh, left by where the post office used to be.'

They looked at him. Clio had a feeling there might be a twinkle in his eye. 'Ladies' hairdresser now,' he added. 'Then go straight on for a mile or so. Look for the gap in the wall.'

'Yes!' whispered Max, as the hedgerow on their right side changed to red brick. 'The wall . . .' He was perched on the edge of his seat now. 'Yes,' he breathed again, 'the gate . . .'

It would have been grand, once—two stone gateposts meeting at the top, like a triumphal arch. On one, a smart little sign said *ARDLEY HALL*.

'OK, Mickey Mouse,' said Oggie. 'Out. And take her with you. You're on your own from here.' No sooner had Max's holdall and Clio's carrier bag of spare clothes touched the road beside them than the Escort revved and Oggie was gone, leaving a cough of dirty exhaust behind him. Max walked up to the gatepost and peered at it, frowning. He leaned back against it wearily and closed his eyes.

'We shouldn't have come,' he said quietly. 'It was *good*, back there on the beach.'

'It'll be better when you've done this,' Clio said.

'Better? Who says what's *better*? Social workers? Shrinks?'

'All the books. I've seen them, at Stella's house.'

'And you've read all about it, have you? While you're babysitting?'

'Yes, actually. I've read a bit. Stella thinks I should be a psychologist. I might do it at A level.'

'Oh, I get it. I'm *homework*. I'm an *interesting case* . . .'

'You know that isn't why I'm here! Max, we're nearly there. We've just got to walk through that gate, and find that swimming pool, and . . . and then it'll all make sense.'

His face froze, as if someone had pressed Pause. 'Max?'

He shook his head. 'Nothing.'

'Something's coming back, isn't it?'

'I said it's nothing.' He shut his eyes. 'You can't *make* anyone do something they don't want to. Not by just *saying* . . . can you?'

'What is it? Is this about the swimming pool . . . ?'

'Nobody *made* him take the car. It's a good joke. He's still laughing, you can see him . . .' Max's voice went fainter. '. . . underneath the water. He doesn't know. He doesn't know he can't get out.' Max turned sharply away.

'Don't stop now,' said Clio. 'Go on!'

'You can see his face inside the windscreen. Laughing! And the windscreen's clouding over—it's still lit up from inside—and he's drawing pictures on it. Smiley faces. And . . .' With a sleepwalker's look Max raised one finger, tracing a shape in the air, and another. Clio watched them. Letters. M . . . A . . .

'Max? He wrote MAX? He wrote your name?'

195

He jerked, as if coming awake. 'You tell me. I'm the liar. You're the shrink.' They stared at each other. 'You don't know what you've started, do you?'

The drive curved gently through the bushes, then came out to a well trimmed lawn. The building was there—with the clock turret over the high front door, like she remembered from the cutting. Everything about the place was very still, as if they were walking into a photograph, slightly faded in the dullness of a winter day.

Clio touched her glasses, just to remind herself who she was. 'Nearly there,' she said. 'Where's the swimming pool?'

Max moved towards the entrance at sleepwalking pace. 'I don't like this,' he said. 'Something's wrong.' There was a quietness in the air that made it hard to imagine any schoolchildren inside those windows—let alone the anarchy the paper talked about. ('Makes me laugh,' said Oggie when they told him. 'All those rich parents paying good money to send their kids to a place like that—doing all the things us anarchists used to do for free.')

They were being watched. Clio scanned the surroundings. Yes, there was a surveillance camera, on a black pole, like the black globe of a streetlamp that did not shed light. Max, though, was looking somewhere else, and she followed his eyes up to a first floor window, where a white face gazed out without moving. A face rimmed by a halo of white hair . . .

Then things fell into place. By the steep steps was a long ramp with stout handrails. As they stood, the doors came open and a very small, very old lady came out, bent almost double on her wheeled walker, with a blue-uniformed carer at her side.

'Old grannies,' Max breathed. 'I'm off.'

'No!' Clio caught him by the hand. The carer at the door had seen them. If they turned and ran now, who knows what she would do? She might call the police.

'Yes?' the carer called out. It did not sound welcoming. 'Can I help you?'

'Old people!' Max hissed. 'They give me the creeps.'

'Come *on* . . .' whispered Clio. She was going to have to do this by herself. 'Uh, excuse me,' she said to the carer. 'We're doing research for a project and . . . and it's about the school . . . you know, that used to be here. We just wondered . . . er . . . if we could look around a bit—if we could see the swimming pool?'

'Swimming pool? Look, I'm sorry, this is a residential care home. Now, if you don't mind . . .'

'Sybil will know.' The small voice seemed to come from nowhere.

'I don't think we should disturb Miss Wilkes,' said the carer.

'Nonsense!' The old lady raised her head, with effort. 'Nothing she likes better than talking about the old school. The rest of us are rather bored by it. She'd be glad of someone young to talk to.' The carer hesitated. 'If I were to tell Sybil that these nice young people had come asking and you'd sent them away . . . well, you'd never hear the last of it.' She gave Clio a startling knowing little wink. 'Sybil knows *everything*. She used to be a teacher here, you see.'

Max was edgy as the bird-frail lady led them to the day room. They had stopped at the reception desk to get their visitors' badges, with names they had plucked from the air. Clio was starting to feel uneasy with the way Max glanced at her from time to time, as if he hoped *she* knew what was going to happen next. The place was hot and airless, with that artificial sweetness you know must be masking something worse. When they came into the room it was like a freeze-frame on a slow, slow film. Old people were dotted in chairs round the edges of the large room, facing in, and some of them—the ones who could hear, Clio guessed—looked up and stayed looking, expressionless and motionless. For a moment Clio could not breathe.

Even in her wheelchair Sybil Wilkes was a commanding presence, tall and thin. Her pale blue eyes held them as she bent her head to catch the whisper of their guide. She nodded. When she spoke, even the old man dozing at the far end of the room jolted and looked up. 'The school?' she said. 'Ah, well . . . What can I tell you? What can I *not* tell you, that would be the question. Oh, do sit down, you two. I'm not in the habit of talking to people who *loom* over me. Here, sit!' She slapped the chair beside her.

'I have to tell you,' she went on, eyes flashing from one to the other, 'that I am not afflicted with forgetfulness, like many of our friends here. Some people—eh, Maisie?—might prefer it if I was. This was the headmaster's study, by the way. Ridiculous, of course, but the only thing he was any good at was impressing the parents, you see, and most of them had mansions of their own. Now, I'm sure . . .' She raised her voice to catch the carer, just retreating to the door, '. . . one of the staff will be happy to fetch you a wee cup of tea. Now—don't mind poor Mrs Hunstanton here, she's deaf as a post, in a world of her own, but very pious—now . . . what were the details you wanted to know? Come on, I haven't got all day.'

Three chairs away, Mrs Hunstanton raised a soft, pink, vaguely smiling face towards them. 'Do not interrupt,

198

please, Mrs Hunstanton,' Sybil said. 'Let these young people get a word in edgeways.'

Clio gave Max a glance, but he was as stiff as a rabbit in the headlights of a car. 'Uh, I'm sorry,' said Clio, desperately. 'There are so many things to ask—we don't quite know where to start. Uh . . . You must have been working at the school some time ago, before . . . what happened. I mean, the accident. The swimming pool . . .'

'I know what you mean. It's the only thing anybody ever asks about the poor old school—that and the narcotics and the Head's unfortunate predilections. But, Heavens, what makes you think that I was working here *before*? I might be ancient—and I am eighty-five, I'll have you know—but I was here the day they shut the school. I thought of it as an early retirement, being fifty-seven at the time.'

Now Max was staring at her. 'I'm sorry?' he said. 'Fifty seven . . . eighty-five . . . But that's nearly thirty years.'

'Indeed! I can still do my arithmetic, even if young people nowadays cannot. Nineteen seventy-six, the year was, as I'm sure you know. What is the matter, young man? You look as if you've seen a ghost.'

'Nineteen seventy-six?' said Clio. 'It's just that . . . my friend here, he was sure he came here . . . to the school, I mean . . . when he was younger.'

Sybil's laugh was as sudden as a playground whistle. 'Pardon me,' she said, 'but I thought it was only we ancient relics who had trouble with the memory. Maybe his father could just possibly have been here, though . . .' She looked at Max, her head on one side. 'I cannot say I recognize any likeness. No, my dears, the school was over and done with long, *long* before either of you were as much as a twinkle in your mothers' eyes.'

Max was on his feet now, swaying slightly. 'Excuse

199

me,' he said. 'I need to get some air.' As he turned, the silently smiling Mrs Hunstanton reached out a soft pink hand and touched him on the arm.

'I know you,' she said sweetly.

'I don't think so,' Max said.

'Oh yes. Your name is Legion. Mark five, verse nine, you know. So nice to meet you.' And with a smile she clicked back into the reverie from which she had come.

Outside on the steps, Max was trembling. As fast as she could make both their excuses, Clio came after him and sat down by his side. 'Max?' she whispered. 'Say something.'

'*Say something!*' His voice was quiet and very hard. 'I've just remembered something. That's what you wanted, wasn't it? Well, I've had this incredible flashback. I remembered that I used to have more sense than this!' Clio stared at him. 'This was all your idea,' he said.

'But . . . I thought we agreed . . .'

'*Agreed!* It's all coming back now—how I knew from the start this was stupid—just something you'd read in a book—but because it was you . . .' He took a breath. He was quivering. 'Because it was you I believed you. I even let myself *want* it to be true. How stupid is that?'

'But the cutting . . . ?'

'So? I keep lots of things—good stories. Maybe someone gave it to me, some other silly do-gooding little girl like you?'

'But the car . . . The poor kid in the swimming pool . . . ?'

'Heartbreaking, isn't it? Brings tears to my eyes too. It does . . . except it isn't bloody true!'

'I don't believe you. You weren't lying.'

'You still don't get it, do you? It's not lying. It's just

200

how it is for me. Stories, memories—it's all the same. Maybe I *can't* remember—like those sad old crumblies who don't even know who they are. I should be locked up in a place like this!'

'*Stop it!*' Clio clamped her hands over her ears. When she looked up, Max was striding off towards the gate, not looking back. She stared after him, speechless, then went after him. *Don't run*, she thought. At the windows behind them, eyes were watching, and they had acted strangely enough as it was.

He heard her feet behind him, and walked faster. They were at the gate before she caught up. 'Max,' she called, as they came round the corner, out of sight of the building. 'Max, this is *me*!'

'Oh, I remember,' he said coldly. 'Little Clio with her fairy stories. Dressing up. Playing house on the beach. Go home. Grow up.' He turned away. As she reached out he spun back, slapping her hand away, hard. She clutched it, and the tears rose up behind her eyes.

'And don't you *dare* come running after me,' he said. 'Oh, and if it's any help, it's my fault,' he added, without warmth or mercy. 'I made a fool of myself. I trusted you. And the one thing I remember is: I've always, always known, since I was *that* high—trusting is what stupid people do!'

201

23

Promise

It came at her like a hailstorm—cold, hard, every worst thing he could think of, cruel, unkind, unfair. It lashed her until she was numb.

For a long time Clio could not move, but only watch Max's figure get smaller and smaller down the road. Her heart was shrinking with it, down to almost nothing. The stupid glasses were steaming up with tears, and she stuffed them in a pocket. When she looked again, Max was out of sight. Only then did she start to run, but it was too late: just past the bend was a crossroads. Footpaths forked off. For a while she stared, willing him to reappear, but she knew: she had blown it. Their last chance . . . and she had staked it on some half-remembered, half-baked theory out of Stella's books. She hadn't been thinking about *him*—she'd been thinking how clever she was, how she was going to save him. And she'd called *him* arrogant!

There was a thought, a warning, like a telephone ringing in her mind. Their bags! She had brought them out onto the steps. They must still be there. If one of the carers found them, they would have Stella's clothes, the ones from her police description; they would have all Max's things. They would have his book.

Clio ran. Never mind what had just happened. She would think about that later. All she knew was that no one—nobody but her—must get their hands on the book. As she came through the gate she willed herself to walk, walk—panting, heart beating hard. She was back in the slow-motion world. The bags were on the steps. She saw the front door opening, and a couple of porters coming out, in no hurry—on a tea break maybe, just stepping outside for a smoke. Slowly, slowly, they were heading for the steps. Ten paces and the bags would be right at their feet. If she could run, she might just make it, but it was like a dream where the air has turned to water.

The main door opened; a carer looked out and called after the men. One of them turned and went back. As the other swung round for a last word—*See you, mate*—he stepped over the bags and went off round the building, with his mind on other things. Clio reached the steps, and the hardest thing of all was not to clutch the bags and run. She unzipped Max's bag, felt round inside—spare trainers, socks, some odd things . . . and the book. She patted it, for comfort, then zipped her own carrier bag in with it and—taking deep breaths—walked away.

She glanced back once. No one was following. Only, at that upstairs window, she was sure she saw that same pale face that had watched them earlier. She could feel its unmoving gaze on her back, all the way to the gate. She saw herself through those sad eyes—diminishing, as Max's shape had done—getting smaller and smaller until she was gone.

With Toby at school, Stella sat in the house and was very alone. It sounded like a bad joke now, those times she had longed for *a bit of peace and quiet*. To sit with her feet up for an hour, doing nothing—luxury! Well, she had that hour now . . . and another, and another, till she could scream at the thought of it. It was just her and the phone.

After Rob's call, she had nearly pulled the damned thing out of the wall. *Don't*, Dawn had told her. *Leave it on the answerphone. If you get anything dodgy, don't pick it up. Let me know.* So she listened, and jumped when it rang. Sometimes, not often, it would be a friend, but once or twice it clicked off when the answerphone cut in. Stella rang for the number, and there never was one. Then she sat and thought of the car on the corner, and the sound of footsteps, and the eyes she felt watching her, every time she scurried to the school and back.

The phone rang.

Stella was on her feet, listening. She heard her own recorded voice click on. *Please speak after the tone . . .* Then a pause, and a faltering 'Oh . . .' Stella grabbed up the phone.

'Clio? That's you, isn't it? Don't ring off. Clio, please . . . Say something.'

'Hi, Stella,' said the faint voice. 'It's me.'

'Thank God. Where are you? Give me your number, quick, I'll phone you back.'

'No. I need to talk for a minute, that's all.' Clio's voice was hoarse, as if she had been crying.

'Tell me where you are. I'll come and get you.'

'No! Please, Stella—don't rush me. I've got to think . . . And I'm OK, don't worry—I've just got to . . . to make up my mind.'

And that was when the coin ran out. The phone beeped. There was an awful silence, and a click and whirr.

'Clio? You still there?'

'Yes. I haven't got much change, so listen. You haven't got anyone with you?'

'No, no.'

'And you won't tell anybody after.'

'Clio . . . I've got to tell your parents.'

'No! Promise you won't, or I'm putting the phone down now. I mean it. Promise!'

Stella swallowed. 'All right. Promise. Where . . . ?'

The beeps started again. 'It doesn't matter . . .' Silence. *Please have another coin*, thought Stella. Then clunk: there was her voice again. 'If I'm coming back—I mean, *if*—I'm going to do it myself. Nobody's going to *bring* me. Do you understand? Thanks. It's just that . . . Max . . . he isn't with me.'

'Thank God.'

'Don't say that. I'm *worried* . . .'

'You should be. Come home. You can do your thinking here.'

'I'm not sure. Not yet . . .'

'Clio, listen to me. I've had some time on my hands—you know I've been suspended . . .'

'I know. I'm sorry. It's my fault. You trusted me.'

'I trusted *him*. It doesn't matter now. Thing is, I've done some reading. Have you ever heard the letters NPD? No? *Narcissistic Personality Disorder*. People with it tell lies all the time.'

'They aren't lies,' Clio said. 'Not Max's. Not like ordinary lying.'

'Exactly. People with NPD aren't ordinary liars. They're fantasists. They *believe* what they're saying. And the rest of us get taken in.'

'*I'm* not taken in,' said Clio. '*I* know when he's lying, and he knows I know. That's why he wants . . . why he wanted me with him.'

'They're very persuasive, people with this syndrome.'

'He never tried to persuade me of anything. He kept telling me to go home.'

'So why didn't you?'

There was a pause. An indrawn breath. 'I love him.'

205

'No!' said Stella. 'Don't. Just . . . don't. That boy is sick. It's an illness.'

'Can't they . . . cure it? Can't he take pills or something?'

There was a pause. 'It isn't like that, Clio. It goes deeper. These people, it's their whole personality.'

Then Clio was shouting. 'What's the point of it, then? If they can't make him better, what's the point of your stupid psychology?'

It was too much. Stella felt her own voice rising. 'I'm trying to help! Think of me, Clio. Think of Toby. Think of your poor mum and dad—they're going mad with worry . . . while you're off on some . . . little holiday!'

There was a hush at the other end.

'Oh, sorry, Clio, love. I didn't mean it. Everything's . . . such a mess.'

'What do you think we've been doing,' said Clio, coolly. 'Playing sandcastles?' Then the beeps were going, and the line went dead. Stella sat for a minute, for five minutes, hoping. But it did not ring again.

Clio sat at the bus stop in the village feeling like a ghost. No one had stopped in the street and pointed, no one called the police. A car had slowed to let her cross the road, so she wasn't invisible, though she felt it. Everybody was busy with their own small lives, their stories in which she and Max didn't figure at all.

It was the same with the bus driver. He took the £10 note with a grunt, but he didn't look up. She realized that she hadn't thought about the glasses since Max left her, and it just hurt to think of them now. He'd picked them for her. He'd carried her face in his mind.

She was almost the only passenger on the bus. From the small amount of change, she guessed it was going to be a long ride back to Milbourne. And so it was. The bus wound in and out of villages with names she had only ever seen on signposts. *Home. I just want to go home*, she thought, and settled back, and everything that had happened rose up in her mind like waves.

It had seemed so logical. All the clues had been there, as if he had scattered them through the book on purpose: *Come and find me*. The way the memories had started coming back . . . the way he started telling stories when it came too close. It was—she could hear Stella saying it—*a textbook case*.

Except that she'd been wrong. Maybe his real school had been like that, or maybe the opposite, or maybe he'd borrowed it from someone else, and the more he tried it on, the more it seemed to fit. Just like everything did.

It's deeper . . . When Stella said that, it sounded like a life sentence. *It's their whole personality* . . .

Clio wished she could sleep—close her eyes so when she opened them she'd be home and this would all be over. She wrapped her arms around the bag and clutched it tighter.

The book . . . What would he do without it? What if he tried to go back to the Hall for it? And a worse thought: would he even care about it any more? She tried to keep her eyes open, watching the endless fields and hedges, anything to stop the picture that kept forming: Max, rocking himself like a hurt child on the wall above the waters of the Rip. She'd stopped him, and what good had it done? She'd made things worse. What if he had headed back there now?

The bus stopped. She kept still, with her face down, as someone got on. For a minute she did not want to look, she was wishing so hard: it might be him. But it wasn't and the bus moved off.

207

Let's go back . . . It was good on the beach . . . He'd said that, a few hours ago. It was true. He'd meant it—more than he'd meant the terrible things at the end. If only she had listened, they could have been back there by now, in their hut, the snug nest of their loft, with a feast of tin cans spread out round them on the floor. She saw them sitting among the wreckage of their midnight feasts, laughing at one of his stories—laughing at nothing, sometimes, just because that was how it felt, with him.

I made a fool of myself. That was the worst thing—he didn't just want to hurt her. He wanted to hurt himself more. *I was so stupid, I trusted you!* Clio found her fingers stroking something, stroking till it felt as warm as real live skin. The book . . .

Would he still want her to look at it? In the early days he'd warned her: *Never touch.* Would he feel like that again now? Would he just not care?

I'll always come to find you, she'd said.

Promise?

Promise.

She opened the book.

TO CLIO

There's a girl behind your eyes
nobody sees,
behind your smile, behind you saying
Thank You, Sorry, Please,

behind your lips and finger tips,
behind your eyes and hair,
your secrets, silences and moods,
she's there, she's there,

at the bars of one small window
far away and very small

she's trying to be smaller, trying not
to be at all

in case one day they find her,
point at her: Get out,
you've got no right, you're not the one
this story is about

and send her back into the dark
from where she came
where no one has a family
and no one has a name.

You've guarded her behind her eyes
so long, so carefully.
But Clio, I can see that girl.
She can see me.

No village seemed to be too small for the bus to make a detour to it. When they reached the outskirts of Milbourne it was much the same, weaving round through streets and duller streets of bungalows. At the back of the bus a face stared from the window and no one—not even the girl herself—could have guessed what was going on in her mind.

The bus came out on the coast road, where windswept bungalows faced out to sea from a low cliff. A little further was the misty view of Watchman's Down. The face in the window stayed motionless, then, just as the bus was about to pass the only stop, jumped up and pushed to the door. 'Make your mind up,' grumbled the driver, then the bus was on its way.

On the coast road there was no one but a driving instructor and his learner staring blankly at the wheel. She looked like someone about to give up. Clio pulled her hood up and strode past. A handful of gulls were hanging on the wind at the edge of the cliff, and the one lone dog-walker was half a mile off, heading home to his tea. Clio cut across the rainswept grass towards Watchman's Down and beyond it, the Spit.

Max might be there. He just might. It was a small hope, but if there was one chance in a thousand that he might have gone there, she would take it. And if he *was* there, he might rage at her again . . . or, one chance in a thousand, he might open his arms and say *You came!* That made one in a million. OK. Until she had tried that one chance, there was nothing else she could think or do.

She took the steep slope up the Head. Not once in their time at the hut had they been up here, but she wanted to avoid the road past Oggie's hut. The Down was rough ground, almost moorland, and as she came near the top her instincts took over: she kept low, skirting round beneath the skyline. When the beach huts came in sight, she dropped into a hollow and peered over cautiously.

She saw no one moving. Oggie's car was there. Apart from that, the place looked dead, deserted. She could not help glancing out to the Rip. She wiped that thought from her mind, for now. Clio lay in her dip, and on a sprig of gorse in front of her a delicate, almost transparent snail slid, somehow, over the spikes, testing the air with its feelers. At the edge of the sprig it felt into the space around it, and recoiled, and stretched again, then found another sprig and poured itself across, shell and all.

Dear M,

Here I go again, wanting to ask you that same question: when was the moment things tipped — when everything after it had to happen like it did? I didn't know the bus would come that way. I could have not got off . . . but there was the poem. Was that the moment that clinched it, when I read it? Or when you'd written it, days earlier, maybe that was it?

Even then, I could have turned back from the Down. Yes, there was our beach, but it looked empty, not like it did with you there. I think I nearly went back . . . only then there was this snail. That sounds really crap, as if I think it was some kind of message, like the Scottish bloke in his cave with the spider and Try-try-again. My English teacher would say: Ah, a metaphor! Except it wasn't. It just made me smile, that's all.

So, Max, when was it? Please tell me, or I'll be asking the same thing for ever. It doesn't make any difference really — just that it feels like if I find the moment — the place that's not real, like the end of a rainbow — somehow I might find you there.

24

All That Matters

*T*he sound of a house when there's no one at home . . .
It was Stella who had said that, when Clio
wasn't meant to be listening, telling Mum and
Dad about the night her husband left. *I just opened the
door and . . . you know the sound of a house when there's no
one at home . . . ?*

The words hadn't made much sense to Clio at the
time, but she heard it now. That sound. It wasn't silence,
because the sea was grinding shingle and the wind
slapped a wire on the metal flagpole, clack, clack, clack
. . . She did not go straight to their hut. She had a
feeling—superstitious, really—that if she tried all the
unlikely places first, then when she came to the last
place he might just be there. So when she put her hand
on their door handle, she hardly dared to turn it.

It opened. Not locked. 'Max?' she called. '*Max?*' She
stepped inside, still calling. She climbed to the loft, and
back down, before she could accept the truth: there was
no sign of him. Oggie had forgotten to lock up, that's
all. Everything was just the way she and Max had left
it when they had been here last—a few hours, and light-
years away. Clio curled up on the tatty sofa with her
legs tucked up and cried.

When that was done, she set herself to tidy up. Bill
and Mary might come back, at least. Clio found herself

imagining it. They were old, so maybe one of them had died, and she thought of the other one coming back alone, and she did not want them to find the place messed up. She cleared the used cans in a black bag, went to empty the bin, and there behind it was the tangle of her cut hair.

For a minute she held it in her hand, above the swing bin, then she looked in the cupboard till she found an empty biscuit tin. Christmas Selection, it said, among holly leaves and reindeer. She laid the hair in carefully and closed it with an airtight hiss. Then she went on with the job, sweeping the sand and dusting shelves like she and Max had never done before. She stood at the old dresser with Max's message-in-a-bottle in her hand.

She could open it now. All it would take was a crack with a stone. At the thought, she shuddered. If I break it, he'll be dead. She tried to tell herself that was a silly thought—creepy, illogical—but in Max's world where cormorants were dragons, who knew what might be true?

On the ends of the groynes, among the waves, the dragon birds were still on duty, staring out to sea.

Max might come back. Maybe not straight away. Maybe he needed time. Maybe one day . . .

He would. If he was anywhere, if he was still OK, this place would pull him back, like it had her. Well, then, she would leave it ready for him. He would find his book in the loft, under the pillow on his mattress, waiting. After a while she went out on the beach. If he came at all, he was bound to come here, to the little rise where they had sat together. Then he would find something else—a secret garden, in among the wiry dune-grass, where nothing would grow.

She found nuggets of glass like amber, or like cloudy jade, tumble-milled smooth by the sea. She marked out a border with these. In between she placed shells, especially the white ones with their inner spirals exposed by the sea. She took a shred of bright blue hawser from the tide line and unravelled its threads, teasing them out fine and finer, till they looked like a flower from the moon. She planted them beside some creature's dried egg cases in a clump, like the moon-plant's papery seed-head. Best of all, in the centre she placed a prize find from Bill and Mary's shelves—a knobble of flint with a cavity and, in that hole, a smaller pebble, just too large to slip out, so it rattled when you shook it. Her mum had shown her one, once, on another beach and called it (wistfully, it seemed to Clio now) a *mother-stone*.

She worked on the garden till it grew too dark to see, then she dragged herself inside. Tomorrow, she supposed, she would go home. She could phone her parents now . . . but she would not. She'd have one more night, before all this was history.

She climbed into the loft and fell asleep.

Clio could not tell how much later the voices woke her, but they made her sit up, tense with fear. They sounded drunk, laughing in that braying, brawling sort of way. There was a shatter of glass—someone was smashing bottles, laughing, as if littering the beach with splinters was a really cool game.

She pulled the blanket round her and kept still.

It was an hour before the noise grew blearier and softer, then there was only the sea. She couldn't sleep, but lay stiff and wakeful, listening. The loud voice had been Oggie's, she was sure.

Footsteps crunched on the shingle, just outside. She sat up, as the front door shuddered. Someone fumbled

with the handle, then she heard the floorboards creak—
indoors, downstairs, right beneath her. Oggie must have
been watching her, toying with her, biding his time. She
should have pulled up the ladder after her, but it was
too late now. It shook as he stumbled against it and
began to climb.

She was trapped. Wildly, she felt round for something,
anything, some kind of weapon to defend herself. Can
you smother a drunk man with a pillow? Her fingers
tightened on the square hatch cover, and she crouched,
trying to focus on the opening she could hardly see.
When the man's head appeared in it, she would have
just a second to slam it down on him, as hard as she
could.

The ladder lurched, and she could hear his breathing.
It was louder, it was nearer . . . now!

She hoisted the cover, for a good swing, and her
knuckles cracked against a rafter. She cried out. The
hatch lid clattered from her hands. Clio doubled over,
seeing stars of pain, and smelt alcohol breath and felt
its warmth above her.

'Hey, who's . . . What? Clio, is that you?' The voice
was unsteady, but it was not Oggie's.

Max had come home, as she'd always known he
would.

'It's all right,' she said over and over. 'It's going to be all
right.'

She touched his hair, his face, his lips, and he touched
hers, as if neither of them could quite believe it. Then
they held each other tight—not like lovers, but Babes
in the Wood. 'I knew you'd come,' he said.

'Did you?'

'Of course. You promised. Forget what I said at the

215

old people's place. It was that old bat, she spooked me.'

'She was just a teacher. Teachers talk like that!'

'Not her—the other one. *Your name is Legion.* Weird stuff from the Bible—you know, demons. I couldn't take it.'

'It's OK,' she soothed him. 'Quiet . . .' He was talking too fast, all slurs and jerks and jumbles.

'That textbook stuff of yours . . . it just doesn't apply— not to me—because I'm something else—you know what I mean . . .'

'Ssssh,' said Clio, 'sssh . . .' She pulled him closer, till his mouth was stopped against her shoulder. He was suddenly calm as if whatever he'd been on, out there with Oggie, had just worn off. 'Yes,' she whispered in his hair. 'You're something else all right.' *This is it*, thought Clio. *This is all that matters.* She held him till he was fast asleep.

'There we are!'

He spread a newspaper out on the table, in the morning light. 'Barcelona! I've always fancied Barcelona . . . and look, somebody's seen us there!'

He was impossible. Even yesterday, running away from that disaster at the old folks' home, he had picked up a paper somewhere, to check if they were still celebrities. Far from having a hangover from the night before, he had woken her early with a playful, careful kiss. The fact that it was *careful* was the only sign that yesterday had ever happened.

'I knew you'd come back,' Max said. 'Couldn't manage without all these home comforts.'

'Actually,' said Clio, 'I *was* going home. I just forgot for a moment where *home* was. Good thing nobody else except us knows it's *here*. Except Oggie, I suppose.'

'Don't worry about him. He was a bit surprised when I showed up, but he came round in the end.'

'How many bottles of whisky did that take?'

'Enough! Anyway, I told him you'd be back.'

Clio looked at him, shaking her head. Yes: impossible. 'Hey,' she said. 'Come outside. Shut your eyes.' She led him on to the sand, keeping her fingers gently on his eyes. 'I made it for us.'

At the sight of the garden, Max laughed out loud. For a moment she wondered if he was laughing at the childishness of it, but then he was running down the beach, scavenging the tide line, like a kid on holiday. He came back with an armful, grinning, and the two of them set to work on hands and knees.

The most beautiful thing so far was the seaweed— *ghost weed*, Max said, balancing a frizzy clump of it on his palm. Dried to crispness, almost weightless and bleached by salt, the weed branched finer and finer out towards the edges, like a map of the vessels in the brain. Clio threaded several of them on a silver twig to make a glassy bonsai tree, and Max crumbled some beads of expanded polystyrene in its branches, like fruit.

At the base, he laid a crab's pincer—not the workman's-pliers or nutcracker sort of a claw, which always made Clio feel squeamish, but a delicate long pink one like a watch-mender's tool. They went off again, and she came back with a smooth flat stone. When they looked closely, it was like a porthole into a grey prehistoric sea, with the fossil prints of stalks and stems of plants that died a million years ago. Max turned up with a splinter of plywood from a packing crate, with a few words not quite washed out on it: THIS WAY UP. They planted it proudly, like a welcome to their garden, upside down.

Max and Clio stood back, hand in hand, and admired it. 'Pity it won't grow,' she said.

'It will, it will. Every storm, it will. You wait and see.'

Max washed his hair again. With each rinse the black dye faded and he laughed out loud at the mirror. '*And when they found him next morning . . .*' he intoned in a quavery horror-story voice, '*his hair had gone COMPLETELY GREY!*'

It was true. His soft fuzz was the colour of ashes. 'See, I'm old! I'm forty years old. I *could* have been a pupil at that Ardley stupid Hall.' He peered close into the mirror. 'I could be anybody. Cool. No problem. That's where your theory was wrong, admit it.'

'I don't even want to think about that place.'

'Admit it!' Max came up and grabbed her from behind. 'I'm going to squeeze you till you do.'

'Uh-huh,' she said, and leaned her head back against his. She could admit it, easily, but now he had both arms around her waist, and that was all that mattered.

Stella got out of the house. She had to, before she went mad. Ever since she had been off work the place had felt like a prison—one she locked herself in every day.

And now it was worse. They had moved in a policeman, just *to keep an eye on things*.

It was her own fault, really. She had tried to keep the promise she made Clio on the phone. For twenty minutes she had sat, or paced to the kitchen and back, and could not stop her mind from playing back every word of Clio's, every pause and sigh. At last, she'd phoned Dawn. She did not dare call Mike and Jen.

'I just wondered,' she'd said, 'if there's been any . . . news? About Clio?'

'No,' Dawn had said, then, 'Stella, is there something you're not telling us?'

To be fair, the officer they had moved in to monitor the phone and watch the street had tried to be as unobtrusive as he could. He even brought his own tea in a flask. But it was a while since she'd had a man in the house, and every time he moved, she heard. She felt guilty, too: he was doing his job, and she just left him up there, in the box room, with the paper, feeling bored.

'I'm going to fetch Toby,' she called up the stairs.

She was early for school, but she had to have some air. Since the police had been there, she had lost the slightly unhinged feeling that there was somebody watching, round the corner, all the time.

She would not hurry. She had never had time to be one of the mums who chatted at the school gate, and now wasn't a good time to start. Her picture had been in the local paper—under those of Clio and her anguished parents. Nobody ever mentioned it to Stella, but everybody knew.

She took the long way round—partly to avoid the main gate, where the other parents stood to gossip. She enjoyed the path through the allotments, under the embankment, and it helped to take her mind off things. The allotments looked a bit sad, in December, but she liked the way each one had its own small hut—a kind of Wendy house for old men. Maybe she would get one, if the enquiry went badly and she lost her job. She would grow their own veg—she and Toby could be self-sufficient. That would be hard work, at least. It was the doing nothing, trying not to think about it, she could not stand.

She was planning the first year's crop as she turned in to the subway tunnel beneath the embankment, and she was halfway in before the figure stepped in front of her. He must have been waiting in the shadows. With the light behind him he was just a silhouette.

'You just stay calm, OK?' It was just a whisper, resonating in the dark. 'I just want some answers, right?'

'I've got nothing to say,' said Stella. 'I've made my statement. The police . . .'

'The police will sit on their arses and do nothing. And I'm not a reporter, if that's what you think. I'm an ordinary bloke. I want a bit of justice for my family.'

There was a tremble in his voice, on the word *family*. He sounded younger than she'd thought. It occurred to Stella that he might be almost as afraid as her.

'Let me pass,' she said. 'People know I'm here . . .'

'I'm not going to hurt you. An answer, that's all I'm after. That kid, who said he bombed the Complex . . . you're his friend.'

'Not friend.'

'I know what you are.' The voice was harder. 'Bloody social worker! Everybody knows you were the one who let him go.'

'I made a mistake.'

'You bet you did. But you can make up for it. You know where they are.'

'No. Truly!'

'You've had phone calls. See? Nothing's a secret round here. I've got friends in the cops.'

'Two calls,' said Stella. 'That's all. She didn't say where they were. I'd have told the police if I knew.'

'Maybe. You're soft on that kid.'

'No, Clio's my friend. And they aren't together now.'

'Oh yeah? So where is *she*, eh? No, either you've been

stupid and they're stringing you along . . . or you know something.'

'No! Believe me. If I knew where they were I'd . . . I'd go and drag them back myself.'

For a moment there was silence. She could hear him breathing through his teeth. Then he swore. 'OK, so I'll believe you're stupid—stupid Ms Do-Good seeing the best in any little creep or crook. You'd just better not be lying—and you'd better not mention this to anyone . . . because I'll know.'

And he was gone—a silhouette, head down, in a woolly hat, disappearing back into the light. Stella steadied herself, trembling, against the dirty subway wall.

25

No Free Lunch

Oggie stood in the door. How long he had been there, Clio could not tell, and the big man did not speak. He turned and went back out without a word, as if this was his place, and he did not have to explain himself at all.

'Can't he just leave us alone?' Clio whispered.

'Ignore him.'

'I'm serious. I don't like it. Max, I don't want to be alone when he's around.'

'You won't be.' Max looked at her straight, and she remembered the shock of his pale eyes, the first time she had seen them. 'Whatever happens, I'll look out for you.'

'Promise?'

'Promise.'

Sometimes, without warning, Max would be on edge. 'Someone's watching, I can feel it.'

'Oggie?'

'No, no. There are people over on the quay.'

'Not Psykes and Franko?' she said.

'No, just . . . people. They're using the telescope.'

'Are they looking this way?'

'They're pretending not to.'

222

To Clio, the people looked like a middle-aged couple out for a breath of sea air. 'If anyone knew we were here,' she said, 'they'd have come and got us.'

'That depends,' said Max, annoyingly.

She looked again, and the people had gone.

This would happen from time to time. One moment they would be talking, playing house, laughing about nothing . . . this wary look would cross his face. 'We've got to be more careful. They could be watching from across the harbour. They could be on a boat right out to sea.'

'You keep saying *They*,' said Clio. 'Who . . . the police?'

He drew her back into the hut. 'Remember what we said about your family—not the one in Milbourne, the one . . . back there? How the father sees a picture in a foreign paper . . . ?'

'That's your story, not mine.'

'No, think about it. He's a powerful man now. All those fighters—the commanders, I mean—they're in the government now, or they're big criminals, sometimes both—smuggling things, drugs, people, you know, it's always in the news. Well, this man wants his daughter back. His princess. So he comes to find her . . .'

'I'm not listening to this.' Clio got to her feet and barged outside. A sheet of rain moved in across the sea but, very faint and far out, she could see the squat shape of a tanker. She shivered. Going back in, she found Max making coffee. She carefully lifted his arms from the sink. 'Hold me,' she said. 'Don't let go.'

She was still trembling. She would have liked to say that it was just the cold.

The storms were best. Then the world beyond the sand spit vanished. There was nothing they could do but huddle, listening to the rain. Now and then she thought about Mum and Dad, but that was another world, another Clio. *That* Clio had been back in Milbourne all this time. She hadn't got off the bus on the coast road, or she'd never met Max at the café, or she hadn't gone round to Stella's . . . Whatever, she was doing what she'd always done, and everybody was happy . . . and that left *this* Clio free to be here, doing what she had to, with Max and the sea. If the two Clios had met in the street, the old one would not have recognized the new one, and the new one would have quickly walked away.

The other good thing about storms was you could run out in them, shouting as loud as you could. You could scream or swear or hoot with laughter, or do crazy karaoke with the wind. Above all, you didn't have to be careful. They were careful the rest of the time.

They kept up the lookout routine. The more time passed, the surer Max was they were being watched. It was hardly a surprise, she told herself, if he'd got a bit paranoid in all those years of telling lies. The trouble was, it seemed to be catching. When she felt it coming over her she would sit beside him, in their lookout place, and neither of them said a word.

She read his book most days now. 'It's yours too,' he said. 'I'd have lost it without you. Only, please . . . no more psychology.'

I'm cured of *that*, thought Clio, curled up on the sofa. She toyed with the ornamental conch shell, putting it to her ear for the sound of the sea. *Their* sea was better. She tried opening his book at random, scanning for new entries in among the old. On one page were what looked like quick notes, scribbled and crossed out, almost illegible. Clio looked again.

Keep the door on the chain when you answer it. We're OK together LIE.

Mummy's having a bad day, that's all. LIE.

Tell them I'm out. At the shops. Or asleep. They'll go away. LIE.

Oh, say anything. Smile. They always believe you. LIE.

Don't touch that, it's mummy's medicine. LIE.

They can't take you away from me, I'm your mother. LIE.

Let us in. All we want is talk to her. It's for her own good. LIE.

She's coming back as soon as we've made her better. LIE.

Everything will be all right then. LIE. LIE. LIE.

Clio laid the book down, with a sick feeling. Not long ago she would have pounced on that. Now she wished she hadn't opened it. *I shouldn't have intruded*, she thought. Then she looked up, and there was a shadow, leaning at the door.

'Don't mind me,' said Oggie. 'Aren't you going to say hello?'

Clio got to her feet. 'Max is just outside if you want him.'

'I know where Max is.'

In the pause that followed, Clio saw the inside of the hut more clearly than ever before. How little gap there was between the sink, the benches, and the table. How just by taking two steps Oggie blocked the way, the only way, between her and the door. 'Can I get past?' she said.

He smiled. He was drunk, but not too drunk to watch her steadily. 'Standing in your light, am I? Sorry.' He took one step closer. 'Then again . . . I can stand where I like. It's my place. I moved here for the views. I'm enjoying one now.'

'We promised we'd stay out of your way,' said Clio. 'We do.'

'I don't think you get it.' He was within arm's reach. 'This isn't a free lunch. You want to live on my patch, rent-free? I'll need payment in kind.'

As she backed away, he moved forward, penning her into the corner by the disused toilet door. She wondered, wildly: could I barricade myself in there? But he saw her glance flicker that way, and he grabbed for her. Clio dodged and tripped over a deckchair, bringing it down with a crash. The noise seemed to stop the big man for a moment and he swayed over her, chuckling quietly. He did not turn, not even when Max came through the door behind him. There was a second in which Max could have spoken; instead, he took everything in and acted, springing forwards, grabbing something from the sofa. Before Oggie could turn, Max slammed the thing down, two handed, hard, like a blade in the back of his neck.

Oggie's eyes opened wide, as if a great idea had just occurred to him. His hand let go of Clio and pulled back, very slowly, to feel what had bitten him, and his mouth came open in a roar of rage. As he started to turn, Max raised the conch shell and hit him again.

It caught the side of his head, with a sick wet sound. This was not a cartoon knock-out, where a neat red lump comes up and all the birds start tweeting. No, the weak part of the skull, the temple, just behind one eye, had caved in. Even as the man crumpled, Clio saw his face was not the same shape any more.

The noise that started as a roar became a groan, as Oggie dropped to his knees. He was still shuffling forward, with his big hands groping out at Max, at Clio . . .

Max hit him again.

Then the Ogre was still, and in the hush that followed Clio thought this must be the sound that Stella meant—

the sound of a house that's empty, where no one will ever come home.

Clio stared at the heap on the floor. It could have been a sack of old clothes bound for the charity shop. That's Oggie, she thought. That was. There seemed to be more of him now than when he'd been alive.

Max was thinking on his feet. 'Towel,' he said. 'Quick.' When Clio did not move, he shut the door, then darted to the sink. He came back with tea cloths, which he pushed under the lolling head. They reddened slightly, but most of the damage was beneath the hair and skin. Max dabbed at a stain on the floor, before it could soak into the wood.

Clio was still staring, motionless. Max had found a bin bag now, and he pulled it down like a hood over the dead man's head.

Suddenly the words burst out of Clio. 'We . . . we've got to tell someone. Don't look at me like that. We've got to. I'm going to call someone right now.' Max caught her by both arms before she reached the door. 'Let me go,' she said, 'we've got to, we've . . .'

'Clio . . .' he said, very gently, and it stopped her like they say a slap in the face stops someone with hysterics. Her eyes opened wide.

'Oh, God . . .' she whispered. 'What have you done?'

'I promised,' he said.

'What?'

'I said I'd look out for you. *Whatever happens*. You made me promise, remember?'

Limply, she nodded. 'But we can't just . . . I mean, we can't . . . can we?'

They both stared at the pile on the floor, as if it might have an opinion. 'Nobody will miss him,' Max said. 'He was a mean old sod.'

'He must have family, something . . .'

227

'The man's a hermit. He hates people. The only ones who'll even notice are the dealers . . . Oh, come on, you must have worked it out by now. Those little *deliveries* of his—off the boat, into the city. Yeah, a few of them are going to be out of pocket when he doesn't come round with next month's gear. You feel sorry for them?'

Clio gazed at the body in its bin-bag hood. 'I suppose not.'

'Well, then . . . We might even have saved a few lives! Look, he was nothing. A creep, a dirty old man, a drunk . . . He hated everything—himself included. He won't be sorry it's over.'

There was a feeling Clio often had with Max—as if there must be a logical argument but . . . She had felt that at the railway tunnel, when he'd explained why it didn't matter that they could have died.

'Or you can go back,' he said. 'Tell the police. I mean it: you can do that. Up to you.'

'What about you?'

'If you go,' he said, 'I don't care what happens to me.'

'Don't say that! We could go back together. We could explain. It was self-defence, wasn't it?'

'Sure! It wasn't you who hit him.'

'Oh . . .' Everything round Clio seemed a bit further off than it should be—like on a really icy day, when you feel numb but things are very clear. 'It *could* have been me,' she said.

'Not from that angle. Not if it was self-defence.'

'No, I mean . . . that night. When you came back from the school . . . I heard you climbing up . . . I thought you were him.'

They stared at the body. There was an unpleasant smell around it, though it couldn't have started to go off so soon. It was just the smell of Oggie.

'You should get out,' said Max. 'He's no loss. Me neither. Lost souls. Get out while you can.'

'Max,' she said, 'whatever happens—I mean *whatever*—I'm not leaving you.'

26

An Unnatural Position

Clio did not know much about undertakers, but she knew they put a person in the cool-box pretty soon. Max seemed to know more. 'Best be quick,' he said. 'The longer we leave him, the more . . . you wouldn't want to know.'

Bury him: it was easy enough to say it. Did Bill and Mary have a shovel? Not that they could see. 'The office?' Clio said. 'He was, like, caretaker. Bound to have tools.'

The office was locked. So was his hut. 'He keeps the keys on him, doesn't . . . didn't he?' They looked at each other.

'No,' said Clio. 'Not me. I'm not touching him.'

Max shrugged. 'Doesn't bother me.' Still, he came back looking paler than he had. But he had keys.

The office had a filing cabinet and a couple of locked drawers . . . but no shovel. 'His hut, then,' said Clio. She did not sound keen. They unlocked the door and stepped in gingerly. Empty, it was just a squalid little room. How many years had he lived here, Clio wondered, and not bothered to pick up more than one threadbare armchair, probably from a skip, and that pathetic portable TV? The place smelt like old people's houses, only stronger, with the stale smoke and spilled booze.

'Look at this!' Max had opened a drawer by the bed. 'He wasn't poor, then . . .' Inside were various bottles of unlabelled pills . . . and wads of bank notes. Max pocketed one wad, casually.

They found the tools all mixed up with the kitchen things, as if he might have used a power drill to mix his soup. There were a couple of wide flat spades for shifting sand. While they were at it, Max picked up a chisel and a screwdriver, a Stanley knife, bolt-cutters . . . all they would need, he explained with a smile, for a little light breaking and entering.

A few of the huts kept old rowing boats, upended, on the sand outside, but the ones into expensive gear like sailboards, wet suits, and scuba kit kept it locked up in compartments under the floor of their huts. Most of them would have taken it home for the winter, but Max kept searching till he found what he was after: a two-wheeled sort of trailer for taking a boat down the beach. Clio did not have to ask what that was for.

Where to dig, that was the question. Just behind the toilet block, between it and the shingle, seemed possible—as long as they kept close to the building, they would be out of sight even from prying eyes on Watchman's Down. All they had to watch out for, said Max, was boats at sea.

No sooner had he said it than there was one. It looked like a fishing boat, but . . . 'Max?' whispered Clio as they hid. 'When Oggie gets *deliveries* . . . they come by boat, don't they?'

'Not in daylight,' Max said, but he did not sound too sure. They crouched and watched as the boat passed down-coast, very slowly. When it was out of sight, they set to work.

In the next hour they discovered what any sand-castling child could have told them: fine sand isn't good for digging. The flat spades might be good for clearing porches, but for a two metre hole . . . ? The harder they dug, the more the sides collapsed—like digging water, only slower. Soon they were sweating and bad-tempered. Then they hit the shingle underneath.

Max stared at the shallow crater, in the gathering dusk. 'We could just lay him flat,' he said. Clio had a vision of the seaside game most little children play at some time, called Burying Dad. She used to cover all of hers with sand until only his head and toes were showing. Then he would pretend to be trapped, and struggle . . . then lie still . . . and suddenly rear up and chase her, with a scary roar.

She stifled the thought. What rose up from the sand, in her mind's eye, was Oggie.

'I've got an idea,' she said. 'It was something *he* said. Something about if you want to disappear, jump in the Rip. He said the currents take a body out to sea, for ages.' Max was watching her with interest. 'And . . . I don't know what's, you know, *left* of a body after a few months in the sea, but . . . maybe they couldn't tell what happened any more? I mean, he could have jumped. Knocked his head on something. He could have . . . Oh my God, I don't believe I'm saying this!'

'Don't stop,' said Max. 'You're doing just fine.'

They couldn't do it yet. The tide would have to be going out, or who knows where it would take him. It could dump him right in Milbourne, by the Complex. Max studied the tide table in the warden's office, and the clock. Two a.m.—that should be about right.

Which left about six hours, he reckoned, as they dragged the trailer back to the hut. All they had to do was wait. 'We could get some sleep,' Max offered.

'Sleep! With *him* there?'

'We can go upstairs. We could make each other . . .

232

comfortable.' He reached a hand out, gently. As he touched her shoulder, Clio flinched.

'Sorry!' She stared at Max's hands, the hands that had touched Oggie. 'I'm not staying in that hut with him.' She shuddered.

'You can't stay out here. You'll catch your death . . . oh, sorry!' And before Clio knew it they were laughing, too hard, and holding each other, just a bit too tight.

Inside the hut, they got a lamp lit. The thing on the floor, with a bin bag for a head, seemed larger than it had been, but that was the shadows. Oggie had crumpled forward, arms reached out, as if hunting for a contact lense, then rolled against the table. That was how Clio tried to see it, but when you came down to it, it was still Oggie, a great lump of Oggie, dead.

'We've got to get over this,' Max said, stepping over him. 'Be rational. It isn't like he's . . . *there*. It's just like meat. Sorry—I know, you and red meat . . . For God's sake—if we don't do it now we'll never be able to. Look . . .' Max got hold of a cuff and lifted the stiff arm. The fingers of the hand were slightly curled, and as Max dropped it Clio heard the click of fingernails on floor.

'There! No problem. You try.'

Not the hand. Maybe the middle of the back . . . As she touched the cloth she pulled back as if stung. 'He's warm. They're meant to be cold. Max, you don't think he's . . . still alive or something?'

'It takes days. One degree per hour . . .'

'How do you know things like that?'

'You're not the only one who reads books. Look, there's *nobody there*.' Max grabbed the dead man's shoulders and gave him a shake. 'Hello, Mister Oggie? Yoo-hoo. Anyone at home?' He pulled the bin bag up and for a second, before Clio turned away, she saw the face. It had gone slightly pop-eyed and the cheeks were

233

blotchy like some nasty rash, but the worst was the tongue. It poked out slightly, like a child being rude behind the teacher's back.

Clio swallowed hard. Behind her, quite suddenly, she heard Max being sick.

Somehow, that seemed to help. They held each other's hands a moment, then they nodded. 'Let's just do it.' He took charge of the hood. She found a ball of string. Max wound it round and round the neck and tied the bin bag tight. Then they made themselves reach under the armpits and, crouched awkwardly, they levered up the weight, just enough to drag it a few paces. The head leaned sideways, as if it was listening.

They heaved and dragged again. There was a grating sound, and something clattered behind them. They froze, then saw Oggie's legs, bent in an unnatural position, had hooked round the table leg, and the colander was rolling on the floor.

By the time they were outside, Clio felt sweat chilling on her skin. They rolled the body to the edge of the decking, then on to the trailer. Oggie landed face down, in his awkward crouch. Max threw a blanket over it— a blanket, Clio thought, they would never, never use again. Even so, one of the hands reached out with stiff bent fingers. Max took the string and lashed the body into place—round and round, till it looked like something in a spider's larder.

'Maybe we should stay and guard him?' Max said.

'You can do it if you want—on your own.'

'OK, OK.' They wheeled him to the darkest place between the huts. 'Don't blame me if the land crabs get him,' Max said.

'That's not funny.'

Back indoors, she boiled a kettle, filled the sink and rinsed and scrubbed until her skin was raw.

234

They huddled on the sofa, with a blanket round them. There was a coldness in them that a mug of tea could not shift. Clio tried to think a thought, any thought, that did not end with Oggie.

The wind blew, and the sea was a steady growling, like a cage of creatures ready to be fed.

'Should he have weights?' said Clio.

'What?'

'There were divers' things, sort of belts with weights in them, where we found the scuba kit. That might make sure he . . . stayed down there.'

'Good thinking,' Max said. 'But . . .'

'What?'

'He might go straight down and stay there—here in the Rip.'

'Oh, God . . . We've got to stop talking about this.' It was somewhere near midnight, and they had talked about nothing else. 'I can't stand this.'

'Yes you can,' Max said gently. She let her head rest in the curve of his shoulder and for a long time neither spoke.

'I nearly didn't come back,' she said. 'After the school . . .'

'I bet you wish you hadn't.'

'No! Can you believe that? Even with . . . all this . . . I'm glad I did. *Can* you believe that?'

He was quiet for a long time. 'That's strange,' he said. 'That is *really* strange. Thank you.' He held her tighter, and Clio felt warmer inside than she had all night.

'It was your poem,' she said after a while. 'That's why I came back. I don't know how you could have known . . . about the little girl.'

'She's just you.'

'Yes, but the window—the little window with bars on it. That's true. I remember it. It came back when I read

235

the poem.' Clio nestled closer. 'I don't remember much, not from before England—I was really very small. But I think there's something—just one time. There was this long room—lots of iron beds in it . . .'

'The orphanage.'

'I suppose so. It's not like any school I've seen here. Though Mum and Dad, they could have described it, I don't know. How can you tell?'

'What happened?'

'There was this girl—about my age but prettier—she was a kind of princess, or she seemed that way. Someone important's daughter. I don't know how she got there. But she had this lovely purple ribbon in her hair, and I wanted it, wanted it so much, I just grabbed it, and we had a fight, and then . . . We got called downstairs.'

'Go on.'

'We all went down in the courtyard, because there were people coming to look at us, and I still had the ribbon in my hand. I couldn't tie it, but I sort of balanced it behind my ear, and . . . I don't remember if it was Mum and Dad, because I didn't know them yet, or if it was people from some charity but . . . they picked me.'

'Good for them. So would I.'

'It's not a joke. Don't you see? It could have been the ribbon. That was the sign. It was meant to be the other girl they took, not me!'

There was no sound but the grinding of the sea. 'You told your parents this?' said Max, after a while.

'Of course not. I thought they'd send me back, if they knew.'

'No one will send you back,' he whispered. 'Ever.'

For a couple of hours she slept, his arm around her. Every now and then uneasy dreams would make her whimper, and he would wake her gently, and hold her again.

236

Then it was time. He roused her gently, and like two sleepwalkers with a wheelbarrow they heaved and dragged the trailer to the Rip. It stuck in the fine sand, but once they found the concrete path it trundled smoothly. Sometimes they hit a rough patch and the stiff hand poking out would quiver or twitch.

Clio could not have said how long it took. It was one of those dreams which last for ever . . . until suddenly they were at the edge, and heard the water hissing close below. Max struggled with the string that lashed the body to the trailer, but all the knots had tightened, or maybe Oggie had begun to swell up. It was better not to think. 'Shit!' he breathed as his fingers went numb.

Clio ran to the hut for the kitchen knife. When she got back she put it in his hand, then tried not to look as he sawed and sawed the string. Sometimes the knife slipped, slicing with a soft sound into something else. At last he bundled the cut string together with the bin bag and the blanket. 'We can burn that in the morning.'

'Burn it? What about the smoke?'

'Oggie has fires. We'll do it down by his hut, like we're him.' He looked back at the dark and baggy heap of Oggie. 'I've just had a thought,' Max said. 'You aren't going to like it.'

It was true. Years ago, doing lifesaving classes at school, Clio had learned that people falling overboard should keep their clothes on. They'd played at ballooning their wet T-shirts up like floats. 'We've got to get his things off him,' Max said. 'Sorry, but we've got to. Once the . . . you know, gases start coming out, he's going to be like a balloon.'

Afterwards, Clio did not like to think about the next bit—struggling with the zips and buttons, trying not to touch. Under the drenched clothes, she could feel the skin was still not cold. Once, a button popped off, and

Max had them both down on their hands and knees, fumbling on the dark ground for it. 'Evidence,' he said. 'There mustn't be any evidence at all.' After that, he just carved at the clothes and they worked together to rip them off in strips. Each time, Clio could feel the dull give of the flab around the body, till the cloth gave way. Oggie's beer gut appeared, pale even in the near-dark, apart from a line of hair down to the navel. Then the horrible jeans, too tight and stiff as a board . . . Max sawed through the waistband, and they peeled him, inch by inch.

'Can we leave the underpants?' said Clio. 'Please!' Max nodded, then turned to the edge of the quay and doubled over and was sick again.

They manoeuvred the trailer as near as they dared, and tipped it sideways. The body rolled off and lay there, with its stray hand hanging over, pointing to the Rip below. They braced themselves, put a foot against its back and pushed.

It might have struck a beam on the way down, from the dull sound. Clio did not look . . . until Max said, 'Good. That's it.' Then she looked, and there was only rushing water, and the two of them pushed the trailer back to its hut. Max explained the plan, quite calmly. When it was light, he would give Oggie's hut a going over—check there was no evidence there, nothing *awkward*—leave it ready for the day, one day, when somebody really came looking for him.

Clio looked at him. Suddenly, it all felt simpler. She was an accomplice, an accessory. Whatever Max was, she was, and there was no going back.

27

The Garden of the Lost and Found

Walk straight to school and back. Keep to the main road. We've got a car to watch out near the school at going-home time. Stella had to give it to the police. Whatever they'd said about the things she'd done so far, they were doing their best for her now.

It was just after dinnertime she had the phone call from school. Toby's teacher . . . Stella felt the fear well up in her again. It must be something serious because the teacher did not want to say it on the phone.

They sat in the Head's room with another woman, whom the teacher introduced as Marjorie, the Educational Psychologist. 'We've been concerned about Toby for a little while,' she said. 'It's been difficult for him . . . this situation you're in.'

'What's happened?' said Stella. 'Is he all right?'

'He's fine, physically. We found him crying. There'd been a bit of teasing. We've spoken to the children involved.'

'Teasing? You mean . . . Oh, God, he's being bullied, isn't he? Because of me.'

'You mustn't blame yourself,' the teacher put in. 'You know how these things build up, then blow over. It's down to the parents really, not the kids. We can sort it out, given time.'

'We had been wondering,' put in the psychologist, 'if

maybe he could benefit from . . . a little quality time with you.'

Stella bridled. 'We have *hours* together at home.'

'I know. But things at home aren't easy, are they?'

The thought of *home*, with a policeman in the box room, made Stella's heart sink. She thought she had managed to protect poor Toby from most of it. At the back of her mind was the worst thought: what if Toby's father had been on to them, behind her back, dripping poison in their ears? 'We're doing fine, me and Toby.'

'Of course, of course. But he has seemed withdrawn, a bit disturbed—not like himself. And then there was the artwork.'

Stella looked at the drawings the teacher pushed across the desk. She would not have recognized the face, with turned-down mouth, round glasses, and spiky short scribbles in place of hair, if it had not been for the letters beside it—*cLIo*

'Who is it?' Stella said.

'He says it's Clio.'

'No, no, he must mean it's *for* Clio,' said Stella. 'When she comes home.'

'That's what we thought at first,' said the teacher. 'But he says it's Clio.'

'No, I know how he draws her. He starts with the hair.'

'That's what worries us. We think he might be expressing a deep anxiety. Cutting off her hair might be . . . symbolic.'

'I'll ask him about it.' Stella got to her feet. 'I'd like to see him, please.'

'That's what we thought,' said the teacher. 'We thought you might like to take him out for the rest of the day. That's if you're free.'

Free! Stella sighed. All she wanted was to run—to

wrap her little boy up in her arms and take him somewhere far away from all this—to the nearest place to
nowhere you could get to on a Tuesday afternoon.

'Aren't we going home?' said Toby, in the car.

'Aha. No. An adventure.'

'Not shopping again?'

'We're going to the sea. This is a mini holiday.'

'Ice cream?' said Toby, smiling for the first time. 'Yay!'

They drove through the outskirts, on their way to the
wildest, most nowhere place she could think of within
reach of Milbourne.

Stella had half hoped there might be an ice cream van
in the car park under Watchman's Down. There was
nobody, no cars at all. Above the Down grey clouds
hauled past on the wind, and Stella wanted to be up
there in it, letting all this blow away.

'Wrap up warm,' she said, tucking his scarf in. 'We're
going for a walk.'

'A *walk*?'

'OK, we'll go hunting.'

'Tigers?' Ever since that story of Max's, Tigers had
been Toby's form of Hide and Seek.

'Toby,' said Stella, casually. 'Mrs Boult said you'd been
drawing nice pictures of Clio. Without her lovely hair.'

'That's how she was,' said Toby.

Stella felt a coldness up her spine. 'Pardon?' she said.

'When I saw her. Only I didn't.'

'Slow down, Toby Trouble. You saw Clio?'

'Sort of. You know Arlie's party—his Mum took us
all to Superquest and we had ice cream after—and I had
three different flavours . . .'

'Go on,' said Stella, very calm. 'You saw Clio?'

'It was funny. She looked into the window of the ice

241

cream shop, and I waved and then I looked again and
. . . and it wasn't her, because she had glasses and short
hair.'

'So you didn't see Clio—not really. You've been
thinking of her so much you imagined it.'

'I miss Clio,' Toby said, and Stella gave him a hug.

'Let's do Tigers,' she said, and he wriggled free. He
was off already, heading from the thickets of gorse that
speckled the side of the Down. 'Slow down,' she called.

He turned and called back. 'You're the tiger!' Then he
ducked behind a bush. She felt that chill again. Children
can vanish, just like Clio, just like that. She scanned all
round them, right back to the car park. There was their
car. And another at the far end. Children can run past
a stranger's car, and a door swings open, and . . .

'Toby!' she yelled. 'Don't go out of sight!' His face
popped out behind the brambles nearby, puzzled at this
new rule for Hide and Seek, then decided she was only
teasing, and zipped out of sight again.

It had been a good night for the Storm Garden, with
the sea still stirred up from the last few days of wind.
Clio and Max came out in the grey morning light to see
what the waves had brought. She hardly dared look, in
case the sea had not liked Oggie either and had given
him back. It hadn't. Not yet. Max was crouching by the
tide wrack, picking it over for the latest finds.

The garden grew.

Clio found the best piece of driftwood she had ever
seen—like a dancing figure, white and sparkly with salt
. . . or like two figures dancing so close that you could
not tell how many arms and legs they had and whose
was whose. She stood it upright in a corner of the patch,
and Max set to work with miles of unravelled cassette

242

tape, blowing from the figure's raised arm like ribbons. Clio looked at the label, but it was home-recorded and the ink had washed off. 'Listen,' said Max. 'You can hear the voices.' True, there was a whispering as the plastic quivered in the wind.

The next time Clio looked, the figure was an angel. They often found feathers, but last night's tide had brought a whole gull's wing. It should have been gruesome, but the fine white bones and the delicate fan of feathers were a thing of beauty, and Max placed it on their figure's back, its wing half spread. Clio knew that most things in their garden were dead or abandoned—like the sad rubbery baby-doll with an empty socket for its arm—but she and Max were giving them another life. It made her think of a phrase her grandma had used, years ago, and it had stuck in her mind—about a place in the paper for unwanted things: *The Lost and Found*.

The worst thing in the garden was the slim syringe. Max came up the beach holding it carefully. 'Get rid of it,' said Clio, but she could see he had a plan. He wedged it in the angel's right hand like a spear. 'That's horrible,' Clio said. 'It's dangerous.'

'Deadly, probably. It'll keep the intruders away.' When his back was turned she balanced a shell like a sheath on its tip.

The most precious find was not really a find at all—unless you count poking around in other people's huts as beachcombing. 'Eyes closed,' Max said. 'And hold out your hands.'

'What is it? It's not one of your gross things, is it?'

'Trust me.'

What he placed on her hands was so light that Clio almost dropped it. He closed her fingers round its crisp and slightly spiky edges, gently. 'There!'

243

She opened her eyes to find a sea-urchin shell—rosy pink, with lines and white stipples, like a flower folded in for the night. Max lifted her hands up to between their faces, and blew across the little opening in the empty shell, so it made a wistful little sound. 'It's lovely,' said Clio. 'So fragile.'

'Not as fragile as you think. The sea hasn't broken it. Squeeze.'

'No! I can't.'

'It won't break—like an eggshell. It's a perfect shape.'

She squeezed a little, and a little more, until her fingers were trembling. 'Can I stop, please?'

Max laughed. 'If you want. Squeeze me instead.'

It was getting colder. They kept the heater on day and night, and did not worry when the canister ran out. With Oggie gone, there was no reason not to get whatever they wanted from the shop. 'Hey,' Max grinned. 'We could put in central heating!'

'Wha-a-at?'

'Sure. You don't think I left all that loot of Oggie's lying in his hut.' He took down the china donkey from the dresser and lifted its hat. The whole inside was crammed with rolled-up wads of notes. 'They're bound to search his hut one day,' Max said. 'If they found that lying round, and him gone, it's alarm bells straight away.' Clio stared at the cash. She was trying to remember why the stuff mattered so much to so many people. Somewhere in her mind a voice said *That's stealing* but it was a little girl's voice, far away and long ago. Besides, was it stealing if they weren't going to *spend* it? The last thing they were going to do right now was go out on a spree.

In fact, the less they needed to go out, the better. Max stashed gas bottles, large and small, out of sight in the chemical loo. They raided the shop for towels, T-shirts, even swimsuits they could use like thermal underwear.

244

When they found flat sheets of expanded polystyrene padding, they took them home and packed them round the loft for insulation, as if they were digging themselves in for a freezing winter or a siege.

Most of the time, though, they were children, in and out of the other huts—not stealing, just plundering cupboards for old family games—Monopoly, Risk, a complicated plastic thing that didn't work called Hungry Hippo . . . Half the children who had played them might be middle-aged by now. Max studied the rules as if he was swotting for an exam, then played fiercely, to win. Clio glanced at his little frown of concentration in the gaslight, and he was easy to love. Blink: he looked grown-up, with a fine fuzz round his chin. Blink again: it was as if he'd never been a child but he was learning now.

Once, she nearly asked him about the little boy with the door chain, lying for his mother. Those jottings lay in the skin book like a raw wound. Then she looked at him, soft in the gaslight, and thought: *Leave it. Don't try to change him again*. Wasn't that what we *all* wanted—for someone to love us just exactly how we are?

Sometimes it was difficult. He was surer than ever that someone was watching, but not saying it in case it worried her. She knew what he was imagining: that someone was after her, out of her past, only now it was not her family, but the family of the girl with the purple ribbon, who had been thrown back in the orphanage and died because of her. The most innocent dog-walker, he thought, might be one of Them.

Or he'd say, out of nowhere, something like, 'Shall I see if I can make that kettle boil?' He stared at it fixedly.

'You could try a match,' said Clio.

'I did it with the Complex,' he said.

She looked at him. He wasn't smiling. 'That was an accident.'

'Yes, but *why* did it happen? My powers! No, I can't do the kettle. I'm not angry with it, that's the reason.' Then he smiled, as if it had all been a joke, and she smiled with him, nervously.

Another time he said, 'They were right, you know— Franko and Psykes. When the aliens abducted me . . .'

'Max! You made that one up.'

'Maybe I just *thought* I was making it up. How would I know?' He was talking fast—his eyes were wide and bright. 'How do we know *anything*? How do we know that wasn't *me*, in the car?'

'Car?'

'In the school swimming pool! Writing my name on the windscreen: M . . . A . . . X!'

'Max, we've been through all this. It was thirty years ago.'

'Exactly. My last life. That's why I remembered.'

'Oh, Max, I don't like this, I don't *like* it. Stop it.'

He put his arm around her. 'Sorry. Did you ever hear the story of the Flying Dutchman? Not one of mine— it's a big opera or something, so it must be true!' His voice was calm again. 'The thing is, he's this lost soul and he's doomed to sail and sail and sail until . . . until the impossible thing happens.'

'What's that?'

'Someone loves him.'

They took to sleeping in each other's arms, and not only at night. Both of them had dreams with Oggie in them, and dreams in which Clio was Max and Max was Clio, and she started jotting down her dreams in case they might turn out to be his real memories. Sometimes Clio would wake with a feeling like free-fall, nothing specific, just dread. They held each other. Bit by bit, she told herself, he was a little less lost. She must never let go.

Time must be passing, but it did not matter. The days were so dark and so short that sometimes Clio could not tell if it was morning or evening. Since the horrible night, neither of them had mentioned making love; Clio thought it would happen, one day, and that seemed all right, that time was not yet. Meanwhile they would lie for hours, just looking at each other, even when it was too dark to see. She asked him if they should try the portable TV in Oggie's hut. He shrugged.

'Sure, we'll be on the news,' he said. 'We're famous. There'll be people imitating us all over.'

'Don't you want to see?'

'Why bother? This is good enough for me.'

'Really?' said Clio. 'Just this?'

'Oh yes. No one's going to take this away—I'll see to that.'

When they were awake, they still kept a lookout. 'Do you know what day it is?' asked Clio.

'Don't know. Do you think it's Christmas?'

'Can't be . . . can it? No. I think it might be the weekend. There were a couple of joggers out earlier, and there were people on the quay. I think it might be Saturday.'

'If you want it to be Saturday,' Max said, 'Saturday it is.'

He got busy with a little artwork. The day before he had found a cuttlefish bone and now he was scratching at it with a kitchen knife. Outside, the day was slate grey, with clouds blowing past, each like a small night, out to sea. They had taken—borrowed—extra gas lamps from Oggie's hut and office, and Clio had ranged them round the hut like the wall lights Mum thought made their sitting room look 'cosy' at home. The heater made its gentle hiss, and smells of coffee lingered round the stove. Now and then Max would hold his cuttlebone

247

carving to the light, and when Clio bent down beside him she could see the shape—a face, maybe hers, maybe the picture of her he'd had inside him when he chose the glasses—glowing through.

But it would take time, and she did not want to spoil it by watching. She was spending most of her spare hours these days with his book. She curled up on the sofa, under a lumpy old feather quilt they had found in the loft. She had just come to a page where he was on an adventure holiday in Borneo, and there was this giant moth that came by night, and sucked blood . . . Clio smiled. She'd start that later. Right now she was stiff, so she found a cagoule. *Back soon*, she whispered and slipped outside, tucking the book in her pocket, just because she liked to feel it with her.

Any time she went out these days she used the instincts they had been learning by *living like mice*. They had been off guard—she should have kept watch, but the last hour had been perfect: her, the book, and him, bent to the cuttlefish work, thinking of her but not looking up at all.

As she stepped round the side of the hut, she heard a sound. In the wind it was not easy to tell where it came from. There it was again: a voice. Close. She could have darted back then, but she ducked down, watching. People who came to this part of the beach were usually walking with their eyes fixed on the furthest end. But these sounds were different. One of the voices—there were more than one—was a child. A little boy's voice called out nearby . . . from down by the Storm Garden. He whooped, he laughed: *Look, Mum, look!* He had found it. There's no harm in that, thought Clio. It could have been there months, since summer. Anybody passing could have put the things there.

Then she thought: that horrible needle . . . She knew

248

she should have made Max throw it back. A child could touch it.

Clio scuttled forward, keeping low. Round the end of the hut, she heard the voice again—a voice she knew so well that she forgot the hiding instinct. She stood up and looked.

And there, crouched in among their beautiful dead things in the garden was Toby, and he looked up, laughing . . . looked her straight in the eye.

28

Where Stories Get You

Watchman's Down had been wonderful. Wind and sea and wild sky above them: Stella felt it blowing all the nagging fears away. She had not felt so free for weeks. She and Toby had caught several tigers, or been eaten by them—she was never quite sure which was which—then they forged on up the hillside for the view. Stella held tight to his hand near the crumbling cliff edge, but let go as they crossed to the gentler side which looked down on the playhouse-like cluster of huts on the Spit.

'Can we go to the beach?' said Toby.

Normally she would have said *We should be getting back now*, the way parents do. But getting back for what? They were happier here. As they scrambled down and came out in among the huts she thought: *Nothing would matter so much if we lived by the sea*. If she lost her job, so be it. They could sell the house and buy a beach hut.

'I'm doing sandcastles,' Toby said, and set off over the shingle, looking for a patch of sand.

Sandcastles . . . Somewhere an uneasy echo rang in Stella's brain. *Playing sandcastles*. Clio had said that. After Clio's phone call, the police had been on at her to tell them every word she said—on at her so hard her mind went blank. It was only a throwaway line at the end, when both of them had lost their tempers, but . . . Stella wondered if she ought to tell Dawn. She reached for her mobile, but . . . No, she didn't want to think about all that, and spoil the mini holiday. She'd tell them when they got back.

There was a hush behind her, where Toby had been.

'Clio! Clio!' he yelled suddenly.

Stella turned to see him pointing. 'Mum, Mum, there's Clio!' Next moment he was off at full tilt, vanishing between the huts.

'Toby! Wait . . .' she called, but he had gone.

Sometimes a parent's reactions go faster than the mind can think. Stella made for the gap between the next two huts, not where she'd last seen Toby, guessing she might head him off that way. And yes, a figure darted out in front of her. 'Toby!' she called. But as it turned towards her, frozen for a second, it had Clio's face.

Their eyes met. Next moment, Clio doubled back, with a leap onto the decking, not quite judging it right. Her foot slipped on the wet wood and she went down, clutching her knee. As Stella reached her, there was Toby, too, and at the same time the door of the hut came open and the four of them faced each other, speechless.

Max. Clio. Toby. Stella. For a moment each of them looked at each of the others, taking them all in one by one.

'Oh, Clio!' Stella could not help it. 'What have you done to it . . . your lovely hair!'

The girl looked up, blank with shock, and rubbed her knee.

'Are you all right?' said Stella.

'I'm OK. Just banged it,' Clio muttered. Max was beside her now, helping her gently to her feet.

'*I* found her first,' said Toby. 'Everybody's looking for you, Clio . . .' His grin faded and his voice trailed off in

251

the strange hush round him. No one looked as pleased as they ought to be.

'Oh, Toby Trouble,' Clio gave a pale smile, 'come here.' Toby hugged her, quickly, then moved back alongside Stella, watching.

'You'd better come in,' said Max politely.

After the wind, the air in the hut felt thick and humid. Max closed the door behind them with a double click. In the glow of several gas lamps, Stella saw a dingy little room with everything made out of plywood, cheap and makeshift, with no taste or style. It smelt stale, unaired, unhealthy, and it was a mess, with newspapers crumpled on the floor, plates piled in the sink, and clothes draped up to dry on window frames and on the rungs of a ladder at the far end.

'Is this it? Is this where you've been all the time?'

'I can't explain,' said Clio. 'It's too complicated.'

'But you're . . . all right?'

Clio nodded.

'Come home,' Stella said.

'It's too late,' said Clio, almost too quietly to hear.

'What do you mean?'

Clio bit her lip and looked at the floor. Clio, Stella thought, could this be Clio, acting like a sulky adolescent? And the girl looked tired, half-starved, and hollow-eyed. Stella could not stand it.

'Great!' she burst out. 'You're having a holiday. Very nice. And what about everyone else? Do you think you're the only ones who matter? Your mother's beside herself.'

'I told them not to worry.'

'Oh, Clio, Clio! You're a sensible girl. You think about other people. You care what they're feeling. You aren't stupid. So tell me: what the hell's been going on?'

Clio's expression did not change. She went to the wall

cupboard and reached down a biscuit tin, emptying it out on the table. The heap of dark cut curls lay there like a living thing. Stella flinched.

'What's that meant to mean?' she said.

'Nothing. Take it home to Mum and Dad.'

'I don't understand this,' Stella said. 'But it's over now. I'm going to let your parents know.' She reached in her shoulder bag, but Max stepped up behind her, lifting the mobile deftly from her hand.

'I'm sorry,' he said. 'We can't let you do that.'

Stella froze. Her eyes went to Clio . . . to Max . . . to the shut door. She reached for Toby's hand. 'Please don't argue,' Toby said.

Max turned his charm smile on him. 'We're not arguing,' he said. 'We're just explaining why . . . we can't come home, not yet.'

Toby was very still.

'You like Clio, don't you?' Max said. 'You want Clio to be happy. Well, then—this is a kind of a secret.'

'Leave Toby out of this,' said Stella, folding an arm around him. She was facing Max now, with a fierce look in her eyes. 'What do you *want*? Well? You don't *know*, do you?'

'You've made it difficult. You shouldn't have come.'

Stella moved towards the door. 'We'd better be off now, Toby,' she said in a tight voice. She tried the handle. 'Max is just going to open the door,' she said. 'We can come back and see Clio . . . later.' There was a pause. Wind hissed in the shutters and under the door.

'Look,' said Stella. 'There's no need to be stupid. You haven't done anything very wrong. People will understand. Lots of people are . . . on your side, you know that? They think you're heroes of some kind.' She was talking faster, getting short of breath. 'Now, open this door. Toby needs to go home now.' She looked at Clio, but the girl looked down and would not meet her eyes. Max was shaking his head, wearily.

'Max,' Clio muttered. 'Surely . . . if they promise not to tell?'

'I wish it was that easy . . .' Clio was watching him now, her eyes as big as Toby's. With his ash-grey hair and stubble, it seemed to her that he was very old.

'What are we going to do?' she whispered.

'Where's your car?' Max said to Stella.

'Huh—the one you wrecked, you mean? It's miles away.'

'Where?'

'West Parade.'

'By the ice cream parlour,' Clio whispered.

'That'll do.' Max thrust his hand out. 'Keys.'

Someone banged on the door.

They all jumped back together. 'Who's that?' Max snapped. 'Who came with you?'

'No one. I swear!'

'Who knew you were coming here.'

'No one! Honestly. I . . .' Stella stopped in mid sentence as it dawned on her: this might not be the smartest thing to say.

The second knock sounded like a fist, not knuckles.

'Quiet,' Max breathed. 'Everybody. Quiet!' Toby made that creaking sound he made just before crying.

Then the door wrenched open so hard its hinges splintered.

Back in the subway Stella had only seen the man in silhouette, but there was no mistaking him now. He squinted into the hut, nodding as he took it all in—her and Toby, Max and Clio, one by one. 'Thanks,' he said to Stella, pushing past her.

'You lied!' said Max. 'You said you didn't tell anyone . . .'

254

'She didn't,' said the man. 'I just reckoned if I watched her long enough she'd lead me to the right place in the end.'

'You followed me?' said Stella. 'How dare you? Who are you? What do you want?'

'Frankly, it don't concern you. There's only one person here I want to talk to.'

Toby made a muffled sound, his face pressed into Stella's jacket. 'Take the kid out,' the man said. 'No, on second thoughts, hang about. I want everyone to hear the next bit.'

'I was right, wasn't I?' Max said. 'You're from Kosovo?'

The eyes beneath the woolly hat narrowed, then the man laughed. 'Kosovo? Like you're from the moon! I'm Milbourne, Milbourne born and bred—from Marshfield, you know, where little Jade Brown came from. That name ring any bells with you?'

'The girl at the Complex,' Stella said. 'The majorette . . .'

'Shut it,' the man said. 'I want to hear it from *him*!' The *him!* was so sharp that Max staggered back, stumbling against the table. 'Yeah, you're the one I'm talking to. My mate Clive should have done you over that night, while he had the chance—remember him? I wish I'd been there, but I was trying to find my sister. Get it? You're very quiet. I thought you liked telling stories. What's up? Mind gone blank?' Each question was like a prod, a poke, and Max rocked on his feet like a punchball. *Say something*, Clio willed him, but his eyes were empty, as if he'd given up on this scene and slipped away and left his body standing there.

'*Jade Brown*. Don't you read the papers? Go on, *think*!' The man thrust his face towards Max, who crumpled backwards on the sofa, and sat staring at this stranger with a puzzled look. 'Front page news, it was—little girl in hospital with burns. Do you know what it feels like? Do you? Do you know what it *looks* like—third degree burns on a little girl's *face*? A pretty little girl who wanted to be an actress, in the films, like Maylene? Well?'

'He didn't do it,' Clio said. 'It was an accident.'

'I know he didn't bloody *do* it. That's what's sick about him. If he *was* a bloody bomber . . . I could understand it. But he made a joke of it. Our Jade was lying in the Burns Unit and it was like he was standing by her bedside, laughing in our faces. If he was a real sodding terrorist, I mean, like *fighting for something*, I could understand. But with him . . . With him, it's a just a bleeding *game* . . .'

'He didn't *know*!' yelled Clio.

'Didn't know! Well, Uncle Ryan's here to make sure he does. So he knows *exactly* what it feels like, what Jade's going through.' Ryan grabbed the hissing gas-lamp from the dresser, raising it to Max's face. 'The rest of you, out! We two need a private little chat.'

For some time Toby had been quite still, eyes wide, hardly breathing. Now his face began to crumple.

'*Beat it!*' Ryan said.

Stella moved. Very calmly, she backed to the door, steering Toby with her. 'It's OK,' she murmured to him, 'OK. We'll just go outside, and when we're there, you run. You just run to the shop—the one back there, remember?'

'Come with me.' He tugged at her hand.

'I'm coming. I'll be right behind you. Ri-i-ight behind you.' She eased him through the door behind her and set him off with a little push. All this time she had not taken her eyes off Ryan. Nor had Clio. 'Clio,' Stella said. 'You come too. Clio . . . ?'

Very slowly, Clio shook her head.

'Believe me,' said Ryan. 'This isn't just me. Half the blokes on the estate would love the chance to deal with this one. Cat got your tongue?' He jabbed the lamp at Max, who flinched and crouched, at bay. Ryan grinned. He turned the flame up till it sparked and spat.

Outside, there was a wail. Stella turned to see Toby in the middle of the path, stopped rigid. Some way off, a man in a raincoat was trudging towards them but his ugly brown dog was there already, snuffling in circles round Toby, growling and slobbering. Toby wailed. Stella cast a final look at Clio, then she ran.

'Good,' said Ryan. 'You can go too,' he said, without glancing at Clio. 'You won't want to see what comes next.' He made a feint towards Max; Max flinched, but Ryan swung the lamp the other way. It glanced off Max's cheek and he cried out, scuttling back against the dresser, clutching his face with his hands. The ornaments rocked. Two glass animals tinkled down, the china donkey rocked and rocked . . . then, as if in slow motion, fell and smashed. The sight of the money curling out of it caught Ryan's eye, and in that moment Clio made her move.

Afterwards, Clio would never agree that what she did was brave. She simply saw the scene in long shot, with all sound turned off except the soundtrack of the wind outside. She saw the row of beach huts—grown-up Wendy houses—and three figures as small as children in it, playing a dangerous game. Playing with fire. She saw that the man with the lamp was angry, puzzled, scared—almost as scared as the other who was huddled in the corner whimpering. And there was the third, a girl who could somehow stand a long way back and see it all.

'We've got to stop this,' she said, stepping forward. 'Max . . . just *talk* to him.'

257

'Back off, kid,' snarled Ryan. 'This is between me and him.'

'I'm sorry about Jade,' said Clio. 'Really sorry. Max is sorry too.'

'Bloody useless—*sorry*.'

She took another step forward. Max looked up between his fingers. 'He can't help it.' She hardly recognized the calm, firm voice that came out of her lips. 'He tells stories.'

'Yeah, well, he needs to learn where stories get you.'

Ryan turned to face her, and at last Max moved. He scrambled to his feet, and for a second Clio thought he might have jumped at Ryan. But Ryan glanced back, and the lamp flared, and next moment Max was scrambling for the loft. Ryan made a grab, but Clio stepped in, between Ryan and the ladder, knocking his arm to one side. For a second he almost lashed out again, but Clio raised her hands and looked him in the eye.

Ryan took a step back. Stared.

'You're something, you are. Not like him. He's a coward, you know that? He's not worth it.'

'Then neither's . . . what you're going to do. You'll go to jail,' she said. '*That's* not worth it. Jade wouldn't want you to go to jail.'

That was the mistake. His eyes flared. 'Don't you bloody tell me what Jade wants.' He tensed, and Clio grabbed for the ladder. In one quick movement she was halfway up. As he reached for her leg, she kicked out, climbed another step . . . and there was Max's face in the hatch.

'Go back,' he said. 'Get out of here.'

'No!' She reached for the hatch. Her fingers closed on the edge, ready to heave herself up and over . . . and it happened. He kicked her. Max. He kicked her fingers off the edge.

She fell back, crashing into Ryan. For a moment they both sprawled. The lamp clattered somewhere out of sight, and flared. Clio looked up, half dazed. 'Get *out*!' Max yelled again.

Then there was smoke, all round them. As she scrambled to her feet, she saw the newspapers on the floor, already burning, and the gas lamp on its side among them, and the flames already reaching for the feather quilt that had slipped from the sofa . . . reaching for the clothes hung to dry on the ladder . . . reaching for the empty canister they'd changed earlier, except it wasn't quite empty, and it gave a little flash and spurt of flame. Then the fire was all around them, grabbing at everything, taking hold.

Ryan was on his feet now. 'Jesus!' he said. 'No!' Then he was coughing, stumbling backwards from the smoke. He blundered into Clio, nearly pushing her aside, then turned and grabbed her by the arm. For a second she resisted, then a choking spasm took her, and she staggered. Ryan caught her, half helping, half dragging her out of the door.

The cold air hit them like a slap. 'Jesus!' Ryan stared at her, gasping. 'I . . . I just wanted to scare him, that's all.' Clio struggled, wriggling free of his grip. 'Stupid kid!' he yelled. 'There's sodding *gas* in there!'

'Max!' Clio yelled, and stumbled back towards the hut. For a second she could see a world of flames, a small Hell, framed in the doorway. Even the walls seemed to be burning—curtains, wallpaper, the thin partition between the ladder and the disused toilet. At the centre of it was the ladder, ablaze, like some medieval burning-at-the-stake.

She stepped inside. 'Max!' she tried to yell, but doubled over coughing, just as Ryan grabbed her from behind, heaving her round towards the door. There was a soft deep thud, as if all the air around had punched her at the same time, knocking the breath from her lungs. For a long while she was falling, though downwards or upwards or nowhere Clio couldn't tell. There was light all around her, golden, like the clouds of that fantastic sunset she and Max had watched together. And then it was night.

Long shot: the view from the harbourside, Milbourne. No one much is looking, though a couple strolling on the quayside, by the ruined Complex, might be staring out towards the stormy-dark horizon, lost in each other or thoughts of their own. There's a flicker, maybe lightning . . . No, it comes up from the dark line of the Spit, its dragon's-back of beach huts, as if there really was a dragon, breathing real flame. For a moment it hangs in the air, a fist shape, then it spreads out like a great bird's wings. A second puffball of fire bursts, then a third, and then the wind sets in, fanning the blaze and stretching it out lengthways, so it leaps from one wooden hut to the next, bending and curling, flapping like sheets hung out to dry, until the whole stretch of the sand-spit's small encampment is a ragged wall of flame.

29

Nothing That Won't Heal

It was peaceful on the seabed. When she was
younger, Clio had dived to the bottom of the swimming pool and looked up, wondering if that swaying
jiggly ceiling was what fish could see. The water had
gone up her nose so that she came up spluttering. Now,
though, it was calm and quiet—sometimes dark, sometimes light, sometimes shallow, sometimes deep, as the
tide went in and out above her. At low-tide moments
she could see the faces bending over—Mum and Dad,
Stella, several strangers—peering in. She wondered if
she should send them a message somehow, just to say
she was OK. But it was comfortable where she was,
lying still, with a silky-soft duvet of mud wrapped
round her.

Clio . . . Someone said her name, behind her.

Max? she said, struggling to turn.

Snug down here, in't it? Oggie stretched and yawned in
a tangle of seaweed. *First good night's sleep I've had for
years.* Clio tried not to look as his mouth fell open wider,
wider. She broke free of the mud and struggled upwards
as the sea rocked with his laughter:

> *The 'orses stood still, the wheels went around*
> *Goin' up Camborne 'ill coming down.*

*　*　*

'You're going to be fine,' said the nurse. 'There's nothing that won't heal . . . apart from your clothes, that is.'

'My clothes?' said Clio.

'We had to cut the top things off you,' the nurse said. 'We normally do that with burns—you know, so we don't have to drag them up over your head. How's it feeling, by the way?'

'OK. Not bad.' Her head felt sore and numb and sick and floaty, but Clio had something else on her mind. 'My clothes,' she said. 'Where are they?'

'Should have gone home with your parents last night but . . . yes.' She looked in the bedside locker. 'There. They can pick them up when they come in.'

'Can I see?'

'They're a bit of a mess. Are you sure?'

Clio looked at the nurse. She was young, and not as bossy as the others. A couple of years ago, she'd have been at school like her. Now, though, she had just what Clio needed: time for her, and space. No awkward questions. Clio found herself smiling. 'I just want a look, that's all.'

'Well . . . OK, then. Shall I leave you to it?'

'Thanks. That's nice of you.'

When she was alone, Clio reached in the bag. She pulled things out slowly, bit by bit. That top from the charity shop . . . A bra she'd stolen, while Max chatted up the staff . . . Laid on the bed, they didn't look like clothes—more like the shed skin of some insect that had hatched and flown. Then she fished inside the zip-up pockets of the ripped cagoule. She lay back with a long sigh, as her fingers found it. Max's book.

'Nobody blames you for what happened,' said the doctor. The psychiatrist, in fact, but nobody said that. He had little rimless glasses and a kind but worried look.

'And you mustn't blame yourself,' he said.

'I don't,' said Clio.

'You're bound to. You've been through a difficult and confusing experience. We all think you're an exceptionally brave young woman. And a lucky one. You could have been hurt much more badly, if it hadn't been for Mr Brown.'

He paused, as if that was a difficult concept to grasp. 'You do know, don't you, that there is, well, just a question or two to be answered? And there is—I'm sorry, I have to say this—still the question of the inquest.'

Outside, a couple of gulls careened by, against the grey clouds, silently. Clio was finding it hard to keep her mind on what the man was saying.

'Just remember,' he went on. 'You weren't completely responsible for your actions.'

'Who was, then? Max? Are you saying it was Max's fault?'

'He was a very disturbed young man. You do understand that, don't you?' There was a pause. The man looked at her gravely, as if she ought to guess what came next.

'Everyone concerned,' he said, 'the staff here, and your parents, and myself, we all agree that you should not be put under any additional stress. On the other hand, the police do have a job to do . . .'

The window at the far end of the day room was a blaze of light—a blaze like a halo round the large, broad figure of a man. For a moment he was just a silhouette—no face, no features—and Clio froze. Then the figure swivelled round and took a step forward, holding out a hand towards her awkwardly.

'We haven't met,' he said. 'Wayland—DI Wayland. I

263

once interviewed your . . . friend.' He paused. For a big man, an important one, by the look of it, he seemed oddly ill at ease. 'I'm sorry about the way it turned out. A bad do.' Behind Clio, the ward sister had appeared in the door. 'Better sit down,' he said. 'I've promised I won't tire you out. Are you all right?'

'Yes, yes. Just a bit . . . you know,' Clio said. There wasn't a way to say it: *I thought you were Oggie*. 'Bit faint, that's all. Is this about the inquest?'

'Another line of enquiry, let's say. To do with a Mister Ogmore—that name mean anything to you? Site warden. You must have met him.'

Clio nodded.

'Not one of the good guys. And he seems to have done a runner, round about the time of the . . . accident.'

'Excuse me.' The sister stepped in. 'I don't think Clio is quite strong enough for this yet. You did say . . .'

'Fair enough.' The big man nodded and, unexpectedly, smiled. 'I've waited thirty years. I can wait a few days more.' He turned to Clio. 'I can see this isn't the moment. Just . . . think about it. Anything you can remember. Anything that comes back to you.'

Clio nodded. 'Sure,' she said. 'I'll think about it.'

In long shot, there's a splash of colour in a grey day. A young woman leaves the clinic by the side door. Round her head, draped like a turban, is the purple scarf she will be wearing till the hair grows back. The wind blows the bare trees and she pulls her black coat around her. She looks round, as if she has not quite decided yet which way to go. Across the car park, her mother's face watches from the windscreen of the family car. The young woman walks with firm steps to the car and climbs in.

264

All right? says the mother's look.

By the automatic barrier at the exit gate, a security camera waits for them, impartially, the way it watches everyone who passes through its one-eyed angle on the world.

She glances up and nods to it, in passing. She thinks of what it must know, this world-wide web of cameras— CCTV, home digicams, video phones. (*We're film stars now, Max, all of us.*) Except, she thinks, they don't know anything. They have the data, bits, bytes, megabytes, gigabytes of it, but . . . but it isn't a story.

All right, says the girl's look and she gives her mum a quick kiss. *Thanks.* And off they go.

Dear M,

Midnight. That time again. Our time, with wind in the trees. The one time I can get out the book, and be with you.

I visited Ryan. We were both on the burns ward together at first, though I got out before him. They say he'd pulled me round before the first explosion hit us, so he took most of the blast.

He's not a bad man, Ryan. I just thought you'd like to know. He swears that he never meant to hurt you. He just wanted you to be so scared you'd never forget. I don't think they believe him — not with everything Stella told them about that day, and besides, he and Jade come from this really crummy estate. No one knows if they're going to charge him with something really serious — manslaughter or something. If they do, I'm going to stand up and tell them exactly what happened — that it was a kind of an accident. I think that's true.

Mostly, though, I don't talk much. Some people want

to know everything, some try not to mention it at all. They're all doing their best — Dad included! Now and then I catch somebody looking at me — Rachel's mum, for instance — as if she's not sure who I am. (And then she looks at Rachel, sort of wondering, too.)

You're still famous. They say it was a great show from the harbourside. It would have been even better at night, like with the Complex, but there were dark clouds in the background for effect. Trust you. Half of Milbourne came out to watch, like it was bonfire night again, thanks to you. When I imagine it, I see you there among them, mingling with the crowd and watching. You were always kind of doing that, weren't you — watching yourself from a distance, watching your life like TV? At the end of the show, I see you slipping away, before the credits.

(How crazy is that, then? As crazy as you.)

The psychiatrist used a good word. He said what we did together was a 'folie à deux'. I like it—sounds like a kind of dance in ballet. They've got names for everything . . . but they haven't got a name for you.

Stella's gone. Moved away. I can see why. Everyone's making excuses for me (though I don't want them) —not for her. She sent me a text to say she was sorry I won't be seeing Toby for a while, and that it wasn't my fault. Sorry about what happened in the end, too. Sorry about you. She said she just knew it was time for things to change, and wasn't that what I'd felt, when I met you. She said she hoped she'd be as brave as me.

She couldn't say that we were right, of course. (Who could?) But, Max, I think maybe she understood.

Milbourne's OK, for the time being. It's not Ibiza or Los Angeles, but everyone's got to live somewhere. I know the secret now: everything, everything that matters most, can happen anywhere. And everything that happens matters. That's what this book of yours — of ours — is for.

And this is our time, with the wind in the trees in the garden, the rain coming in from the sea. Half the people in the world asleep, half the countries dark, half the languages not being spoken, except in their dreams. Our time. It doesn't matter if it only lasts an hour — it's all the time in the world.

There are plenty of pages you left blank. Quite soon, I'll tell it all: not just the answers to the questions they ask — policemen, psychiatrists, Mum and Dad, my friends at school. I mean all of it: the whole truth. About Oggie. How that came to happen. How you hit him once — to save me, like you'd promised. How that might have been (in some sad, awful, helpless way) OK. How you hit him again, and it wasn't. No. Could you have stopped then? Could you, ever? Could we have stopped — yes, me too — anywhere along the way?

The answer's in there somewhere, if I can just write it. No more secrets, Max. I'll tell it — in my own way. How you died and I came alive. All the incredible things. The true story of you and me.

Me, Clio-with-an-I.

The Muse (Remember? The one who doesn't make things up?) — the Muse of History.

Philip Gross was born in Cornwall in 1952, the son of an Estonian wartime refugee and a Cornish schoolmaster's daughter. He has been a writer and teacher of writing for twenty-five years, visiting schools and colleges all over the country. As professor of Creative Writing at Glamorgan University in Wales, he divides his time between there and Bristol, where he lived for many years and brought up his family. He has won many awards for his poetry, and *The Wasting Game* was shortlisted for the Whitbread Poetry Prize in 1998. He has also written plays, radio stories, and opera libretti, and enjoys working with people from other art forms—dancers, painters, and musicians. *The Storm Garden* is his fourth novel for Oxford University Press.

www.philipgross.co.uk

Other Oxford books by Philip Gross

Going For Stone
Marginaliens
The Lastling

The Storm Garden